MURDER COMES TO EDEN
A **CRIME CLUB** *Novel*

THE Eden of Spig and Molly O'Leary was a lovely, peaceful place. There the O'Learys acquired a home, largely through the sudden generosity of Miss Celia Fairlie, an odd, vague and unexpectedly shrewd old lady who had taken a great liking to small Tip O'Leary. When Spig is already involved in preserving this idyllic spot against industrial encroachment, another, older story begins to unfold: a story that goes back into the past of Miss Celia Fairlie, concerning a mysterious death many years before. In both stories—the present crisis and the secret of the past—Spig O'Leary becomes involved; in his bitterness and anger he blunders badly and even his marriage seems threatened. This brilliant new story moves at a dazzling pace. Even the greatest admirers of Colonel Primrose will forgive the author his absence from *Murder Comes to Eden.*

MURDER
COMES TO EDEN

by
LESLIE FORD

WILDSIDE PRESS

Murder Comes to Eden

Published by Wildside Press LLC
www.wildsidepress.com

CHAPTER I

Tipton James O'Leary had his war all taped out. Mission: no entangling alliances. Method: off duty, stick strictly to those spots where you don't run into any. It was a conclusion he'd come to the sixth time he was best man at a hasty wedding, fortified every time he saw a girl with a lost look in her eye and a kid in her arms waving good-bye on a station platform. He finished his last year in college and enlisted when he was twenty-one. He was a staff sergeant in a cadre at Fort Bragg when he was twenty-three, dropped in at a USO dance for a minute because he was fed up with a crap game, and that was that. She had red-gold hair and a green dress. She was standing over in a corner all by herself, like something cool and lovely that had slipped up from the crystalline caves of the sunlit sea.

" Who is that girl? " he asked the hostess.

" That's Miss Dulaney. Shall I take you over to meet her, Sergeant? "

" No, thanks," said Sergeant O'Leary. He went over by himself. " I'm Tipton James O'Leary. Spig, for short," he said.

She looked up at him, laughing. Her eyes were greenish brown, flecked with sparkling gold, and there was a faint almost milk-blue transparency under the long golden lashes that shaded them.

" I'm Mary Margaret Dulaney. Molly for short."

" May I have this dance, Molly—and all the rest?

5

Then I'd like to take you home, if your father the Sea
King doesn't mind."

"You may have this dance," Molly said. "More
than one's against the rules. And my father the Sea
King's coming for me at half-past twelve."

"You leave the rules to me," said Spig O'Leary. "A
sergeant can do anything."

At twelve-thirty he took her out. The Sea King's car
was khaki-coloured, with a flag on the fender, a flag with
two stars on it. He got out, giving his daughter a testy
glare.

"Daddy, this is Staff Sergeant Tipton James O'Leary
—Spig, for short.—My father, General Dulaney."

Spig saluted. The general returned it. He was a short,
peppery man.

"'Spig'" he said. "No relation to old Spig O'Leary,
West Point '16?"

"My father, sir."

"Ha. Where is the old horse?"

"Washington, sir. War Production Board."

"Ha." He looked at Spig's GI uniform. "What are
you doing in that?"

"Backbone of the Army, sir. Save money. No uniforms to buy."

"Sounds like old Spig himself. Too bad. Loss to the
Army."

"Eight kids to feed, sir."

"Tough going with three, myself. Give him my best.
Hurry up, Molly."

"I'd like permission to see your daughter again, sir,"
said Spig. "Immediate mission: matrimony."

The general started. "No way to save money." He
glowered around at his daughter. "I told your mother
she was a fool to let you come here." He looked at his

watch. " Now you're here, the sergeant can walk you home. I had to leave the only Christian hand I've had all night. Your mother'll be delighted. Daisy Tipton was one of our bridesmaids."

He returned Spig's salute and got back in his car, and Spig kissed Molly then in front of a streetful of cheering soldiers.

Spig O'Leary was six feet one, his hair, what the barber had left of it, ginger-red, his eyes grey, his mouth wide, his lips thin, his jaw round but appearing square.

" I don't know what our kids are going to look like," he said. " Have you had biology? What do two reds make—any idea? "

" Blue, I think," Molly said. " But I only got as far as frogs."

Two weeks later they were married.

" It's a mistake," the general said. " Nineteen's too young."

" He'll have to take a commission, now," said Mrs. Dulaney.

" We need the money," Molly O'Leary said. " I've been in plenty of officers' clubs. The backbone of the Army, Daddy. I've heard you say it. And he's leaving so soon, Mother, you won't be embarrassed long. Oh Daddy, I love him! I'm going to get an apartment in Washington. Maybe he can hitch a plane back once or twice. . . "

" A sergeant can do anything," the general said.

Sergeant O'Leary made it five times—once, just before Normandy, for twenty-seven minutes on a darkened airstrip in Virginia. In May, 1947, he came back to the Sea King's daughter and two small kids—older, tougher, quieter, profoundly happy, profoundly in love. Molly had a three-room apartment in a rabbit warren of brick with " Keep Off " signs on the patch of grass in front of it. He'd been home two weeks the morning she plunked the coffee pot down on the table, her eyes flashing, the gold flecks tinder-bright.

" Spig O'Leary . . . we can't stand this! " she said hotly. " We've got to have a bigger place to live. That box you threw in the garbage yesterday had Tippy's leaves in it, the ones he's been collecting all spring every time we took a walk. This marriage has gone beautifully all the time you were away. It's going bust in six months unless——"

" Not ever, Mrs. O'Leary. This marriage is never going bust."

" It is unless we get a little room to move around in. And Tippy's just got to be outdoors. Look, Spig. We've got thirty-five hundred dollars we've saved. We could buy a little piece of land and get a GI loan to build us a small house. Just *some* place. On the water, maybe. Maybe down in Devon County where the Camerons are. Joe commutes. You could do it. Mag Cameron says there are lots of places down there. It's Garden Pilgrimage Week. We could go look . . . just *look*, anyway, Spig."

They put the two kids in the car and went down to Devon County. It was forty miles and the roads were narrow and winding. But it was lovely. The dogwood was in bloom and the honeysuckle sweet all along the barbed wire fences. They took their lunch and had a picnic under an oak tree in somebody's field. Tippy wouldn't eat. He was too absorbed in gathering violets, leaves and blades of grass. He was such a minute and perfect image of his father that Spig laughed every time he looked at him.

" I know who his father is, all right. I'm not sure about his mother. But what I really don't get is this Nature Boy stuff. Doesn't he ever whoop it up like other kids? You didn't just sit concentrating on Socrates, did you? Or some big wheel in botany? "

" You're being the heavy father before he's even out of nursery school," said Molly. " I don't know what we've produced, but it's something special. He adores things that grow. That's why we've got to have a place with a yard of some kind."

A few miles along they saw the sign: " Devon Manor —Waterfront Lots—$250 and Up." The ones on the water were " Up " $500.

" They're beautiful, Spig."

" We're planning a club house, with dances Saturday nights, oyster roasts and crab feasts," the man said.

" Well, let's not rush it," Spig said. " Let's look at one House and Garden—and have a drink with the Camerons." He looked at the Pilgrimage guide folder they'd picked up at a service station. " Here's one. ' The Garden of Eden. Miss Celia Fairlie, owner. House not on view.' That's fine. The kids won't break anything. Maybe they'll have the snakes on view, up the apple tree."

" Do snakes live in apple trees? " Tippy asked.

" No. Just a joke, son. About another Garden of Eden."

" I'd like to see the apple tree," Tippy said. " I've seen snakes at the zoo."

They went through Devonport, a quiet little town with a courthouse square and nobody much around. The green arrows tacked to the trees led them out a narrow road through pastures and newly planted tobacco fields. The gate marked " Eden " was a couple of miles from town. They followed a lane for half a mile between oaks and beeches, the fields on either side gleaming through shimmering masses of dogwood and shining green holly. There was another gate set in a serpentine brick wall, beyond a small Greek Revival building where a woman with a cigar box came out to take their money.

" I'm sorry—no children," she said with a toothy smile of no regret. " Miss Fairlie wouldn't want the flowers trampled. Now, this building is the old estate office. John Eden landed here on the *Devon* in 1729. That's why it's called Eden's Landing. Miss Fairlie is a direct descendant; her mother was a Miss Eden. Just the gardens. The house isn't on view. It's supposed to be haunted." She laughed. " Now, if you'll just park by the gate. The children can get out, but they must stay on this side."

Molly looked at Spig. Spig looked at his son and felt a sharp tug at his own heart.

" Let's not bother, then," he said. " We'll go some place else."

" No," said Tippy. " We'll stay by the car. We can see it when we grow up. We can look at the trees on this side."

But it took all the fun out of it for Spig and Molly. It wasn't as if the place were crowded. There was only one other customer, a tiny old lady in a white dress, with a stiff, white sailor hat and white gloves, and a parasol standing by the iris border near the gate. She and an old, coloured man in his Sunday suit guarding the house were the only people in sight.

" We'll do it quickly," Molly said. " Then let's go and buy the lots."

" Right," Spig said. The lost expression on Tippy's face had decided it. They went rapidly along the turf walk between the borders, hardly seeing them, and both looked back then as their son's earnest treble reached them across the peonies. He was through the gate, his sister by the hand, talking to the old lady with the sailor hat.

" Lady, do you think it would be all right if we stood here and looked at the flowers, if we didn't touch anything? "

" I don't see why not," said the lady.

" I'd better go back," Spig said. But Molly was suddenly pale green. He got her over to a white iron bench. " You sit down till I get them back in the car." He was still hearing his son's voice.

" My name is Tipton James O'Leary, Jr. My mother calls me Tippy. My father calls me Tip. I'm four and a half. This is my sister Kitsy. She's only two."

Spig was starting towards them when he heard the lady's voice.

" I'm Celia Fairlie. I'm sixty-one. And I'm very happy to meet you and Kitsy, Tip. I hope you will enjoy my flowers."

" Thank you, Celia Fairlie," Tip said.

Spig grinned and came back to Molly, sat down and took her hand in his. " He'll be all right." They could still hear his voice.

" We don't have a place for a garden where we live," he was saying. " It's very small. It was all right till my father came home, but he's very large. That was my father and my mother we came with. We're going to have another baby, but we don't know whether it's going to be a boy or a girl till it's born. We don't know where we're going to put it. It's a present for my father, because he's been away a very long time."

Spig got up hastily. " Look, the rat . . . Couldn't you tell him to tell people I was home for a week six months ago? "

" Sit down," Molly said. She was blushing and less green now. " I'll be all right in a minute. Let's go and get our lots then."

But even Molly was startled when they heard Tippy go on. " Have you any children, Celia Fairlie? "

They didn't hear Miss Celia Fairlie's reply. The three were moving away behind the boxwood.

" We'd better go," Molly said. " I feel fine. It was emotional, I guess. He was so disappointed. Let's go get our lots. You find him."

But Tippy refused to go. " I'd like to stay with Celia Fairlie," he said. He slipped his hand into hers as Kitsy toddled back to her father.

" I'm sorry, Miss Fairlie," Spig said. " We thought the children were staying outside."

" I like them inside," said Miss Fairlie. She was very small and very erect, with pale, faraway, blue eyes. Her voice was faraway, too. " If you have some other house you want to see, Tip may stay here till you come back. Tell the woman at the gate so she doesn't charge you a second time. Very grasping."

Molly and Spig looked at each other, avoiding their son's eyes.

" I'd like very much to stay," he said soberly, but there was a little catch in his voice. " Miss Fairlie says she'll show me the apple tree. She says they do have snakes, but down in the water, not in the garden."

" He could stay a little while, then," Molly said. " We can come back on our way to the Camerons'. We'll take Kitsy."

" I'm not sure about this," Spig said as they got in the car.

At the little, white-pillared office the toothy lady

stopped them, smiling officiously. " The little boy . . .
where is——"

" He's staying with Miss Fairlie a while."

" Oh . . ." She looked very startled indeed.

" She said he might."

" Oh, well . . . I mean, I'm sure it's all right. David—
the old coloured man—he was there, wasn't he? "

" Down by the house," Spig said.

" Oh, well, it's quite all right, then." She smiled
brightly. " I just wanted to check, that's all."

They went on three or four miles. " Spig," Molly said.
" That woman. What do you suppose she meant? "

" I guess she thought the old man'd keep him off the
flowers."

But Molly was disturbed. " Let's go back, Spig."

" Oh, he's all right. They were doing fine, I thought."

They went on, but just as they got to the sign Molly
put her hand quickly on his arm. " No, Spig, I know
I'm being difficult. But I'd be a lot happier . . ."

" Okay." They went back. The woman at the gate
smiled at them cordially.

" He's quite all right. I've kept my eye on them."

And he was all right. He and Miss Fairlie came
around the turf between the borders, walking very
solemnly. Then Tippy ran to meet them, his eyes shining
like brand new stars.

" Miss Fairlie says she has lots of land and lots of
water! " He stopped breathlessly and ran back. " Didn't
you, Miss Fairlie? Didn't you say that? "

" Yes, I did," Miss Fairlie said.

" I told her we didn't have very much money. But she
said that's all right. Didn't you, Miss Fairlie? "

Spig and Molly stared at them. Miss Fairlie came up,
her pale childlike eyes resting on them quite definitely a

moment before the far away look came back. She stood there, her white-gloved hands folded in front of her, blinking vaguely a moment before she spoke.

"Tip said thirty-five hundred dollars. Is that correct?"

"That's . . . correct," Spig said.

"Then you may have that piece on the other side of the Cove." She turned and pointed across the gardens. "The house is old and very small. But if you paid me two thousand dollars, you'd have enough left to add on to it. There's several acres. It goes to those trees you see this side of Mr. Sudley's tobacco fields. There's a pleasant piece of beach the children would enjoy, I think."

Neither Spig nor Molly could speak. Tippy's face had no need of words.

"There's a great deal of honeysuckle. In fact, it's completely overgrown, except around the cottage. I've kept that clear. You'd have to fix the road, but you could use mine as far as the old wagon trail. I've kept the bridge repaired. I don't think you'll mind the blood. You can hardly tell it unless you know it's there."

"She says you can hardly see it now, anyway," Tip said urgently.

"That's . . . wonderful, Miss Fairlie. But——"

"No. Blood disappears. It's like everything else. Time is all it takes. We can go look now, if you like."

"I don't know. My wife——"

"We can go through the gardens. It won't be too much for her."

"Let's go, Daddy! Please, Daddy! Please, Mother!"

There was a narrow, white bridge at the bottom of the garden.

"This isn't the bridge I was talking about," said Miss Fairlie. "This is my own bridge. The other one is over that way." She waved vaguely out through the jungle of sassafras and locust, all matted with fox grape and honeysuckle. " The wagon trail is under there." She indicated the jungle again. " We take this path."

A moment later a small whitewashed cottage, windows and doors heavily shuttered, came into view. Through another tangle of vines and swamp myrtle in front of it they could see a glimpse here and there of the shining blue water of the Devon.

" I let it stay like this to keep fishermen and hunters away," Miss Fairlie said. " We must go now, I think. You can come back and take the shutters down. There are two rooms. The blood is on the table. I'd like for Tip to live at Eden. I think he'd enjoy it very much. If the price is too high . . ."

" Oh, no. It's not high enough. It's——"

" But Daddy, it's what she said. Isn't it, Miss Fairlie? You *do* like it, don't you, Daddy? And you like it, Mother? Don't you? " Tip's face was passionately alive with pleading, but his voice still its sober self.

" Of course, darling. It's wonderful. But——"

" Then don't talk any more," Miss Fairlie said. She turned and led the way back into the gardens. At the gate she stood, blinking absently for a moment. Then she said, " I must go away now. Good-bye, Tip."

She put her hand out as gravely as he took it.

" Good-bye, Miss Fairlie. Thank you very much for the house and land. I enjoyed the gardens very much, too. You'll take care of my little ducks till I come back, won't you? "

" Yes, I will."

She turned and walked down the oyster shell drive, around a circle of boxwood, past the old coloured man, and into the house.

" She gave me six little ducks," Tippy said.

They got to the white-pillared office where the ticket taker was counting her cigar box of money by the door. She smiled at them.

" There's a hundred and ten dollars, we made to-day. Everybody came very early in case Miss Fairlie suddenly changed her mind. It's the first time Eden's ever been opened." She looked at Tippy. " I see you got him back. I didn't mean to alarm you, but Miss Fairlie's very . . . well, I expect you could see it. She's quite mad, as mad as a hatter, really, you know. It was all right with David there. He watches out for her. Well, good-bye. Come again, won't you? "

" Miss Fairlie wasn't mad, Mother," Tippy said, when they were on their way through the shaded lane to the outer gate. " She was glad. She liked us there. She told me so. She said she didn't let people come in her house because they made a noise and there was a child asleep. But I don't make a noise when Kitsy's asleep, do I, Mother? "

" No, Tippy. She's asleep now, so why don't you take a nap too? "

" Yes, because we've had a very hard day," said Tippy.

Neither Spig nor Molly said anything till she looked back and saw him sound asleep.

" I can't bear it, Spig," she whispered. " I just can't. How can we explain to him? It'll break his heart."

" I know. I'm sorry. We should have got out of there when she started talking about the blood. You could see she was bats . . . the look in her eye. Do you want to go to the Camerons'? I don't."

Molly shook her head. When they got to the Devon Manor sign, she said, " No. Somewhere else. Virginia, maybe. I wish we'd never come."

She cried herself to sleep that night in Spig's arms, and he felt like crying himself. He couldn't get the hurt, completely not-understanding look on Tippy's face out of his mind. " I'll go to a real estate agent in the morning," he said, and he was shaving, getting ready to go, when the phone rang. Molly had taken Kitsy to market, and Tip with with them.

" Devonport calling Mr. Tipton James O'Leary, Senior."

" This is Mr. O'Leary."

" Go ahead, Judge," he heard the operator say, and a dry, precise voice came on.

" Mr. Tipton James O'Leary, Senior? "

" Speaking."

" This is Judge Nathan Twohey in Devonport. I understand you were at Eden, Miss Celia Fairlie's place, yesterday."

" That's correct."

" I understand you were offered a tract of her land? "

Judge Nathan Twohey sounded as if O'Leary had not only been offered it but had picked it up and carried it away with him and Judge Twohey wanted it back at once.

" Right," said Spig.

" Then I must ask you to come to Devonport and discuss the matter here in my office."

Spig's jaw tightened. It was not a request but an order. He was just about to say, "And I must ask you to go to hell, Judge Twohey, sir," when he thought of Tip's face. Even if they had to pay more than two thousand— even if they could only get a piece of it . . .

" The property *is* for sale, is it? " he asked instead.

" That's a matter I prefer to discuss in my office."

" I'll come down right away."

Don't count on this, he said to himself in the mirror.

B

He scribbled a non-committal note—" Business. Back around five. Love, Spig "—and went down the service stairs so he wouldn't meet them coming back from market.

CHAPTER II

HE DIDN'T see the dingy yellow line on the kerb when he parked in the somnolent tree-shaded square in Devonport. The courthouse was a faded brick building with a squat, rusty, gold cupola and a porch with pillars, like the little Greek Revival building outside the wall at the Gardens of Eden. There were broken-down green benches under thirsty trees whose exposed roots ribbed the dry ground where a few unhappy blades of grass struggled to live. He went up the uneven brick walk. A big man with curly black hair and deep-set dark eyes was lounging against one of the weater-beaten pillars in the sun.

" Can you tell me where I'll find Judge Twohey? "

" Other side." The man shoved a big fist out across the square. " That little round arch in the wall, upstairs to your left. And that heap you've got. It's parked on a yellow line. I can make you a deal, if you want to turn it in. I won't give you a ticket this time." He grinned at Spig. " I'm the law in these parts. Yerby's the name. Tell the judge I killed the fellow stealing his wife's chickens. He's a black snake about seven feet long. Don't forget when you want a car."

" I'll remember when I get the dough. My name's O'Leary."

" Oh." Yerby looked at him with alerted interest.

" You're the guy. Well, good luck. Be seeing you around
. . . maybe."

Judge Twohey was behind a beat-up oak desk across
one corner of a musty room lined with old law books and
dog-eared file boxes. He was very old, very neat in his
black poplin suit, fragile and semi-transparent as a potato
shoot in a dark cellar. But all Spig was aware of were
the eyes examining him, intensely alive, unfriendly.

Judge Twohey spoke abruptly. " Here is the plot of the
land you propose to buy."

Spig took it. He looked at it. " Oh, no," he said, his
heart taking a sickening nose-dive into the pit. " Oh,
no. There's some mistake. She said several acres, not
fifty. She said a . . . a pleasant piece of beach—not
thirty-three hundred feet of it. She said two thousand
dollars . . ."

" You're not interested in the property, then." Judge
Twohey's voice sounded a shade less hostile.

There was the sudden, sharp taste of tears in Spig's
mouth. " It's not that, sir. We are interested. But we
don't have that kind of money. We couldn't expect to
buy . . ."

" It's your opinion that if Miss Fairlie wishes to sell
you this land for two thousand dollars, she hasn't the
legal right to do so? "

" Not that, sir. Not if she's of sound mind." He
flushed. " I'm sorry. I didn't mean that. Except that
there was this dame with a lot of teeth taking tickets out
there yesterday said Miss Fairlie was mad. Mad as a
hatter."

" That dame was my wife, Mr. O'Leary."

In the silence, of the kind commonly called abysmal,
the sweat trickling down between Mr. O'Leary's shoulder
blades was very cold.

" My second wife. A capable and efficient woman with only the normal dentitional complement, I believe."

" I'm sorry, sir."

" Quite. It does suggest the practical wisdom of keeping one's big mouth shut."

" You're understating it, sir."

Judge Twohey smiled a little. " Also, here in Devon we say 'eccentric,' not ' mad,' Mr. O'Leary. But you needn't have any anxiety on the score of Miss Fairlie's eccentricity in financial affairs. She has an uncanny gift. A good many people think she has second sight. Her tenants especially. If she plants early, there's never a frost. If she doesn't put tobacco in, that's the year of the blue mould. Yesterday's the first time she's ever opened the Gardens of Eden . . . and if I were superstitious, I could easily believe she knew you were coming."

He picked up a typed letter. " There is one stipulation. In case of resale, in whole or in part, during her lifetime, Miss Fairlie must approve the vendée or have the option to buy the property herself at the price you're now paying, plus any actual cash you've put into it."

" That's more than fair," Spig said.

The judge looked at him intently. " This land may increase greatly in value."

" It's still fair. We're very grateful to Miss Fairlie."

" Gratitude is highly volatile, Mr. O'Leary," Judge Twohey said dryly. " In my experience, it seldom withstands the impact of hard cash. Miss Fairlie asked only for your word; but I've put it in the form of a written agreement. There's no legal obligation . . ."

" There's a moral one." Spig read the letter and signed it.

" I'm glad you say that. Because it's my duty to tell

you that such a stipulation is not legally binding. At most, it could be used only to show intent." He looked steadily at Spig. "I'm asking you for your solemn word, as well as your signature, Mr. O'Leary. There must never be any threat to Eden during Miss Fairlie's life-time."

"You have my word, sir."

"Thank you. May I say I'm greatly relieved about you? Miss Fairlie has refused a good many offers for this tract—one recently from her neighbour Mr. Sudley of one thousand dollars an acre. I didn't know what form of hypnotism——"

"Not mine, sir. My son's. Age four and half."

"Ah," Judge Twohey was silent for an instant. "Yes, that would explain it. In any case, there was nothing I could have done about you. Short of a touch of cyanide."

He went over to the dingy corner cupboard and got a bottle and two small glasses. "I did ask Yerby to stand by. He's the sheriff. Just back from the Marines. If necessary, he might have persuaded you Devon wasn't the place . . ."

Spig grinned. "He said to tell you he'd killed the seven-foot black snake stealing your chickens. I'm only six."

"My wife's chickens," said Judge Twohey equably. He took the stopper out of the bottle.

"One other thing, sir." Spig's face had sobered. "I don't know how to put it. Miss Fairlie's . . . eccentricity. My wife and kids'll be out there all day. There was something said about blood . . . and the big house being haunted."

Judge Twohey stood with the bottle stopper motionless in his hand.

"There was blood, Mr. O'Leary," he said quietly.

" A great deal of blood. And possibly the house is haunted. It well may be. But the blood was a long time ago, and as you're not living in the big house, its nature is no concern of yours. You'll find many tongues anxious to relieve your curiosity. But Miss Fairlie took you on faith. She makes no inquiries about you. That's all, Mr. O'Leary. Take the property or leave it."

" I'm sorry . . . we're glad to take it."

The judge's face, grave as he poured the liquor into the glasses, lighted with a sudden flicker. " I'll tell you why my wife thinks Miss Fairlie is crazy," he said amiably. " She and another estimable lady, hell-bent on good works, went out to Eden one hot September day. The gate was padlocked. They climbed it. They walked the half-mile to the garden gate, sweating virtuously. They were climbing that when Miss Fairlie let fly with a bushel basket of rotten pears, one at a time. My wife's corset caught on one of the pickets."

He handed Spig a glass. " This court may feel that the defendant acted hastily and without due regard for the plaintiff's position, socially or physically. But you the jury must consider the provocation and weighing the undeniable fact of trespass, it will be your duty to determine the credibility of this witness."

He raised his glass. " To Miss Fairlie's continuing eccentricities, Mr. O'Leary. And to your own long life and happiness at Eden, sir."

" Thank you," Spig said. " No cyanide? "

Judge Twohey smiled. " On the contrary." He put the bottle back in the cupboard and took out his black straw hat. " We'll finish our business after lunch," he said, still smiling. " The Board of County Commissioners meet to-day. We'll see them at Devon House." He stopped at the desk, looking down at the plot.

" Actually, you have nearer sixty acres than fifty here. This is a very old survey. The marsh you see indicated has filled in. Mr. Harlan Sudley had his line resurveyed last February. He found his fences well over on Eden's side. But Miss Fairlie said it was a reasonable exchange, as the land that filled the marsh was Sudley land, due to Sudley bad farming practice."

He put the plot in a desk drawer. " Malice, I'm afraid, is a sin not even old age can cure." Spig thought it was Miss Fairlie's malice about Sudley farm practice he meant until they got across the square to Devon House and he met the six commissioners. They were eating in a small dining-room with Rotary and Lions club banners under the flag over the piano in one corner. Harlan Sudley, president of the board, was at one end of the table.

Miss Fairlie's neighbour, the one who offered her a thousand dollars an acre and had had his land resurveyed. Spig noted as they shook hands. Sudley was a big burly man with a soft voice, grizzling sandy hair, a ruddy sunburned face and shuttered pale blue eyes.

The judge took his place at the other end of the table, Spig beside him.

" Mr. O'Leary has bought the Plumtree Cove tract," he said very casually—by way of explanation, Spig thought, until he heard the crashing silence, and the loud burst of guffaws that broke it. But not from the president of the board.

" Hear that, Harlan? " The man sitting next to Sudley gave him a boisterous thwack between the shoulder blades.

" I did. I'll be glad to have Mr. O'Leary for a neighbour."

That took a definite effort and brought another round

of hearty mirth. This was the malice Judge Twohey meant. It was friendly, but it was malice just the same. Sudley had really wanted that land; an unknown young man had got it. Spig was too dazed at the miracle of the O'Learys having it to think below the surface. All he could think of was getting back to Judge Twohey's office, writing his cheque for two thousand dollars and then calling Molly . . . when it was done and nothing could possibly slip. He could see her face and Tip's there in front of him as he ate, with no idea what he was eating. It never entered his mind to ask why Judge Twohey had insisted on the stipulation, or Sudley had offered a thousand dollars an acre for the tract, or why the silence and the loud guffaws.

Nor did he listen to the sharper warning three months later when he and Molly—with a new son named John Eden O'Leary—their hearts full to overflowing, bursting to share their boundless good fortune, decided to give Molly's sister Kathy the ten velvet acres for a wedding present.

" This is seven hundred feet of waterfront you're giving away, Mr. O'Leary," Judge Twohey said. " I strongly advise you to keep it. It may greatly increase in value. Family dissension over land and money is as bitter as it seems to be inevitable."

" Not this family, sir. Miss Fairlie's seen Kathy and she's agreed. Kathy's wonderful. Stan Ashton, this lad she's marrying—he's one of the best. He's an idealist. I don't think he even believes in money. He's a sociologist, works for the Town Planning Commission in Washington. He can drive back and forth with me. Kathy'll have their car and be down here with Molly. It's the perfect set-up for all of us. None of us'll ever have money enough to fight about, anyway."

" Perfect set-ups have a way of becoming imperfect. Life and circumstance—both change." Judge Twohey shook his head. " Well, Mr. O'Leary, I understand that God takes care of fools and children—my experience to the contrary notwithstanding. I wish you'd listen to me. But if you won't, you won't."

CHAPTER III

IF SPIG O'LEARY had asked, no one would have told him. The site of the bridge that was to cross the Devon River, picked by the Corps of Army Engineers, and the location of the super-highway, Devon County's link in the new coastal defence system, were top secret in the hands of the State Roads Commission. There were rumours in Devonport, but Spig O'Leary was clearing honeysuckle, week-ends and nights when he got home. It took him another three months to find out that the bridge site and almost a mile of the dual-lane approach to it were on the Plumtree Cove tract, on the Eden's Landing side of Harlan Sudley's fence line. The reason for Judge Twohey's warning was also clear. The bridge site and a good two-tenths of a mile of the approach were on the ten velvet acres the O'Leary's had given Kathy for a wedding present—very velvet for Kathy and Stan Ashton. The bridge, fifty feet from Sudley's marker on the shore, took two hundred feet of the Ashtons' beach. The two-tenths of a mile right-of-way on it took four of their ten acres. The Ashtons took eight thousand dollars. The next section of right-of-way was five acres belonging to the O'Leary's, but it was through the filled-in marsh and not good for much. The O'Leary's got the standard fifty dollars an acre.

But there wasn't any dissension. The O'Leary's could have used the eight thousand dollars. They were a little rueful, but they weren't bitter, and by the time the cheque came, they were glad it gave Stan Ashton the chance to take a couple of years off and write his book, " Safety Factors in Highway Control."

" It'll make him famous and we'll all be so proud of him . . ." Kathy was starry-eyed and confident. And it did make him famous, but not at once—not until a paper-backed edition of the book was brought hastily out when Kathy was killed in the first hideous accident on the new two-million dollar bypass around Devonport. Coming home from a strawberry festival at the church, she put on speed to pass a gasoline truck in front of the Breezy Inn as six punk kids roared out into the road, cutting directly across in front of the truck. Seven people were dead, before or after the truck exploded no one knew, and the driver died that evening. That was just three months after the Governor had come down to open Devon's link in the new highway. The O'Learys were bitter then, not about land or money but about the road and about Stan Ashton and his book. It had a new title, " Death Takes the High Road," with a lurid picture on the front cover, maybe not Kathy but somebody like her, and a sub-title, " An Author's Personal Tragedy," with a note about the author's three-year-old child. Maybe none of it was Stan Ashton's fault, but having a best seller certainly eased his personal tragedy. The O'Learys and Molly Ashton, the three-year-old who'd come to stay with them, saw him on television but seldom in person. Until one Sunday afternoon, not a full five months after Kathy's death, he came out driving a

Cadillac convertible that belonged to the blonde girl in the seat beside him.

" This is Anita," he said happily. " I wanted her to meet you. We're going to be married Wednesday. You'll put her up overnight, won't you? She couldn't stay in that flea bag in town, and you know my stand on motels." As an afterthought, he asked, " Where's little Molly? "

" She's with our kids," Spig said. " They're having a picnic supper over at Miss Fairlie's."

" Well, then, don't bother," Stan said. " Anita can see her later. She's got a kid of her own. Lucy. She's sixteen."

" Fifteen," said Anita. She was slim, sleek and self-possessed, not as young as she'd looked in the car, dark-eyed, with long hair in a knot of glittering gold at the nape of her neck. She was polite and detached, a transient at a convenient inn. She tossed her floppy black hat on the sofa and tapped her lips to smother a yawn. " Don't you get horribly bored, way out here? "

" We love it," Molly said.

Stan lighted a cigarette with a new gold lighter. He was tall, on the slender side, clean-cut and boyish in a sort of academic way, with his steel-rimmed spectacles. The quiet shyness that had been one of his most attractive qualities seemed to have got swallowed up somewhere along the line.

" We'll just mosey on over and have a look at my place," he said. " Anita's got plans for a house she wants to build. We're going to turn the old shack into a garage with a guest studio upstairs. Anita knows a lot of top-flight artists. They can come down and work, be company for her while I finish the new book. They'll be a bit of leaven for the local dough-heads."

A little towards the woods between the two places, he left Anita and came back. " I knew you'd be crazy about her," he said. " Her first husband was a louse, stinking rich, but her father's a lawyer, so she got enough to do as she pleases. You'll probably want to get some of the neighbours in, but let's keep it small—just the Camerons and Potters. We brought some Scotch in the trunk. We won't be long."

The Camerons and the Potters had the only show places, except Eden itself, out on the peninsula known as Eden's Neck. The rest of the neighbours were people like the O'Learys, with jobs in Washington, people who wanted a place for their kids and had bought two or three acres when Sudley sold off a worn-out farm across from Miss Fairlie's gate on the old road.

Spig tried to avoid the pale shattered look in Molly's eyes as she stood there, a white line around her lips. Then he went over to her.

" I'm all right." She turned abruptly away. " How could he? Oh, how could he! " she whispered. " What's happened to him? He used to be so——"

" Don't, Molly . . . please." Spig was sick himself, and then angry, at the callous nonchalance of Stan Ashton's announcement. " And I'm damned if we're going to call the Camerons."

" Yes." Molly's eyes kindled. " Yes, we are. We're not going to be rude to her." She turned quickly back to him. " Spig—she won't take Molly A., will she? I couldn't bear . . ."

" I don't think we need to worry."

" Then you call the Camerons. Ask them to lend us some Scotch—I wouldn't touch theirs. And ask them to bring ice—the kids took ours to Miss Fairlie's."

They thought about Kathy's child, but they didn't

think about Kathy's property. Not till later when Joe Cameron and Spig were out in the kitchen. Over the pink geraniums on the long window sill they could see the airy silver structure of the bridge, soaring gallantly out across the Devon, white sails like a flock of shining sea birds resting on the blue, sunlit water beneath it. Its landfall was hidden at this end by the pair of great chestnut oaks on the Ashtons' shore. The only sign there was a highway over there was a wide gap in the tree tops, in front of the taller beeches and willow oaks that filled the shallow arc between the road and Sudley's fences.

"Lucky for us old Stan's a Town Planner and a big wheel in highway improvement circles," Joe Cameron remarked. He was a big, red-faced man with light hair and stupid, ox-brown eyes, as steady as an ox and very shrewd. "The little lady looks more like Bailey's Beach than Plumtree Cove to me, and that's a nice fifty feet Stan's got between the bridge and Sudley's place. And about three hundred yards along the road? Might be a temptation to cash in . . . if she didn't like it down here."

Spig shook his head. "That's all settled. We're giving that little strip between the road and Sudley's fence to the State for a picnic area." *A sort of memorial to Kathy*, he would have added before Anita came. "If she doesn't like it here, we'll buy back the four acres this side of the road. That's the agreement. It's in a letter of stipulation Stan signed after Kathy died. Like the one we signed for Miss Fairlie. We pro-rate it at what we paid her, plus the cash he's put in."

It was that simple to Spig O'Leary.

"Let's hope the house they're talking about isn't too fancy, then," Joe Cameron said. "I still wish to God we could get the Commissioners to pass a zoning law for this county. Nobody's safe until they do. I don't see why Sudley can't see it. The road isn't a year old and look what's happened to it—right up to his own cow pasture. It's a crime."

It's worse than a crime. Spig O'Leary told himself that twice a day, five days a week, driving back and forth to work in Washington. Coming home, he didn't need the Colonial signpost in the parkway planting of dogwood and laurel to tell him he was entering Devon County. Dave's Drive-In (For White) on the left and Cab's Overnight and Eatery (For Coloured) on the right were like a pair of watchtowers on the county line, where the Governor had cut the broad, white ribbon, officially opening the new highway around Devonport to the bridge. " My friends of this great and lovely county in this great and lovely State . . ." Spig could still hear him as he stood bareheaded, scissors in his hand, flowers on his tongue. " Be ceaseless in your vigil, tireless in your guardianship. Let this magnificent artery of peace and prosperity be a boon and a blessing. Do not let it become a menace to your children, a curse to you."

And Devon's answer stretched from the county line to the Sudley pastures, for five miles on both sides of the road. "Devon Death Strip," the Washington and Baltimore papers called it . . . a nightmare in flowing neon, red, green and shocking pink. Liquor. Beds. Beer. Dance. Soft Drinks. Gas. Oil. Fried Shrimp. Package Goods for Fishing Parties. TV. We Never Sleep. Nor did anyone else within range of the sonic attack from the jukes, the callipoe at Colby's Carnival and the perpetual grind of the slot machines. Five miles of taverns, motels, gas stations, wooden shacks and cut-rate liquor stores had erupted like atomic mushrooms almost before

the concrete was dry. The merchants of Devonport
had rushed out to help reap the golden harvest. There
were super-markets, hardware and farm implement stores,
new and used cars, a branch of Sudley's bank cheek by
jowl with the Breezy Inn. Along both sides, five miles of
cut-throat competition, the turf in the centre parkway
chewed up with tyre gouges, littered with beer cans,
paper cups and empty bottles, from the county line to
Bill's Live Bait, Blood Worms and Peelers next to Sudley's
winter wheat on the left, across from the Three D (Your
Last Chance to Dine, Drink and Dance) next to Sudley's
cow pasture on the right.

From there, the highway ran between Sudley's new
white-painted fences, mile-long ribbons, to the woods
of Eden's Landing and down through them, fifty feet
from Sudley's line, into the Plumtree Cove tract to the
bridge crossing the Devon—a little over two miles in all.
That was what was left of Devon's highway that was not
a shambles.

And it was safe. Sudley loved the land and by Devon
standards was a rich man. Old Stan Ashton was the
high priest of highway sanctity. Miss Fairlie was eccentric,
but not eccentric enough to chop down the woods of
Eden to build a shopping centre two hundred yards
from the gate on the old road that she still padlocked
every night and all day Sundays. At Sylvan Shores the
Home Owners' League was fighting off a boat repair
yard, and at Chapel Creek a canning factory. But the
O'Learys and the people like them who'd socked their
last dime into the homes on Eden's Neck—they were safe.

Or so they thought until Monday evening the second
week in June.

Spig O'Leary saw the men putting the signboard up
in the corner of Sudley's buttercup-gold and green

pasture as he slowed down, blinded by the sun glinting on the blue glass octagon of the Three D (Your Last Chance to Dine, Drink and Dance). He took it for granted it was the sign for the County Fair, held every year on the Sudley Farm. The red light blinking on one of the sheriff's cars at the front door of the Three D caught his eye, and he saw the sheriff himself then, standing by a yellow convertible with two kids in it, neither of them more than seventeen. He saw Spig and motioned to him to pull in.

". . . If I catch you in this county again," he was saying. " Now get going, punks. Get the hell out of Devon County and stay out. You hear? "

The driver gunned the motor and the car roared out into the road, across the parkway, ripping the turf open, both of them laughing, not hearing Buck Yerby's bellow.

" Damn them," he said violently. " I wish this road had never come here. I just dropped in for a pack of cigarettes or Nick'd be on the floor with his head open. He caught 'em putting slugs in his slot machines and that punk driving had a bottle ready to brain him."

" No use blaming the road," Spig said. " It's these joints . . ."

" Yeh, I know." Yerby was still burned up. " I heard you at the commissioners' meeting Thursday night. I don't need you or the Home Owners' League to tell me what goes on. Look—when I took this job, I had one part-time deputy, ran myself an automobile business and went fishing Saturdays. Now I've got eleven full-time deputies, twelve radio cars, uniforms, what-have-you. You don't have to tell me—I've got kids same as you. All I stopped you for was to tell you I need a new deputy out here on Eden's Neck and you're it."

" Not me, I'm not," Spig O'Leary said.

" You. O'Leary, the hot shot of the Eden's Neck Branch of the Home Owner's League. There's not one of you people contributes a damn' thing except to live here and bellyache. You could all go to hell for me. Except Miss Fairlie. I'm worried about her, with this new set-up."

" What new set-up? "

Yerby looked at him. Then he shrugged. " Why don't you take a week off and stick around, O'Leary? " he said sardonically. " You might get the score. But you be in at eight to-morrow morning and take your oath. And take it seriously. I don't pass out any gilt badges just for laughs."

He started to his car and turned. " And thanks, Spig. I sure appreciate . . ."

" You go to hell." O'Leary's grey eyes lighted. " You don't have to rub it in."

Buck Yerby grinned. He looked at his watch. " How about a quick drink on it? You got time? "

" Not for this lousy joint, I haven't."

There was a sudden, smouldering fire in Yerby's eyes. " I figure it doesn't hurt the Three D for the sheriff to drop in for a drink if a drink doesn't hurt the sheriff," he said evenly. " Nick's a citizen. He's got his place over on Shad Creek. His kids go to school with yours and mine. Maybe he is a Greek with lousy taste in blue glass—like that ex-brother-in-law of yours says he is. But you couldn't print what Nick thinks about Stanley S. Ashton. Kathy was a friend of Nick's when he had that Greasy Spoon on Church Street."

O'Leary's face flushed, the heat smouldering in his own eyes. " That's no business——"

" Right. And it's no business of Ashton's if Nick likes blue glass, and you can tell Ashton the quicker he gets

c

out of here the better everybody's going to like it. And there's a lot of people think you're just as big a heel as he is a louse, O'Leary—sounding off on Sudley the other night. So what if he doesn't believe in zoning laws? There's nobody in Devon hates gambling and the slots the way he hates 'em. He's done a lot more for this county than any of you people. And personally, I don't think you're a heel, O'Leary. I think you're a plain sucker."

He opened his car door. " You think you're down on Sudley. Well, that's nothing to how he's down on you." He got in and slammed the door. " If you haven't seen that thing " (he made an angry gesture towards the signboard in the corner of the pasture) " you better take a look at it. That's what Sudley thinks of you, O'Leary."

The loose gravel peppered Spig's legs as the car shot forward. He stood there staring at the sign he'd taken for granted was the sign for the County Fair. He shut his eyes and opened them again. There was no mistake. There it was—and with it an empty hollow where his stomach had been.

" For Sale. For Industrial Development. 600 Acres. 2000 Feet of River Frontage. See H. Sudley, 19 Church Street, Devonport."

Spig O'Leary stood staring at it, the bottom dropping out of everything important to him in Devon County. That was Sudley's answer to the people on Eden's Neck and the petition for some kind of law to protect their homes. It was so stupefying that the people waiting to get to the gas pumps had to sound their horn twice before he heard it and moved.

The green and gold of the winter wheat and the flower-embroidered tapestry of the pastures behind the white

ribbons of mile-long fences were a blur on either side of
him. He drove slowly, still a little dazed. *That's what
Sudley thinks of you, O'Leary.* But there was nothing he'd
said nor anything he'd done that could possibly be taken
as a personal attack on Sudley. He came to the end of
the fences where the highway curved gently into the woods
of Eden, fifty feet from the side of Sudley's tobacco fields
stretching down to the river-front behind the shallow arc
of beeches and willow oaks that they were going to give
the State. He turned left into the cross-way, half-way to
the bridge, and waited for the traffic to clear for him to
go across into the gravelled side road marked " Plumtree
Cove " that ran between the back woods of Plumtree and
Miss Fairlie's fields in her section of the bridge approach.
The narrow strip for the roadside park, behind him as he
waited in the cross-way, was the only thing he could think
of that could have offended Sudley as deeply as Yerby
said he was offended. Having the whole side of his place
bottled up behind a lousy fifty feet, with no access out
to the bridge and its approach, might be what had infuri-
ated him. There was nothing else, certainly.

A sudden flush of adrenalin made the blood tingle at
the back of his neck. He crossed over into the gravelled
road, jerked to a stop at the mail box and got out a letter
to Tip from the county agent and the evening papers.
The sound of a tractor was coming from Miss Fairlie's
field. He drove on around the bend and jammed his
brakes on to keep from hitting a green truck standing
tail-on in the middle of the road. It was Sudley's truck
and his tractor up in the field, with his seventeen-year-old
boy Charlie at the gears. Sudley himself was leaning on
the fence in front of the truck.

He turned as Spig opened his car door and got out.
For an instant his pale blue eyes were not shuttered. The

sudden, naked violence in them was so intense that Spig stopped motionless. It was Sudley who spoke first.

"Good evening, Mr. O'Leary." His eyes were shuttered again, his voice soft as it always was. He turned back to the fence, cupping his hands to his mouth. "Keep your contours smoother, son!" he shouted. "Narrower in the dip!" He dropped his hands to the fence rail. "I like a pretty field. Miss Fairlie's tractor's in the shop, so I thought I'd help her out. Gives the boy extra for that car he wants. His mother wants to give it to him—he's her baby, spoiled rotten. I say he's got to earn it."

Across the field Sprig could see the boy swinging the red tractor in a graceful arc to narrow the dip in the rib of the contour. His face was taut, his full mouth sullen, his dark eyes stormy with resentment as he whipped the tractor back up the field.

"Fine boy you've got, Mr. O'Leary," Sudley said. "Glad I don't raise vegetables—he'd run me out of business. Tells me he's eleven. That's the kind of boy I like to see."

"Tip's okay," Spig said shortly. He tried to keep his voice as even and as affable as Sudley's. "Look. I just saw this sign of yours."

"I figured you'd see it." Sudley interrupted him calmly. "And I figured you wouldn't like it, Mr. O'Leary. I know you and Mr. Ashton got the idea nobody's got a right to sell land—except you and Mr. Ashton."

Watch it, Mac. He's needling you. "Ashton and I aren't selling any land, Mr. Sudley," Spig said quietly. "We're giving the State that little strip along your fence."

"I've heard you say that."

"You wouldn't be calling me a liar, by any chance, would you?"

"You're putting it that way, Mr. O'Leary." Sudley's

eyes met his steadily. " We've got different ways, here
in Devon. You new people here on Eden's Neck—you've
got fine ideas. But you've got jobs in Washington, or
money so you don't need jobs. We find it sort of hard to
tell people in debt with no money they can't sell a mite of
worn-out tobacco land when they're offered a big price
for it. Or tell a widow with five kids she can't sell beer
and soft crab. As long as it's beer and soft crab she's
selling, Mr. O'Leary. We don't much go for double
dealing, here in Devon."

Watch it, O'Leary . . . watch it. " I'm afraid I don't
understand, Mr. Sudley. It isn't because we never gave
you access to the bridge road, is it? Or are you really
opposed to a couple of picnic tables under a beech tree? "

" Did I ever ask you for access to the bridge road,
Mr. O'Leary? " Sudley asked. " And I'm not opposed
to picnic tables under the beeches. I'm opposed to people
who talk about picnic tables on one side of the bridge
to cover up the deal they're making on the other side . . .
with an outfit I wouldn't touch with a fork I used to
spread manure."

" Stan Ashton's the only person who could make any
kind of a deal this side of the bridge," Spig said quietly.
" And he's the one person you could count on not to
make a deal."

" Mr. O'Leary! " There was a sudden flash of anger
in Sudley's eyes. " Do you think any big-time gambling
outfit comes into a small county like this without sounding
out the county commissioners, cutting them in on building
and maintenance contracts, to grease the wheels and keep
the sheriff off their necks? Maybe you and Mr. Stanley
Ashton didn't know that, Mr. O'Leary. Why, that
fellow in the blue silk suit sitting right behind you at the
meeting the other night—what do you think they sent

him down here for? I saw him shaking your hand, congratulating you on a fine speech. Sure, he's all for zoning . . . once his outfit's in. But he'd already talked to us, Mr. O'Leary—about the four acres Mr. Stanley Ashton was selling them, for what they call a ' beach club ' on the Devon."

He got in his truck. Spig O'Leary stood there too stunned to move, his face going from an angry flush to pale to flinty grey-white. The truck moved towards him and stopped. Sudley's voice was charged with passion.

" Maybe you didn't know, Mr. O'Leary. Buck Yerby says you didn't. But I'll tell you this. I hate gambling and everything that goes with it. I love my land and I love this river. All I wanted the Plumtree tract for was to take care of Miss Fairlie and the road and my river. But by God I'll sell every inch of land I've got, I'll drive every one of you people out of this place, before I'll see your cotton-mouth brother-in-law defile it. You tell him. And tell him to keep out of my way. Tell him I'll kill him if he doesn't. Sure as you're born I'll kill him."

The truck moved on. Spig O'Leary stood there blindly, a smoky red haze all around him. " Oh, no. You won't kill him." It seemed to him he was almost shouting it. " You won't have to. I'll do it. The little swine . . . I'll kill him myself, if it's true."

CHAPTER IV

OH NO. *You won't kill him. You won't have to. I'll do it. The little swine . . . I'll kill him myself, if it's true.*

It seemed to Spig O'Leary he must be shouting it, the way his throat was torn. But Sudley didn't seem to hear him. He was going methodically about his business, helping the boy unhitch the disker and load it on to the truck. They were lumbering across the narrow bridge over the drainage run down into Plumtree Cove, going out Miss Fairlie's lane to the old road, when the red haze blinding Spig finally dissolved and he found himself standing there alone.

He got back into his car and drove on to the pineapple-topped gate posts fifty feet along in the woods on the right. There were two signs, one saying " O'Leary ", the other, " Stanley S. Ashton ". He was conscious of a sort of basic numbness in his brain that seemed to transmit itself to everything around him. Superimposed on it was the shameful awareness of his own humiliation, the writhing remains of his self-esteem. O'Leary, the hot shot of the Eden Neck Home Owners' League . . . He could see himself at the commissioners' meeting Thursday night. O'Leary eloquent as all hell, and Sudley and the five other commissioners sitting there, courteously, gravely listening to him sound off on the evils of Devon Death Strip, a menace to our children and a curse to us, quoting the Governor, and the commissioners knowing all about the guy in the blue silk suit sitting right behind him. As Buck Yerby knew . . . and how many others in the crowded room? *They think you're as big a heel as he is a louse* . . . thinking he was putting up a civic front for Stan Ashton to work behind. O'Leary, heel or sucker —which was worse?

He drove in to the fork where the Ashton's fine new road cut off from the O'Learys'. Or the other way around —it made the O'Learys' look like a mud track to an illicit still. A few yards along he put his foot on the brake, looking back at it, a smooth, white ribbon of oyster shell going off through the woods. In November, when the Ashtons were building their house, they used the O'Learys' lane clear in to the dead chestnut tree. This new road wasn't much over a month old. Spig drew his ginger brows together, trying to recall the way Stan had put it.

"It'll give us both a lot more privacy, Spig," he'd said, " if you'll let us have a thirty-foot right-of-way closer to the entrance. I've got the deed drawn up, to save you the trouble and expense. We'll give you back our rights to your lane in to the chestnut. And we'll pay for the clearing and building, and keep it up, of course."

" Big of you, old man." Spig remembered thinking that, amused because old Stan had developed a slightly pompous as well as humourless attitude towards himself and his newly acquired wealth. It explained the business-like efficiency with which he whipped the deed out of his handsome new pigskin briefcase. Or so Spig had thought. Now he wondered. The right to use the O'Learys' lane had been friendly, never put in legal form.

He must have been planning even then . . . O'Leary caught himself sharply, rubbing his hands back over his head, kneading his skull under the short, ginger stubble, trying to think. He didn't know that what Sudley had said was true. People didn't like Stan Ashton very much, but a lot of it was prejudice. Kathy had made a lot of friends.

It was tactless, bringing in a rich, new wife as he'd done it, and Anita's giving most of Kathy's stuff to the church rummage sale hadn't helped. But now he stopped to think, it was obvious that the whole thing was a fantastic error of some kind. In the first place, there was the letter stipulation. Or second place, anyway. First place was Stan Ashton's own name and reputation. That alone would keep him from selling out to the kind of outfit Sudley wouldn't touch with the fork he used to spread manure. Because Stanley S. Ashton's name and reputation meant more to him and anything else he had. The high priest of highway sanctity wasn't going to show any cloven hoof that would kick his own face right off the television panel. Not old Stan . . . not if Spig knew him. And there was still the letter of stipulation in young Judge Twohey's office.

Spig moved uneasily. It was eerie how clearly there for a moment the old judge's voice seemed to come to him, almost as if it were recorded there in the whispering leaves of the oak trees. The old judge was gone now, but Spig could hear him speak again.

It is my duty to tell you that such a stipulation is not legally binding. At most it could be used to show intent.—Gratitude is highly volatile. It seldom withstands the impact of hard cash.— There must never be a threat to Eden in Miss Fairlie's lifetime. I want your solemn word of honour, Mr. O'Leary . . .

"You have it, sir . . ." Spig O'Leary spoke back to him across the years, across the silent bourne, as if he knew some way the old judge could hear him, repeating his solemn word. Strangely, he felt calmer then, able to see the thing much more clearly, the fiery catharsis of his rage burned down to ordinary sanity again. There was no doubt Sudley believed what he was saying. But he was wrong. He didn't know Stan Ashton. The cynic who said that all men were motivated by one of two things—vanity or cupidity—had hit the Stan Ashton nail square on the head, and cupidity was out. Anyone who had seen the fine flowering of Stan Ashton's ego, watered by the life-giving rain of all the publicity he'd got, would know him better than to think he'd do anything to wither it.

"And the poor guy's not a swine," Spig told himself. "Or if he is, he's not a fool. He's not going to commit professional suicide."

He looked at the clock on the dash. It was a quarter to seven, just thirty-five minutes since he'd stopped to talk to Yerby at the blue glass Three D. He started the car and drove on through the woods, past the old chestnut, towards what the O'Learys called the Home Farm, the five cleared acres where the house was, overlooking the Devon River. *I'll go see him. Right after dinner I'll go over.*

He rubbed his face hard to smooth away the outward and visible signs of any inward doubt, and creased his eyes and lips into a reasonable facsimile of the happy grin of the home-coming parent, hearing the kids shouting over in Tip's garden plot as he made the last bend through the woods. He came out into the Home Farm, the grin dying automatically and at once.

The tree-shaded circle behind the house was full of cars. The Camerons' and the Potters' station wagons and the assorted conveyances of the not-so-well-heeled on Eden's Neck . . . the ones Yerby said didn't contribute except to live here and bellyache. And wait until they heard about the sign in Sudley's pasture.

He felt a sharp jolt then in the pit of his stomach. They'd probably heard already, that's why they were here . . . if not about Sudley, about Stan Ashton. Then he saw the foreign, yellow, midget convertible with red leather seats nosed in between the station wagons. It belonged to Arthur Dunning, one of the top-flight artists Anita knew and had down to work and be company for her, be a bit of leaven for the local dough-heads—and a black-bearded pain in the *glutenus maximus* so far as O'Leary was concerned. If it was a home owners' protest meeting, Dunning wouldn't be there. Or would he . . . always turning up where he was least expected. But the kids were shouting, streaking bare-footed in blue jeans across the field to the circle to meet him.

"Daddy! Daddy! I've got a contract, Daddy!"

Tip was yelling it at the top of his lungs. He and a visiting boy were racing ahead, Kitsy, nine now, red pigtails and braces on her teeth, behind them. Behind her was John Eden O'Leary, aged seven, an extravert edition of both Spig and Tip, delayed now because he had to wait for Molly Ashton's chubby four-year-old legs to catch up with him. Mädel, the German shepherd, circled behind her to help her on.

"Daddy!" Tip's freckled face was shining gold, but he pulled himself together with great sobriety. "Dad— this is my friend, Gregory Pappas. This is my father, Greg." He nudged Greg's arm. "Now you say, ' How do you do, Mr. O'Leary?' and shake his hand. We're teaching him not to be so scared of grown-ups, Dad."

Spig put his hand out. "How do you do, Greg?"

"How do you do, Mr. O'Leary?" Greg said shyly. His face was shining too. It was clear olive, finely cut, with brilliant dark eyes under a cap of hair black and glossy as a crow's wing.

"Greg's in my room at school, Dad. He got me my contract, for all my vegetables, Daddy! Every one of 'em!"

"My father's going to buy them," Greg said proudly.

"Every morning I'm going to pick them, and you'll deliver them for me, Daddy? Till I'm old enough to drive?"

"Yes, because it's a long-term contract. Isn't that what my father said, Tip?"

"Yes. You'll deliver them for me . . . won't you, Daddy?" It was only when Tip was bursting with happiness that he said Daddy, not Dad.

"Sure I will," said Sprig. "Glad to. Where——"

"Just down the road," Greg put in. "The Three D. You know, my father's——"

"Hey, wait . . ." But Kitsy was there then. "How's my girl?" Spig caught her up and kissed her, and then came John Eden and Molly A. and he was smothered with small arms and sticky kisses, all sweaty like the little field hands they were, their blue jeans covered with topsoil, streaks of it on their glowing, freckled faces.

Not the Three D. Not after all the stink I've made . . .

The shining pride in all their faces was a stinging barb in his own pride of a baser nature.

"We'll see," he said, as cheerfully as he could. O'Leary would look great knocking on the back door of the Three D with a basket of carrots, O'Leary who was too high-minded to go in the front door.

Tip's face had sobered. "If you don't have time, Dad, Miss Fairlie said she'd lend me the jeep and David could drive me. She says it's a very fine contract. Didn't she, Greg? Mr. Pappas is paying me the retail price, isn't he, Greg?"

"Yes—because they're fresh and Tip's my friend," Greg's face beamed.

"Come on, Tip! We've got to hurry! We're busy, Daddy." John Eden was through with all that stuff.

"And you'd better hurry, too, Daddy," Kirsty said.

" Mother's having a cocktail party. It's Aunt Mag's birthday. Tippy said we could give her some squash if we finish mulching. Didn't you, Tippy? "

They were off then, Mädel the shepherd circling them. Spig O'Leary stood there. He could see O'Leary lugging a bushel basket into the Three D and Buck Yerby standing there, grinning, the big ape. Not O'Leary. Not if he had to buy the whole bloody crop and eat it raw.

Now the kids weren't yelling at him, he could hear the din of cocktail noises coming through the windows from the terrace. They wouldn't be laughing if they'd heard about either Sudley or Ashton. He went into the house through the "hyphen"—the one-room passage connecting the new dining-room and kitchen with the old cottage— put the papers on the table, and went into the kids' downstairs bathroom to wash. It would be better to go in and say hallo to people first—they might see his car and wonder. Then he decided a quick slug would be a good thing to help him face the crowd of cheerful inebriates outside, and went through into the old cottage. It had been two rooms originally. Now it was one, and where they lived mostly, especially in winter with the big, old, whitewashed fireplace glowing green and gold with driftwood from the Cove. The drinking whisky was in the cellarette on the far side, across the pine tap table Miss Fairlie had left with them . . . the table where the blood had been.

You can hardly tell it now unless you know it's there. Blood disappears. It's like everything else. All it takes is time.

" I always keep fresh flowers here, or laurel leaves in the winter," Miss Fairlie said, the day she had the shutters taken down, and the O'Learys had done the same, without asking the reason, nor did she tell them.

There were others who would have gladly, but it was a matter of pride to shut them up. a keeping faith with both Miss Fairlie and the old judge.   Until the day the rector called and they couldn't tell him to shut up he was so sweet and so obviously meant no harm.

"Bless me, there it is . . . how well I recall it. I'd just come to Devonport, my first parish. I knew they were in love, planning to marry as soon as her father was well—he'd strained his heart in the autumn, haying. Poor child. She and her father found him here. It was bitter cold and he'd fallen overboard out at the duck blind. This was the closest place. He wouldn't let his brother Harlan and Judge Twohey's boy Nat come in with him, so they went on across the river, oyster tonging. The fire George made was still burning when I came out with the sheriff and old Dr. John. His clothes were there on a chair drying, and he was wrapped up in a blanket, sitting right there."

He pointed across the bowl of flowers.

"He'd been cleaning his gun, his fingers still numb from the cold. When Celia Fairlie and her father found him, he was lying here on his gun, his great heart blown out, the table a sea of his blood. Never, my dear young friends, believe the terrible calumny some heartless people tried to spread. George Sudley never took his own life. It was a wicked and cruel thing to say."

He shook his silvery head. " It was hours before David, the coloured boy found them. Celia wouldn't leave and her father was too ill to force her. David called us. The sheriff carried her bodily home. You didn't know him— Buck Yerby's father. He was crying. We all loved George Sudley. He and Celia had known each other all their life before they suddenly fell in love. It was like a flame. It was cruel, but God knows best—I must always believe that, even when it's difficult for us to see it. It was very hard. His brother Harlan was eighteen, going away to college. He had to stay home and manage the farm. It changed him, of course. It changed Miss Fairlie . . . But she might have accepted her changed life, as Harlan accepted his and grew with it, if it hadn't been for the terrible tragedy of two months later. But you know that, of course."

"We don't, sir, but we'd rather not," Spig said quietly. "We love Miss Fairlie as she is. We don't want to know anything she doesn't want to talk about."

"That's very wise, and very kind," the old rector answered, not knowing they hadn't known even this much until he told them. "How short is the time of man," he said softly, his eyes resting on the faint, dark stain on the satin surface of the table. "It was terrible, that day. You can hardly tell it now, unless you know it's there."

"All it takes is time, I guess." Spig said, quoting Miss Fairlie the way the rector had unconsciously quoted her himself.

The old man shook his head. "That's not all it takes, my friend," he said quietly. "That is the tragedy of Celia Fairlie. It takes more than time. It takes resignation—which she has never had. It takes pity, and kindness, and there was no one who could give her that, or no one she could accept it from. Except old David. There are stars in the crown that's awaiting him, beautiful stars." He smiled. "And perhaps, in yours," he added. "Or is it your son's? I'm told he is the one who touched Celia Fairlie's heart. She didn't seem quite so remote to me when I saw her last. Perhaps he'll bring her back to us. Who can tell?"

It had been a long time since Spig had thought of

that, as he thought of it now stopping in the door, the nasturtiums in the crystal bowl, there on the shadow where a man's heart had bled, a bowl of fire and gold, alive and glowing in the cool twilight room with its small windows and dim walls of satiny pine.

He started towards the terrace, deciding against a private drink, and stopped as he heard Mag Cameron's husky, downright voice raised a little from the entrance hall just behind the big fireplace.

". . . be a very good painter, Art, but you're the son of a female mongrel hound along with it," she was saying, clearly meaning it. " If you don't like the O'Learys' rum, don't come here. The O'Learys have a liquor budget —with four kids and this place to support they don't have the money for Scotch to pour down your gullet, or ours, either. They're sweet and we all love them . . . and nobody'd miss you if you left right now and stayed a thousand years. And one thing more—you'd better damn' well quit all those psychological passes you're making at Molly O'Leary. They'll get you no place, and they're very apt to get you a lot of bones broken too small to put together again."

" By whom, love? " Art Dunning's voice, amused and mocking, answered hers.

" I could name a dozen. Three ought to be enough. Joe Cameron's one. Hal Potter's another. And then there's Spig. You've heard of him, I expect. He's the big red-headed guy that's married to the girl."

" And hasn't brains enough to see the kind of girl he's married to," Dunning added easily. " He treats her like a plough horse. He hasn't the slightest conception of what she really is. He married her before she was old enough to have any idea of it herself, and kept her producing these brats . . . buried out here, cooking, and cleaning and making beds, without the faintest idea of what life really is."

" And you're planning to show her? "

" I'm not discussing my plans with you, Maggie. And I'd think you'd quit being the earth-mother and worry a little about yourself, sweetie. Or did you know Joe Cameron simply slathers every time he looks at the gal? "

" Joe Cameron and every other male on Eden's Neck," Mag Cameron said calmly. " That's why I'm warning you. It's all open and above board. The idea of termites would offend them horribly."

" Mag, you're divine, you really are. It's you I'm in love with. You must let me paint you." Dunning laughed, the malice crackling underneath. " Such swivets you go into about nothing, honey. Like yesterday at the Potters'. Poor Anita."

" All I told Anita Ashton was to shut up. If she and Stan don't want Stan's child, that's all right. But it's not all right to tell the simple old rector that the poor O'Learys need the money Stan pays for Molly A.'s board and keep—especially when it's a damned lie. Stan doesn't pay them a bean, and never has. Molly A.'s a lucky child—nobody knew how lucky till Anita's own brat came to live here when she got kicked out of that last school of hers. If any sixteen-year-old ever needed the hind end of a hairbrush it's Anita's child, Lucy Bronson. Telling me she's been drinking martinis since she's six years old."

" Five as I recall it. She was very precocious . . ."

" I'm sure of it. But she's not drinking them at my house and not snitching nary another one when my back's turned. Our kids aren't precocious, thank God. They're just ordinary oafs that stay home nights, and that's the way I'd like to keep them. And I don't want to hear any more about Lucy's tricks or Anita's marriages, past or present. Not from you. You're such a malicious little toad you'd knife the only friends you've got without greying a hair of your black, old goat's beard. And where are they, by the way, your friends the Town Planner and his bride? Molly said——"

" Oh, Molly invited them," Dunning said. " But they're busy, packing. To go abroad. Or didn't you know? "

" I didn't," Mag Cameron said. " When? "

" Oh, pretty soon. Old Stan's been invited to lecture in London. They say."

" You mean he hasn't. Come on. I'll listen to this one. I know you're dying to tell it. What's the catch? "

Dunning laughed. " Maggie mine, I wouldn't tell you for all the yellow bees in the ivy bloom. You'll find out. I won't spoil the show. As a matter of fact, Stan is giving one lecture. His publishers arranged it, by request. Anita's.

" You mean they're getting out. Is that it? What for? "

" To avoid the stink, I presume, love. For old Stan, I mean. Anita would adore it. But you don't have to worry. It won't hurt you people way over your side of Eden's Neck."

"It's this side it's going to hurt?" Mag asked sharply. " Spig and Molly? And you think you're in love with Molly? And this is the way you show it? "

" Oh, don't you worry, Maggie. I'll be right here to pick up the pieces. I'm keeping the studio till fall. Or till I finish my gallery of you rural types. That you're going to love, Mag. My New York show. We'll send you a card."

" Look, Art Dunning," Mag Cameron said. " White
things squash. Excuse me now, will you? I'd like a
drink. Some nice, clean, antiseptic rum."

" I'll come with you, honey. That's henna you use,
isn't it? Not meant to deceive. So different from poor
Anita's peroxide. It's very hard to stay twenty-nine
with a sixteen-year-old around and not admit you were
a child delinquent. But don't be alarmed. I'm just
fixing you in my camera mind. You and Miss Crazy
Fairlie—then my gallery's almost complete. There's still
Molly, but . . ."

Spig O'Leary's knuckles were white where he gripped
the hand-hewed chestnut mantel as Dunning's mocking
voice lost itself against the backdrop of laughter from the
terrace. There were white ridges along his jaw and a
cold nausea in the pit of his stomach. It was a good thing
he'd mastered his first impulse to go out and throttle
the bearded little bastard when he started talking about
Molly. Dunning could wait. He dropped his hands and
stood a moment longer then turned and went very quietly
back through the children's hyphen and out the kitchen
door, keeping in front of the native cedars so that neither
the people on the terrace nor the children up in the
garden would see him, until he reached the woods and
made his way along the trail to the Ashton's garden. He
went around it on the grass to the front door.

CHAPTER V

THE NEW, bright blue convertible was standing there in the drive. The door was open but the screen hooked. He raised his hand to press the bell when he heard the phone ringing, and stopped when he heard the maid's voice that did not sound like a maid's voice.

" Baltimore calling Mr. Charles Sudley. Is Mr. Charles Sudley there? Baltimore calling."

He heard her then in an apparent aside, " Who's calling, please? " Then she said, " Lorton's Used Car Sales calling Mr. Charles Sudley."

Spig understood then. It was a country line shared by the Ashtons and the Sudleys. To get the other party on the line you had to dial a code number and hang up for the ring. The O'Learys did that when they called Miss Fairlie.

The maid, still in the character of a long distance operator, said, " Mr. Charles Sudley? " Then she giggled and said, " Okay Charlie," in the character of herself. But the girl had been born and raised on the Sudley place, and anyway it was no business of Spig's. He put his hand up to press the bell, and stopped again at the sudden urgency in her voice.

" Listen quick, Charlie. She had to go to Washington with her mother. She said to tell you the same time, same place. And lookie, Charlie—you kids got to be careful, hear? You know what your father'll say if he catches you. It'll be me that . . ."

Spig moved back and scraped his feet on the flagstones,

reached out and pressed the bell. The girl's voice changed instantly. " Yes, ma'am, I'll tell Mr. Ashton you called. She expects to be home around nine o'clock. Good-bye, ma'am."

She came to the door, a very neat, competent, serenely composed, coloured girl. " Oh, Mr. O'Leary. I hope I didn't keep you waiting."

" I heard you talking to Charlie Sudley, if that's what you mean."

The girl swallowed, the bloom on her glossy cheek bleaching a dull liverish grey.

" It's okay with me," Spig said. " It's Charlie and Lucy's business, not mine. You'd keep out of it yourself, if you were smart."

" It's Mr. Sudley—he'd be blood-mad. But Lucy's just crazy after Charlie, Mr. O'Leary. He's got a right to have a little fun. You won't tell his father, will you ? "

" I said it was no business of mine. It's Mr. Ashton I want to see."

The colour seeped back into her eyes and skin. " I'm sorry, sir. He's busy writing. He's not seeing anybody else, to-day."

" He's seeing me."

She hesitated, glancing sideways down the hall to the living-room.

" All right." She unhooked the screen. " But don't say it was me let you in, will you ? I don't want any trouble from him, either. The long distance wasn't my idea. It was Lucy's. That's——"

" You'd be in trouble just the same."

" That's what I keep trying to tell them." She pushed the door open. " Mr. Ashton's back there in the living-room." Her eyes met his directly. " He's not busy. He's not writing."

Spig went deliberately down the jade-green carpeted hall.

And he's not seeing anybody else to-day—or next week. Not when I get through with him. Stan Ashton's treachery was beyond any further doubt. He wasn't going to kill him . . . half-way through the woods a sudden return of sanity showed how senseless that would be. But Ashton was going to stay here. He wasn't going sneaking off to Europe to avoid the stink of his own making. It was the first time in Spig O'Leary's life he'd come in cold blood to beat the living hell out of any man, least of all a man he'd called his friend and brother.

The double doors in front of him opened on to a small landing. He put his hand out, turned the heavy, brass knob, pushed one wing of the door open, stepped in, pushed it shut behind him, moved forward to the three broad steps going down into the panelled room spread out handsomely, and stopped.

Mr. Ashton was there. He was not busy. He was not writing. He was not seeing anybody else that day. Or if he was, he was seeing them in triplicate, with wavering and densely foggy edges. Mr. Ashton was drunk as a skunk.

He was sprawled out in a deep chintz chair in front of the marble fireplace, his feet up on a Chinese mirrored coffee table. On another table by the arm of his chair was an almost empty whisky bottle, a tipped-up glass beside it. A yellow rubber ice tub was knocked over on the floor, quietly adding to the pool of liquid spreading out into the jade-green carpet. It was the first time Spig had seen him near a whisky bottle. One martini was the most he ever took, or one bottle of beer, leaving half of it.

Spig came down the steps and across the room. Liquor

was slopped all over the front of the yellow, raw silk sports jacket and the yellow tie Ashton had yanked to one side to loosen the collar of his moss-green shirt. His face was flaccid, mottled a sickly grey, saliva oozing out of his weak mouth under the small, delicate moustache he'd recently grown. The whole face that had once seemed so boyish and clean-cut was the sodden portrait of a weakling, mask off, naked to the pitiless impassivity that observed him.

A stertorous snore punctuated his spasmodic breathing, and Spig bent over quickly and picked up the arm dangling limply, his fingers searching for the pulse. There was a book sprawled open, face down, on the floor where Ashton had dropped it. On the glossy red and white jacket cover the title was brave and blue. *Town Planning: An Ethical Approach to an American Problem.* It was Stan's new book, just out. On the glossy white of the jacket back was a picture of the author. Spig already knew what it said in the fine print below it.

"No abstruse visionary is author S. Seton Ashton. Known to his friends as 'Stan,' he has taken an active and effective part in preserving the natural beauty of the highway in his own lovely County Devon bordering the Chesapeake. Town Planner Ashton is shown here on his own estate, instructing the neighbouring farm children in the difficult art of netting soft crabs from the Devon River."

Except that one of the children was his own and the other two were Tip and Kitsy, the last statement was essentially correct—except that it was Tip and Kitsy who were instructing the Town Planner in an art he alone was finding difficult. If you called the six acres he had left an estate. But Stan Ashton at least looked a whole lot better in the picture than he did right now.

His wrist was clammy cold under Spig's fingertips. His eyes opened slowly, in a glazed stare, and he gave a sudden lurch, kicking one leg off the coffee table, knocking a jade cigarette box shattering on to the hearth. He shook his head, blinking, trying to focus.

" Spig . . . tha' you, Spig? " he mumbled. He began to sob. " Fin' her, Spig. Fin' Kathy. She's awrigh'. Kathy's awrigh' isn' she, Spig? " The tears were pouring down his mottled cheeks.

" She's dead. Kathy's dead."

Spig's voice was harsh. The brutal impulse to kick him was almost too strong to resist. *The swine. The rotten, little swine.*

" I wan' Kathy. Nobody cares . . . nobody unnerstan's. I won' do it, Spig. I won'. I'm too fine. I'm too 'mportan'. I won'. They can' make me, Spig! I won' do it! "

He waved his hands, fighting off an unseen enemy. " Keep away from me! Kathy! Kathy! "

Spig started. The door had opened, almost as if Kathy had heard and come. Spig turned. Joe Cameron was on the steps, his big, red face showing mild surprise but nothing more.

" What gives? "

" He's drunk."

Cameron came down the steps. Ashton lurched to his feet, swayed a moment and pitched forward, smashing the mirrored table into shivering rainbows as he crashed on down to the floor, out cold.

Cameron crossed the room. " What were you going to do? Kill him? " he asked dispassionately.

" Not quite."

" Good thing he was drunk. We saw your car. Mag

figured you might have heard Dunning. What's the deal? "

" He's selling this place to a gambling outfit. Sudley told me. He thought I was in on it. He's got a sign up to-night next to the Three D. Six hundred acres for sale. For industrial development. Two thousand feet on the river."

Cameron was silent for a long moment. " I saw him in the bank Friday . . . knew he was sore about something out here. If Stan doesn't sell, will Sudley change his mind? He's a fanatic about gambling."

" I don't know. But Stan's not going to sell. Not to a gambling outfit. Not if——"

" All right, take it easy."

Cameron stood looking around the room until his eyes came to rest on a portrait of Stanley S. Ashton, over the marble mantelpiece. Old Stan was sitting in the foreground at one side of the wide canvas, his book in his hand. It was curiously thin and spidery—like his hands but not like them. The background was a slum street in long perspective, painted in minute, painstaking, brilliant detail. It was not a drab slum but gaily, gaudily alive, flaunting its colourful lack of virtue and orderliness, revelling lustily in it. Ashton looked like a bloodless self-satisfied prig set to destroy it. Two half-naked sailors were lolling in the doorway of one of the shops. On the window was stencilled: " Tattoo Artist—Arthur A. Dunning."

" If that was me, I'd hang it in the attic," Joe Cameron remarked. " Facing the rafters." He turned away. " You'd think Stan could see Dunning's crucified him. I'd kill him, if he did it to me. Ever see him over in a corner grinning when Ashton stands under it when people are here? "

He looked down at old Stan. " What do we do with him? "

" Leave him lay."

Cameron's eyes moved to the book face down on the floor.

" No," he said. " Let's take an Ethical Approach to an American Problem. You take the Town Planner's feet. I'll take this end. His room's through there. We'll dump the little bastard, and you go home. I'll stick around till the maid sees he's alive. If he wakes up and hits the bottle again, he might not be."

" You better get a doctor, then. I want him alive, not dead."

" Good idea. Hang on to it."

They carried him through the door by the fireplace, across the hall into his bedroom, and laid him on the ice-blue, satin cover.

" I was afraid of this when Anita came, but I thought she'd got used to it down here," Cameron said. " Or something. Come around to the office to-morrow. I'll get my lawyer in. See what we can do."

Spig shook his head. " I'm taking a week off. To stick around. I should have done it a lot sooner."

" Okay. Remember this—he didn't get stone blind for nothing. It sort of backs up an idea Mag's got. She doesn't think it's him, or Anita either. She thinks Dunning's the snake in the Gardens of Eden. She's pretty good at calling the shots on people. Except little Lucy— she's dead wrong about her. But you go on. And watch it, boy. He's not worth hanging for."

" You're right."

" And Spig . . ." Cameron stopped him as he started through the door. " I wouldn't get up a tree about anything else Dunning may have said."

" I'm not going to," Spig said shortly.

" You got enough trouble, without making up any extra in your own head. Get yourself a stiff drink, why don't you? "

Spig stood on the terrace for a moment, breathing in the decent air. Two hundred yards off, beyond the chestnut oaks, the bridge rose, delicate and lovely in in the glow of the setting sun. The corner of his mouth moved as he recalled a line from the book face down in there on the floor. " Man's mind creates beauty from concrete and steel: man's cupidity, crouching in the jungle of ignorance, waits only to leap and destroy it." Man, reading his own prophetic words, well might weep and reach for the bottle. Whoever was pushing Ashton, cupidity was in there greasing the skids. Spig was wrong. He'd been counting on vanity as Ashton's compelling force. It had run a bad second if all it could do was get polluted and weep for itself. But the fact that it could still weep meant it wasn't entirely dead.

It was a frail hope, but the only one Spig O'Leary could see, as he quickened his pace abruptly half-way along the trail. He must have heard the dog barking before he was consciously aware of it. A silent dog who never spoke without meaning, she was barking now, her sharp danger bark, and Spig, running, cutting swiftly off the trail towards the field, saw her before he saw Tip, out in front between him and something that was over in the O'Leary's corn, the other side of Tip's garden. She was barking savagely, hackles up. He saw Tip then, and Greg Pappas, hurling clods of dried clay at the thing in the corn. Tip was shouting angrily—Tip who was never angry. Spig cleared the woods out into the field. The clods were flying. Then he heard what Tip was shouting.

" Keep out! Keep out of my garden! I hate you! I'll kill you if you come in here! You keep away from my mother! I'll kill you if you don't! "

For a blank, incredulous moment Spig O'Leary stopped dead in his tracks. Across the end of the corn was a black-bearded face and a blue denim jacket. It was Arthur Dunning, ducking through the corn to the raspberry bushes to get out of the barrage Tip and Greg were sending after him. It was so fantastic that Spig's feet were paralysed, until he saw a clod hit and shatter.

" Tip! *Tip!* For God's sake, what do you think you're doing? "

He sprang forward across the field.

" Daddy! Make him keep out of my garden! I'll kill him if he doesn't! "

He hurled another clod before Spig could reach him. Tears of rage were furrowing muddy lanes down his face, flushed and swollen as he swung round to his father, a sturdy little figure facing him, confident of support, the tears nothing but the impotent outrage of a small boy defending his rights. It stopped Spig's hand. This was a Tip he didn't know existed. It called for wisdom, not anger.

" All right. Put that down now," he said quietly.

" I won't! I won't! Not till he gets out of here! I hate him! "

Spig saw his hand tighten on the clod. Dunning was standing erect now behind the raspberries, smiling, lighting himself a cigarette.

" Move along, will you, Dunning? " Spig called. " Sorry. I'll be over in just a second."

" Right," Dunning said. " So sorry . . . I didn't mean to upset the Lord Proprietor."

Before Spig could catch his arm Tip let fly again. The

clod caught Dunning between the shoulders. He jumped and turned, smiling as before.

" Quite all right, O'Leary. The Artist has been stoned throughout the Ages."

"Just beat it, will you?" Spig was getting sore himself. "All right now, old fellow." He put his hand firmly on his son's trembling shoulder. " Let's take it easy. You know better than this. What's the trouble? What's he done? "

" He won't tell, Mr. O'Leary." Greg Pappas had retired, a little pale, on Spig's arrival, but he came forward now. " He won't even tell Kitsy."

" I won't tell anybody. I hate him! He's got to keep away from my garden . . . and he's got to keep away from my mother! I'll kill him! I'll——"

" That's enough, Tip." Spig took a cigarette out of his pocket. " We'll let it go for now," he said quietly. " Put your tools away and let's go for a swim and cool off. You go in. I'll be with you in a second. Scoot, both of you."

He moved off, lighting the cigarette, not sure he was going to be obeyed. He wouldn't have believed this if he hadn't seen it. Tip, who never raised his voice, never lost his temper, made him and Molly ashamed when they lost theirs—he'd been an enigma to Spig ever since he'd come back home. He was always reasonable, like the time Molly A. pulled up two whole rows of young carrots that took longer than anything else to grow. " She thought she was weeding, Dad. Just trying to help." At times, he'd almost broken Spig's impatient heart with his child's stoicism in the face of his child's disasters. Now he was an enigma on a totally different level.

He glanced back. The two boys had gathered their scuffle hoes and were racing each other and Mädel down to the house. There were still clods, in a pile at the end of the row. It wasn't a spur of the moment defence—that was clearly indicated by the stockpile of strategic materials.

He crossed the grass through the line of cedars into the drive. Dunning was pulling out, grinning, his vivid, black eyes bright with mischief.

" Good-bye . . . good-bye! " He waved his beret. " Good-bye, you happy savages! Maybe you're not as happy as you think. Good-bye! Give my love to Molly-O! "

He streaked off, bouncing over the uneven drive.

Spig watched the swirl of dust settle as the yellow car disappeared into the woods, his grey eyes flat and hard as flint.

Why don't you take a week off and stick around, O'Leary?

He turned and went into the house. Molly was in the kitchen. His heart gave a sudden lurch as he saw her, still the Sea King's daughter, slender, crystalline cave-cool still, the golden flecks in her eyes warm with laughter. She was his, and he knew what he had whether he had any brains or not. Dunning had better watch himself. The rest of them didn't matter.—As long as she wasn't in love with any of them.

" Hi, darling. The boys'll be ready in just a second, so hurry, won't you? " She shook her head quickly at him, the family signal to skip it now, discuss it later, as she gave Kitsy and John Eden, there in their bathing trunks, a small shove over to the door and out. " I've got a casserole. The kids ate early."

" Won't be a minute."

" We'll wait on the pier, Daddy." Tip and Greg came galloping down the stairs. " Where's Kits? Where's Molly A.? "

They dashed out. The laughter faded from Molly's

eyes. *He's angry about the vegetable contract . . . angry at Tip about the business up in the garden. I wish Art Dunning would go away from here.*

She brushed her red-gold hair back from her forehead, straightened her shoulders and went through the entrance hyphen to get the rest of the glasses from the terrace. She stopped, hearing Spig upstairs. He was talking on the telephone. She couldn't hear what he was saying, but the muted sound of his voice disturbed her again. Then the children began to yell. " Hurry up, Daddy! Hurry! "

A moment later he came down in his trunks, long and lean, the muscles rippling over his sun-browned body. He stopped to kiss her and hold her tight a moment.

" Don't let them stay in long, they're bushed," she said quickly.

Spig nodded. " You put 'em to bed, will you? Leave my supper in the oven. I've got to run in town a minute."

" Spig . . ." She caught his arm. " Not about Tip's contract . . . I knew you'd hate it. But he's so proud, and so is Greg. We can't hurt Greg's pride in his own father. It'd be cruel, Spig."

" Hurry up, Daddy! " It was John Eden shouting. " Hurry up! "

" We'll talk about it. I'm not delivering any vegetables to the Three D."

" Then I'll do it. Mr. Pappas called and asked me if it was all right. You're just a snob, that's all! "

" Look here. I——"

" Daddy! Come on, Daddy! "

" Go on. I'll put them to bed. But you're not going to see Mr. Pappas. Promise me that. I really mean it. I really do."

She moved sharply away from him. " He's coming! "

she called down to the raft, laughing. " First one to the raft's a waterbaby! " It was the signal for them all to dive, and Spig had to dash down.

" Easy, Molly A." The dog was swimming in circles around them.

" Last one's the waterbaby," John Eden shouted, because Molly A. was always last. They tumbled on to the balsa raft and waited for Molly A. to pull her aboard.

" Easy back, and then to bed," said Spig. " Your mother's S.O.P. I've got to go in town."

" My father never swims with us," Greg said, and Spig started at the wistful note in his voice. " He isn't ever home, except early in the morning. He's closed on Wednesday, but he has to go to Baltimore to market to get his meat and things. He can't hire anybody, because there's four of us to go to college. But he's a good swimmer. He learned in Greece. He says the water's bluer there. Blue like the glass at our new place."

A small school of alewives broke water, the soft slap of their silvery bodies very clear on the gently swaying raft.

" What time does your father want the vegetables, Greg? " Spig O'Leary asked.

He drove along between Sudley's white-painted fences on his way back into town. The Three D was lighted now, a sapphire pool down at the end of the pasture on the other side of the road. *Blue like the glass at our new place* . . . Nick Pappas's nostalgic memory of the wine-dark sea. Then the neon lights hit him. Your Last Chance to Dine, Drink and Dance. The last words in bubbling bright red, doing a blatant minuet, dancing on one at a time, all off and all on, then back to a single one again.

" Nuts," O'Leary said to himself. " It's still a lousy joint." That was the trouble with people, thinking with their hearts, not with their heads. He had nothing against Nick Pappas, or the widow with five kids selling beer and soft crab. But he had plenty against making the road a shambles. A menace to your children, a curse to you. But for the first time, he could see there might be a two-way pull for a guy like Sudley . . . none for a louse like Ashton. Sudley believed in what he did; Ashton knew he was a swine. That's why he got himself blind drunk. And the thing to do was catch him first thing in the morning when he'd sobered up and show him the letter of stipulation, before Anita or Dunning had a chance to work on him. He couldn't deny his own signature.

He glanced at the clock on the dash as he turned off the by-pass into town. The young judge, as they called Nathan Twohey the old judge's son, had said he'd meet him at the office at half-past nine. He turned into the courthouse square, not dingy now, the cupola shiny gold in the new street lights, a serpentine brick wall around the sodded yard with herringbone brick paths and green-painted wooden benches under the sycamores. You still went under the small rounding arch to go up to the judge's office, but the walls were painted and the steps new.

There was a light behind the door where the old judge's name still stood in its honoured place. Under it was: " Nathan Twohey II—Private." At the back end of the hall another door now led into a reception room. Spig knocked on the door that said " Private " and opened it. There were two changes, inside. The man behind the desk in the corner would never be the man his father was, they said in Devon. The mould was lost. But there was a shadow of his father in the lively eyes he

E

fixed on Spig O'Leary as he came in. The other change was the dog-eared file boxes covering the walls. They were gone; in their place, a bank of grey steel cabinets under the shelves still filled with the old judge's law books. One of the file drawers was pulled out and had an empty space that had held the file Spig saw now on the desk.

" You've come about this Ashton business, I suppose."

Nathan Twohey was in his middle fifties, his dark hair beginning to frost. He was the judge's boy, son of his first wife, who had been with George and Harlan Sudley at the duck blind that winter morning when George Sudley went overboard and rowed back to the Fairlie cottage to make a fire, dry his clothes and clean his gun.

"Everybody seems to have known it but me," Spig said evenly.

" I advised Harlan Sudley to talk to you. He was so convinced you already knew that I wasn't able to interfere. He called me this evening to tell me he'd changed his mind. I was just calling you when you called me."

He got up and went over to the corner cupboard where his father had kept the bottle of rye and his black straw hat. He opened it. There was a safe now behind the wooden doors. He took out a letter, and came back to the desk.

" This is for you," he said. " My father wrote it last Christmas, just before he left us . . . to be delivered to you in precisely this eventuality. He never trusted Stanley Ashton, not after Kathy was gone."

Spig took the letter. It was a blue envelope, " Mr. O'Leary " written on it, " Personal and Private " across one corner, with a pen that spluttered, in a hand that was old, a heartbeat pulsing in the uneven strokes. There were red wax seals on the flap.

Spig looked at it and started to unseal it. Then he stopped and put it in his pocket.

" It's the letter of stipulation I've come about," he said. " The one Ashton signed after Kathy's death."

" That's what I was going to call you about," Judge Twohey said quietly. " I don't have it, Spig."

" What do you mean, you don't have it? "

Judge Twohey shook his head. " Ashton came in a month ago. I was in court—as he knew, we'd spoken on my way over. He asked my secretary for the Plumtree Cove file, to check his deed. She gave it to him. When Sudley told me about the agent down here last week, I looked for the letter of stipulation at once. It was gone."

" But the one Kathy signed. You've still got that."

" I'm sorry Spig. It's gone, too," Judge Twohey said.

CHAPTER VI

" HE TOOK BOTH letters, Spig," Nathan Twohey said. " A month ago. Maybe longer. But the letter itself isn't essential. If we choose to regard it as in the nature of a contract between you and him for the protection of your property, we have evidence that it does, or did, in fact exist."

" It's the fact he took it that's essential," Spig O'Leary said dispassionately. " If he knew he was going to sell a month ago, he knew it when he got us to deed him the right-of-way for his fancy road through our woods."

" We may be able to show fraud in that case. What else we can do . . ." Nat Twohey opened a faded blue file packet. "These are some notes my father made when you bought Plumtree Cove. He refers to Real Estate Company *vs.* Serio, 156 Md. 229. Our Court of Appeals quoted Murray *vs.* Greene, 64 Cal. 367. ' It is difficult to conceive of a condition more clearly repugnant to the interest created by the grant of an estate in fee simple than the condition that the grantee shall not alienate the same without consent of the grantor. With such a condition, if valid, annexed to the grant, it would be neither a fee simple nor any other estate known to law.' Our Court held that the existence of such a discretionary control would be plainly incompatible with the freedom of alienation which is one of the most characteristic incidents of a fee simple title. He's got a couple of pages of precedents here, but that's the gist of it."

He riffled through the notes before he put them down.

" He must have been convinced any restriction on resale would be held void and unenforceable or he'd have incorporated it in your deed, whatever Miss Fairlie's instructions. His . . . extra-legal methods may have been open to occasional criticism, but never his law."

His eyes rested on Spig's pocket.

" There are times when he tended to be somewhat . . . unorthodox. I'd advise discretion in following any . . . suggestions he may have left you. Considering the circumstances in which they were written."

" Which were what? "

" You remember when he sent for you? "

Spig nodded. It was last Christmas Eve, three days before the old judge died.

" I woke up about two. His light was on. He was at his desk, writing. He told me to go back to bed, and next morning he gave me that to seal and bring down here, to give to you at the first sign of trouble at Eden's Landing. My stepmother was at church at the time."

He gave Spig a wintry smile.

" I asked him if he expected trouble. He said he hardly expected anything else. Ashton had showed a highly developed sense of financial self-preservation and Anita was too obvious a realist to stay in Devon with Molly O'Leary next door to her. Then he said perhaps I hadn't noticed Molly was a damned attractive young woman. He couldn't conceive of either Stan or Anita Ashton putting sentiment above cold cash, and he'd never in any event known a situation in which a second wife had any sentiment not adverse to her husband's ex-in-laws."

" He wasn't too wrong, I guess. And vice versa."

Nat Twohey shifted with some embarrassment. " He

said that, too. But it was Miss Fairlie he was concerned about. He talked about her, or tried to, but it was difficult with my stepmother in and out."

He shifted again, hesitating. " It's a little painful to say this," he went on unhappily. " But my father . . . well, I think his whole inner life was dedicated to Miss Fairlie. That was why he could be so extraordinarily objective with all the rest of us. My own mother died when I was six. I don't remember her, or anything except that the house was always dark and cold until Celia Fairlie started coming and taking me out to Eden, to ride on an old pony of hers. All of a sudden everything was warm and gay, for a long time. Until George Sudley . . ."

He stopped again for an instant.

" With George Sudley dead, I hoped . . . But it didn't work that way, of course." He straightened forward in his chair. " That's neither here nor there. What I'm trying to say is, I'm in a difficult position to advise you. You are the only person who can take legal action in this matter. Whether I'd be advising you to take it in your own interest, or in my interest in trying to protect Eden and Miss Fairlie . . ."

" That's my interest, too," Spig said quietly.

" I know. But I'd be highly culpable if I let you get involved in an expensive lawsuit with an outlook as bleak as this is. I only wish my father had left Miss Fairlie to somebody else. I'm not really capable . . ."

He broke off abruptly. " However, there's no use trying to decide anything to-night. You're angry and I've had a . . . a difficult day. That's a bad combination where litigation is to be decided on." He pushed his chair back. " We'll sleep on it and discuss it to-morrow. If my father were only . . ."

His hand moved in a futile gesture. " I don't know how long I'm going to keep on saying that. I say it a dozen times a day. Molly—what does she think about it?

" I haven't told her yet."

" And Miss Fairlie? Have you see her? "

" I'll see her when I've seen Ashton."

Twohey put the Plumtree Cove file back in the drawer and pushed it shut. " I should have gone to her at once. But I frankly didn't have the courage," he said, taking his hat from behind the door. " Of course, I'm a very pedestrian person. Pedestrian means are all I have. I can only hope you and Sudley will be a little more careful. I understand you're both threatening mayhem. If anybody happened to be listening in on the tirade he gave me to-night, it's probably all over town by now. And after all, my father warned each of you, over and over again—you, Harland and Miss Fairlie. You've nobody but yourselves to blame. I'll do my best, of course, but I trust all of you'll remember that."

He switched out his lights. Spig followed him down-stairs to his car, and stood watching his tail lights disappear round the corner.

Nobody but yourselves to blame. It was a truth that only Nat Twohey was likely to find comfort in, a sort of blanket absolution the old judge had left him. What he'd left to O'Leary remained to be seen. Spig took the letter out of his pocket and moved over under the street light to break the seals. He had an idea that it had been a considerable relief for Nat Twohey to get it out of his possession—the pedestrian somebody had handed a time bomb on his morning walk. He broke one seal and stopped as a car coming from the other end of the square slowed down and pulled up. A woman leaned across the

seat and looked up at the office windows. Spig slipped
the letter out of sight into his pocket. There was too much
light for him to slip out of sight himself.

"Oh, Mr. O'Leary!"

The old judge's second wife might have only the
normal dentitional complement, but she still had a lot
of teeth when she smiled.

"My son's gone, I see. But it's all right. I was just
checking."

"Why?" O'Leary inquired. "Curfew rung?"

"I'm afraid you don't realise that Nat's not a well
man, Mr. O'Leary," she said cheerfully. A capable and
efficient woman, she hadn't aged a day in the seven years
Spig had avoided her whenever possible. If she was any
older than the man she called her son, she was too
indestructible to show it.

"He's not going to spend every night of his life down
here the way his father did, killing himself with worry
about that mad woman out at Eden. And you don't look
any too well yourself, young man. If you'll take my
advice, you'll eat more liver."

She shifted into gear and put her foot on the gas.

"And I'd be very careful about threatening to kill
people, Mr. O'Leary," she said briskly. "The judge
would never have condoned murder, I can assure you of
that. Not even for the sake of old Miss Celia Fairlie.
If you get some sleep, you'll feel better in the morning.
Always try to look on the brighter side of things, Mr.
O'Leary."

She was gone then, and Spig moved along to his car.
If the projected mayhem wasn't all over town by now,
it was off to a nice start, and it wasn't the telephone
operator who'd done the listening in on Sudley's tirade.
He caught a glimpse of himself in the side-view mirror.

If liver wasn't necessarily indicated, a good stiff drink and something to fill the void left by the hamburger he'd had for lunch clearly was. The letter could wait. Nathan Twohey II might be worried about its orthodoxy. For O'Leary the mere physical fact of its presence there in his pocket was in a sense a reprieve. He felt better than he had for several hours.

He drove out of town on to the highway, relatively quiet at ten-twenty Monday night, closing day for most of the taverns and eating spots. Except for the Three D. His Last Chance. It said so in red neon all over the place. He put his foot on the brake and pulled in—his second stop there that evening and the only two he'd ever made. He grinned as he got out. If he was going to be delivering vegetables there till Tip was old enough to drive, he might as well start now. Sudley's sign was over in the corner of the field, the red neon making purple waves over the basic sapphire reflected from the blue glass octagon of the Three D. He read it again, without emotion. Maybe it was the sense of reprieve in the old judge's letter, like an amulet in his pocket; or maybe he'd simply reached a point of anæthesia, too saturated to feel anything else that night.

He crossed the gravel, even Stan Ashton a sort of hiatus in his mind—until he saw the yellow midget sports car with red leather seats, edged unobtrusively along one of the Three D's octagonal sides, below the line of the blue glass, so the light didn't hit it. The absence of any other cars there gave it a furtive air, as if Dunning were afraid to be seen there, afraid to offend the Town Planner by catching a quick one out of bounds But it was like a match dropped on a pile of dead pine needles. O'Leary's grey eyes flattened, his pulse racing. He took an abrupt step towards the door, a red neon flashing on in the

saner part of his mind telling him to get back in his
car and get the hell on home, that basically it wasn't
Dunning, it was simply O'Leary spoiling for a fight. He
pushed the door open and stepped inside.

". . . get out! Keep out of my place! "

Except that it was a man's voice and the accent
foreign, the words, the pitch and the intensity behind
them were such a galvanic repetition of Tip O'Leary
with a clod in his hand that Spig came to a halt, his face
lighted with an instant glow of happy malignance.
He relaxed, grinning, closed the door quietly behind
him, and looked around.

The section he was in was the bar. It was shaped like
a wedge of bright blueberry pie, the bar counter V-shaped,
the blue mirror-glass shelves behind it forming the
partitions dividing it from the dine and dance areas
through arches at either side. There were blue leather
stools at the counter, blue leather banquettes around the
outside wall at each side of the door, slot machines
flanking them. Except for himself the bar was empty.
Nick's voice was coming through the arch at the left with
a small, red neon sign, " Dance," above it.

" This is my place. It's a nice place. You keep out! "
In the heat of the moment nobody seemed to have heard
the bell ring as O'Leary closed the door. " I tell you!
I tell you again! You keep out! "

" I won't keep out and you can't make me. You just
try and you'll see what happens! "

Spig O'Leary's jaw dropped. The hand he was reaching with pleased nonchalance into his pocket to get a
cigarette dropped, too.

" When you get a sign that says: ' No Minors Allowed,'
then you can stop me, but not till you do! If I want to
come in here, I'll come. And try to stop me! I'll make

so much trouble for you you'll wish you hadn't! I'll say you sold me liquor!"

"That's a lie. I never sold you——"

"Who'd believe you? It's me they'd believe. I wouldn't tell my mother—I'd tell Mr. Cameron and Mr. O'Leary . . . they'd love an excuse to close you down."

There was a subdued toot of a horn outside and quick laughter from the girl in the dance room.

"I was just waiting for Charlie, anyway. We're not staying. Who'd stay in this gooney hole if they didn't have to? And you dare tell Mrs. Sudley and we *will* make trouble. 'Bye now."

Spig heard the gaily skipping feet and a door swish open and swish shut again. He went over to one of the banquettes and tilted the blue venetian blind to look outside. Anita Ashton's golden-haired child, Lucy, was in Dunning's sports car, Charlie Sudley at the wheel. It was only the tail-end of the kiss she gave him that Spig saw. But it was enough. The movies could have been the textbook, but there'd been laboratory work on the side.

"Bless me," O'Leary said, the years like great black oxen goading him suddenly from behind. "Well, well."

Dunning's car zipped around the gas pumps and into the road, across the parkway to the other lane. There was something in the way Charlie Sudley drove the yellow midget that made it obvious where his emotions lay. If his date had been on foot, Charlie would have been home in bed.

Spig let the blue slat of the blind fall back into place and turned. Nick Pappas was coming through the archway. He was a short, stocky man in shirtsleeves, with a bar apron tied around his waist. The sweat stood in pinkish-purple beads where the light from the neon

" Dance " sign caught the indoor pallor of his bald head above the rim of greying black hair. He saw O'Leary; and stopped in mid-step. He had looked unhappy before; he looked hopeless now.

" You come after Lucy, Mr. O'Leary? " he asked simply.

" No. I came after a drink and a steak, if I can get it," Spig said.

" Okay." Nick wiped his forehead with his shirtsleeve and went behind the bar.

" Bourbon and water." Spig came over and got on one of the blue leather stools.

" You want I should come after my Greg when I close up? "

" Why should you? He's okay. And I want to thank you for Tip's contract, Mr. Pappas. It's swell. You really set him up."

Nick blinked and rubbed his nose with the back of his hand. Then he wiped his eyes. " It's these kids," he said. " They make the trouble. All the time trouble for everybody."

" I heard what Lucy said. I wouldn't worry if I were——"

" You wouldn't worry? " Nick's hand and voice both shook. " You wouldn't worry? You don't know. They get down on you and you got trouble. My oldest boy— I say he can't run with 'em. He says, ' Dad, I don't run with 'em and you got rocks through your blue glass.' He says, ' Relax, Dad, this is America.' All the time tellin' me this is America. In America you don't push the kids around. No. It's the kids push you around."

His voice rose excitedly. " Plenty places round here got back rooms. Not me. I won't have no back room. And Mrs. Sudley, she comes in. She says I let her Charlie boy in here and she sees the commissioners don't give me no liquor licence and nobody leases me a slot machine. And I say, ' Charlie, you keep out,' and Charlie says, ' Nuts.' You tell their parents and they say, ' You're a liar, Nick.' That little Lucy . . ."

The headlights of a car poked blue lines of light through the slats of the venetian blinds. Nick broke off, wiping his forehead with the sleeve of his shirt again.

" I get your steak. How you want it? "

" Medium."

" Okay. I fix you a table in here and a nice Greek salad, special. Okay? No business Monday night, don't make enough to pay the cook."

He gave Spig's order through the speak-box behind him.

The door opened and a man in a turquoise and orange silk shirt, tail out over green slacks, came over to the bar. " Change for twenty, Mac. Dimes. Rye and water."

" Sucker bait," the woman with him said. She wore blue shorts and a bra top. " Give me a pink gin." She sat there on the stool, staring moodily into her glass, listening to the empty clatter of the lemons and an occasional cherry chink of the proceeds of a cherry or two falling into the pan. " Sucker bait," she said again. She opened her canvas beach bag. " Ten," she said. " Half-dollars. Waste your goddam strength on dimes."

She was back for her fourth gin and fourth ten when Spig's steak and salad came. When he'd finished she'd dropped thirty more and was eating a hamburger, morosely ruminant, watching the man work doggedly through his third twenty at the dime machine.

" Good night, Mr. O'Leary." Nick came to the door with him. The music of the iron maidens had cheered him if not his customers. " Don't say nothing, will you?

I just got all excited. You know how it is, Mr. O'Leary."

"Sure," Spig said. "I know." He went on outside.

A car was parked alongside of his, a man saying, ". . . don't need another drink, honey. And you've lost all your money . . ."

"Nick'll cash me a cheque. I've got a right to have a little fun, haven't I? It's my money, isn't it? I make it, don't I? You go on home if you don't like it."

The girl slammed the car door and ran across the gravel. Spig, stopping to light a cigarette, heard the man's door bang shut and his feet scrunching after her. He glanced up as he heard a heavier, slower step approaching him from the side. It was Harlan Sudley, coming from his field. Sudley saw him and stopped, obviously embarrassed, his face plethoric in the blue and purple light.

"You been in the Three D, Mr. O'Leary?"

His voice was soft but he had to clear his throat before he spoke.

Spig nodded.

"Was—was my boy Charlie in there?"

"No. Nobody in there but another couple and those two."

"Those two got no right to be. They're head over heels in debt already." Sudley moved to go back. "If Charlie was there, I'm not saying it's wrong. It's just his mother, is all. Every once in a while she gets an idea."

"That's bad."

"It is that," Sudley agreed soberly. "She thinks Charlie's white with a blue rim around him. If I catch him playing the slots, I'll whale him within an inch of his life."

As he started away Spig stopped him.

" I'm sorry about this evening, sir," he said. " I couldn't believe it, that's all."

" I'm sorry, too, Mr. O'Leary. You seen Ashton? "

" I saw him, but I didn't talk to him. I'll try again in the morning."

" Well, I'm willing to change my mind if he changes his." It was a soft-voiced concession Spig hadn't expected. " Mr. Cameron was over to-night. It's what I told him. And I told him I'd help see if we could put through a zoning plan. I guess you can't count on people acting right without a law, the way you used to. Well, good night, Mr. O'Leary."

He went back to his fence, climbed over it and headed slowly up across the field towards the house.

Funny, Spig thought, as he drove on home. We're all in the same conspiracy. You know damn well Charlie and Lucy ought to be jacked up sharp. So does Nick. But nobody wants to be a heel. Nobody wants to make trouble. The mores of the first grade. Nobody wants to be a tattle-tale. So what happens to Charlie and Lucy? They got a right to have a little fun, haven't they? All he could see was the woman in the blue shorts, morosely chewing her hamburger. Sucker bait. He grinned suddenly as the car bumped over the rugged lane through the woods. O'Leary and the second Mrs. Twohey ought to get together, hell-bent on good works, and institute a military bed-check for curfew time in Devon. *And begin at home* . . .

His spine tensed sharply and his grey eyes flattened again. He was coming out of the lane into the open, the windows in the entrance hyphen dimly lit in the O'Leary's house ahead of him, before his own long lights scoured it and swung around, the shadows of the trees running before them as they caught a flash of faded blue denim moving off, instantly lost in the heavy shadow under the oaks down along the river bank. It was Art Dunning, in person this time. His back was all Spig could see, but it was enough. Dunning sneaking away in the dark of the night.

It was only the brilliance of the headlights contrasting with the pale moon glow that made it look like the dark of the night, and only the quickly moving beam rounding the circle, losing him as instantly as it had picked him up, that gave the impression of haste. But O'Leary didn't stop to think of that. Nor to remind himself he'd been spoiling for a fight. Nor to examine the strange new compound of bitterness and frustration unleashed inside him. It was eleven thirty-five, the house was dark, Dunning was leaving it. It added up to something it could never have added up to any other day in the twelve years of his marriage. He was angry, bitter and hurt. The living-room lights blooming suddenly, softly aglow as he crossed the drive, were like a knife in his throat.

CHAPTER VII

" HI, DARLING! "

Molly called to him as he opened the screen door and stepped inside. She didn't come out of the living-room. He crossed over to the door. She was pushing back the chairs from in front of the fireplace, a couple of ash-trays in her hand. "Just straightening up a——" She turned to smile at him and stopped, her face blank. "Why, Spig . . . What's . . . what's the matter, darling? "

She stopped quickly and put the ash-trays on the coffee table.

" Spig! " She took a step towards him and stopped, a white line around her lips and her eyes amber pale. "What's happened? "

" Dunning making another psychological pass at you? And you needn't tell me he wasn't here. I saw him leave."

His voice was harsh. For an instant a stunned silence hung there before him. Then it exploded in a searing flash as Molly was transformed into blue ice and golden flame.

" I've no intention of telling you he wasn't here. He was, and we've been sitting out on the terrace waiting for you to come home." Her eyes were molten fire as she turned swiftly and picked up the ash-trays again. " I don't know where you've been, but wherever it is you'd better go back and stay there. I'm sick of all this. Anybody speaks to me, they're making a pass at me. If

Art Dunning's making them that's fine with me. Look up there."

She flashed her hand at the corner of the ceiling. "He mixed paint this morning and covered the whole stain you've been promising to fix ever since the gutter you promised to clean out last fall ran over and soaked through and wrecked it. If that's a pass, I like it. And he took the crab grass out of the terrace that you were going to do on Saturday and went fishing instead. And you come in to-night sore as hell because Tip's selling his vegetables to a Greek you don't like and don't even notice the crab grass is gone—or that Art put a new wheel on the terrace table for the one you broke."

"So you've got yourself a handy man, and you don't see what he's trying to do is wreck the whole place," Spig said angrily. "You don't care about that. You don't stop to see why Tip's throwing clods at him . . ."

"I know very well why Tip's throwing clods," Molly said hotly. "Tips just like you. He's jealous of anybody that comes around here and does pleasant things for me. You both want your whole world fenced and nobody allowed in it. You want me to sit here alone while you spend your evening in town. You're all alike—you and Joe Cameron and Phil Potter and all the rest of you. Just because Art isn't seven feet tall and paints pictures and can talk about something besides the market and boats and horses you all hate him. And I'm going to bed and the less I see of you the better I'll like it. You can turn off the oven and give your casserole to the cats. And you don't have to put the pan under the sink to-night. Mr. Sudley fixed that for me when he brought Tip and Greg home in his truck this afternoon. I suppose Mr. Sudley's making passes at me, too. He pumped out the well pit you've been going to do the last three weeks."

She dumped the ash-trays in the copper basket by the fireplace and went swiftly past him out into the hyphen and up the stairs.

O'Leary stood, semi-dazed for a moment, suddenly sick, sick of himself and the whole bloody mess he'd made of things. It was his fault. He should have fixed the ceiling and pumped out the well pit, and he should have kept his blasted mouth shut about Dunning. He knew then what he'd know when he barged into the Three D, ready to tear Dunning apart. It wasn't Dunning, it was Ashton. Everything shot to hell, O'Leary acting like a schizophrenzied fool . . . He took a deep breath and shook himself, trying to get the blistering scorn in Molly's voice out of his ears.

He reached over and switched off the lights and was half-way up the stairs when he remembered the oven. He plodded down and out through the old cottage to the kitchen to turn it off and take out the casserole. He went back upstairs. His bed was turned down but Molly's wasn't. He listened a moment before he went over to the bathroom and opened the door. She wasn't there and her toothbrush was gone from the rack. He went out into the hall. The guest room door was shut.

" Molly? " He stood a moment, waiting for a blistering response, but none came. He put his hand on the knob. The door was locked. " Molly! I'm sorry. Please, Molly."

She didn't answer.—The O'Learys and the Dulaneys. *What do two reds make? Blue, I think.* Blue blazes and brimstone. It wasn't the first time, but it was the first time she'd ever locked herself in the guest room and refused to answer when he'd knocked, sometimes when the fault was his and a lot of times when it wasn't. He stood there a moment, put his hand in his pocket for a cigarette, and felt the brittle wax seals on the envelope he'd forgotten in the general lack of sanity mucking up the last hour. He glanced at the solidly shut door and the equally solid wall of silence behind it. Maybe it was just as well Molly wasn't around when he read it. If the old judge had any suggestions, however unorthodox, O'Leary was ready to take them. With Sudley prepared to back down if Ashton would, it might even be that Molly would never have to know anything at all about it. *Always try to look on the brighter side of things, Mr. O'Leary.*

He grinned and went quietly back to his room, the reprieve in force again as the long shadow of the old judge's hand seemed to lie on his as he broke the other seals and slit open the flap. He took out the letter. It was three closely-written sheets of air mail paper folded around a second envelope, sealed but without the wax. He looked at it first.

" To be opened as directed—N.T." It was written with the same pen that sputtered, the same heartbeat pulsating in the fine uneven strokes. In the long silence, Spig was conscious of the eerie monotony of the tap he'd promised to fix and hadn't, dripping with a kind of sympathetic hopelessness through the bathroom, as he read the enfolding sheets.

" My dear Spig—I don't know the precise circumstances under which my son will hand you this, as I shall be purposely inclusive and purposely vague in my directions to him. The possibilities I see, and one of which he will remember my discussing with him, are these:

"I. You may have trouble with Ashton. Aside from reminding you of the black snake seven feet long the day you came to Devon, I can only assure you that Nat has a sound knowledge of the law and is not as entirely unimaginative or legally unresourceful as he thinks he is. If there is a way out, he will find it for you, slowly but surely—I hope.

" II. Martha Sudley may finally persuade Harlan to sell the farm so that Prince Charlie won't callous his hands working in the vineyard. In this event, communicate with the eldest son, who is anxious to keep the old Sudley land grant intact, and has great influence with his father, who is a bull-headed man but an honest one.

" III. Old David at Eden may die. In which case you are to open the enclosed letter.

" IV. The determined virgins, married and single, male or female, of this community may decide Miss Fairlie should be sent away, when I am no longer here to prevent it. Open the letter. I count on you and Nat to act in my stead as your heart and his head best advise you, remembering that Celia Fairlie is very dear to me.

" V. Celia Fairlie may die or become seriously ill physically. Open the letter.

" VI. With the rapidly changing scene in Devon, unforeseeable situations may arise. Your own discretion will direct you.

" In the side of your fireplace facing the river, there is a stone that can be removed. Celia Fairlie and George Sudley used the space behind it as a post box. I don't believe that anyone alive when you read this—except Celia, David and yourself—will be aware of its existence. If you have no more securely fireproof place in the house, find it and put the letter where it will be safe and still at hand. Death is a flower that blooms at night. You may tell Molly or not, as you wish. You alone are to open it, but Molly should know that in any emergency you are to be called as immediately as possible.

" I sent for you to-day to give you the enclosed with my own hands, and to tell you what I am now writing. But we were not sufficiently alone, and I should have added base ingratitude to my other many and grievous sins had I made an issue of it at a time when devoted care is the last kindness my family can show me.

" I told you once that if I were superstitious, I might believe Miss Fairlie knew you were coming to Eden that day. As my life draws to its close, I no longer call it a superstition. I have faith that you were sent to finish the task I must leave unfinished. May God in His wisdom be with you, and in His mercy be with you and with us all.

Sincerely,
Nathan Twohey."

The spigot dripped its monotonous threnody as Spig sat there on the side of the bed, remembering Christmas Eve. He and the kids were coming in from the woods with their Christmas tree when Nat Twohey called and he went quickly into town.

" You're not to tire him, Mr. O'Leary." Mrs. Twohey let him in with determined good will on earth and peace to no man if she could help it. " We're just humouring our invalid to let you come at all."

The old judge seemed only a little frailer and a little more transparent, sitting up against the head board of the gigantic four-poster in the front bedroom, his eyes as avidly alive as ever as he watched, ironically amused, the delaying tactics of his second wife before she could finally bring herself to leave them.

" Miss Fairlie is coming to you for Christmas, I hear,"
he remarked then.

" If it isn't snowing," Spig answered. " She told Tip
she doesn't like snow."

" She doesn't," Judge Twohey said. His gaze rested
on the door into the adjacent room, or a room very far
away beyond it. " There was snow. A great deal of
snow."

He said it as he'd once said, " There was blood. A
great deal of blood."

" Have you heard about the snow? "

Spig looked at him, afraid his mind was wandering,
until the old eyes turned inquiringly to him.

" No, sir, I haven't."

" It was in February, seven weeks after George
Sudley's accident." His voice was stronger. " It was a
blizzard followed by a heavy freeze that no one expected,
when we thought winter was almost over. I was a member
of the House of Delegates, home for the week-end. I went
out to Eden before I had to go back for a caucus, late
Sunday evening. That night the snow came. It blocked
the roads and tore down power lines. I didn't get back
out there for two weeks. The thaw had come and taken
out the bridges and flooded the marshes. Eden was an
island. No one worried. Farms were self-sufficient. But
Mr. Fairlie had strained his heart, haying, in the fall,
and Celia was not well. I took a boat and went out there,
just to see that everything was all right."

He was silent a long time, living in a world more real
than the bedroom with the holly and ground cedar,
invincibly cheerful, decorating the mantelpiece.

" The dock was gone. The ice had dislodged the piles
and the planking was washed away. I waded ashore.
The house was shuttered. It looked as if no one had ever

lived there. Then I saw the grave. It was covered with pine boughs. The garden gate was padlocked and there was smoke coming out of the chimney of the little office, but no one answered my knock and the shutters were closed there, too. It was Mr. Fairlie I kept calling, until I went out to the barns and found David. He told me. It wasn't Celia who was dead. That had been my only thought, I'm afraid."

There was a longer silence before he went on again.

" Celia hadn't got over the terrible shock of George Sudley. The second shock was even more terrible in its way. She was devoted to her father, the only person not afraid of him. He was Scottish, a dour, solitary man—or had become one after his wife's unfortunate death. One rector we had used to say the ravens fed him, and the picture of Elijah in my mind is always a tall, gaunt windmill of a man striding across the fields of Eden with a grizzled, red beard, in old riding boots and breeches, a Gordon setter at his heels . . . I'd like a sip of water, please. There in the thermos."

Spig O'Leary roused himself and came over to pour the water. The old judge reached under one of his pillows and brought out a flat pint bottle that wasn't water. He poured a couple of fingers into one of his medicine glasses, smiling at Spig, nodded to him to do the same, put the bottle back under the pillow and used the water either as a chaser or to wash the glass—it was hard to tell.

" Every man commits suicide in his own way," he commented dryly. " Ammon Fairlie, with his strained heart, chose to shovel snow. He went out early in the morning to clear a path to get to his prize stock. David was the only one he'd trust to oversee them, and David was laid up with a wrenched back. He keeled over dead.

How Celia got him into the house no one will ever know. It was still snowing; she couldn't leave him out there. The power failure had taken out the oil burner and the lights. She was there with him in that creaking old house in the freezing dark for three terrible days and nights. A farm boy David had sent down saw her and was terrified when she didn't know him and drove him away. It was three days before he dared tell David. David was the only person she knew then and for a long time afterwards. She and he built a fire under a hog kettle, boiled snow, and thawed out a piece of ground to bury her father in. She wouldn't go back to the house, and David got blankets and made a bed for her on the old leather sofa in the back room of the little office. He was the only person she'd let come near her. I saw her, but she didn't know me. She lived there for five years. David and his wife brought her food and looked after her. Perhaps I should have let them take her away, but David thought it would kill her, and so did I."

He shook his head. " We may have been monstrously culpable in many things. But my faith in the Ultimate Court of Appeals is such that I'm sure David and I will be judged with mercy, as with wisdom. He and I testified at the formal inquest, when the roads were open again. I was executor of the estate under Ammon Fairlie's will, and the Court appointed me Celia's guardian. David ran the farm, with Harlan Sudley's co-management, until one April I was sitting for one of the judges on the Second Circuit and Sudley called me. I got home as soon as I could."

He smiled then. " Celia met me on the porch. David introduced us. She said she understood from him that I had been in charge of things while she was abroad, and in her opinion I'd done a very bad job of it indeed.

Apparently in those five years she'd read all her grandfather's law books, the estate records, treatises on banking
and farming, that are still out in the old office. It was
an extraordinary experience, to stand there and have
Blackstone, Bentham and Mill, to say nothing of Vergia
Georgics, tossed at me one moment, and to be told the
next that I would kindly lower my voice, there was a
child asleep in the house and she didn't want it wakened.
But she was alive again, and that's all that mattered. It's
still all that matters. What memory, if any, she has
of . . ."

He broke off, his eyes sharpening with intense irritation
for an instant before he made a patiently resigned movement of his fragile hands on the patchwork quilt. The
door of the adjoining room opened and the second Mrs.
Twohey came in, very brisk, with a decanter and two
glasses on a silver tray.

" I do hope I'm not interrupting," she said brightly.

" Not at all, my dear."

" I called the doctor. He said as it's Christmas he didn't
think a small stirrup cup would hurt either you or Mr.
O'Leary, Judge."

" Very thoughtful of you, I'm sure," said the judge
without a flicker.

She put the tray on the table, poured a far more
liberal wallop than O'Leary would have expected, and
planted herself, firmly significant, at the foot of the bed.

The judge held his glass, looking at it a long moment.
He raised it then, smiling faintly, faintly sad, faintly
amused:

" A stirrup cup, Spig, my friend," he said.

" He hasn't long, you know," Mrs. Twohey said as she
opened the front door for Spig. His throat was too full
for him to more than nod his head and get the hell out.

He sat in the car until the great white snowflakes plopping softly on his windshield covered it, and he started the motor and switched on the wipers to clean it. He didn't know until then that he was crying.

CHAPTER VIII

JUDGE TWOHEY's breaking off as he had done was like a chord of music left unresolved, his death three days later deepening the frustrating emptiness it was vain to protest. It was seven in the morning when Nat called Spig and asked him to go over and tell Miss Fairlie. It was still dark, but there was a light in the old kitchen on the Plumtree Cove side of the big house. Through a chink in the shutter he could see her, sitting at the table, with a coffee pot and two cups and saucers on it. She had on a white wool wrapper with a shawl around her shoulders, her short, pale hair still uncombed. Spig knocked at the door. She looked up, and in a moment rose and came over. She unbolted the long, green shutters on the door and pushed one of them open.

" You've come." An icy wind was slashing across the crusted snow. She hesitated, glancing behind her. Then she said, " You may come in here. You'll catch cold out there."

He stepped in on the brick floor. It was the first time he'd been in any part of Eden. Perhaps it was neutral territory he was in now. She'd let workmen in to modernise it in part. A white enamelled refrigerator, sink and electric range stood cheek by jowl with the old open fireplace with its crane and iron kettle, and the wood range with a fire burning in it. Generations had added but never removed anything. The hooks for hams still hung from the blackened beams and a few bunches of powdery herbs swayed as Spig closed the door behind him.

"It's about Judge Twohey, Miss Fairlie," he said gently. "He died last night."

"This morning around three," she said. "He came by here a moment on his way."

It was only the completely matter-of-fact tone of her voice that startled him. "Did you see him, Miss Fairlie?"

Her blue child's eyes rested on him a moment.

"Spirit is like thought. It has no substance my eyes can see. I woke knowing he was here. He was passing through. Then I heard your dog barking. I thought perhaps he'd gone your way, too. Possibly we all pass for a moment through the places where our hearts have been. I couldn't go back to sleep, so I came out here."

She went back to the table, her tiny figure erect, her eyes blind for a moment. "I made some coffee. I expect it's cold now, but you may have his cup. You may sit there."

She nodded at the other chair and poured the coffee. It was very cold, but Spig drank it as she sat across from him, her eyes blank.

What memory she has, if any, of . . .

They sat there a long time. Finally, she rose. "You must go now," she said calmly. "Thank you for coming. I think Nathan would be amused at our wanting him to stay when his heart was failing and he could no longer move freely about. It would have been quite intolerable in that house, with that woman in possession, all ears, and Nat hovering around like a sheep about to be shorn. I dare say he was content to leave."

She went over to the big refrigerator next to the hand pump, set in the brick floor over the cistern, and took out a handful of cabbage leaves and a couple of carrots. She handed them to Spig. " There's a red rabbit out in the end border," she said. " Leave them there for him on your way home, if you please. Perhaps I should have reported him, but I haven't done it yet."

" I'd let him go, if I were you," Spig said. " He's not hurting anything, I imagine."

He didn't know who you'd report a red rabbit to, but he was aware he'd already assumed part of the old judge's guardianship—before the letters of patent had been formally issued and delivered to him.

He looked down at them now, lying there on the side of his bed, in the silence compounded of the windrift over the river rustling in the oaks and the voices of the myriad things that speak at night—the bathroom spigot, alien, the loudest of them.

He looked down at Point IV. *The determined virgins may decide Miss Fairlie should be sent away . . . I count on you and Nat to act in my stead as your heart and his head best advise you . . .* Fortunately, the red rabbit had remained strictly *in camera*, never reaching the eager ears of the local do-gooders. One red rabbit wasn't enough to set them off, perhaps, but he'd remembered it with a slight chill every time some character at a cocktail party had clucked lugubriously and said, " Something really ought to be done—it isn't safe for Miss Fairlie, out there in that old house all by herself." It was the sublimated itch of the pack, now the Master of the Hounds was gone.

But it was Point I that was the immediate problem. *Aside from reminding you of the black snake seven feet long . . .* That was the only tinge of the unorthodoxy Nat Twohey had been afraid of—and the rhetorical approach was the only difference between it and the conclusion that Harlan Sudley and Spig O'Leary had come to independently of it. Whether there was time for Nat's imagination and legal resourcefulness to get off its prat and start to function instead of it was something else again.

He got up with a kind of sardonic awareness that whatever the hand arranging the pattern, it was doing okay. This was probably the only time in the last seven years that O'Leary could go downstairs and hunt for a removable stone in the fireplace without interference. He wrapped the air mail sheets back around the sealed letter, put the whole thing back into the envelope, held his lighter to the wax seals and pressed them into place again. Then he took off his shoes, got out a pair with rubber soles and slipped them on.

Molly's door was still shut as he went quietly down the stairs and into the old cottage room. He closed the door, switched on the lights and then, on an off-chance, drew the curtains across the windows. He went over to the side of the fireplace next to the cellarette. The chimney breast was a good three feet thick, to accommodate the crane, cooking pot and dutch oven. It had been white-washed a couple of times since they'd been there. There were no visible cracks around any of the stones. He went to the desk, got the paper knife and came back, and tensed sharply at a rasping scratch on the door across the room. Nervous. He grinned then, remembering the dog, and tensed again. The dog couldn't open the door, not that slowly. The cold prickles skidded down his spine as a single bare foot six inches off the floor moved, edging the door open silently, inch by inch. He relaxed as he saw the wrinkled pyjama leg attached to it. The door swung open then and there was Tip, eyes wide, face pale, the dog beside him, at ease, wagging her tail.

O'Leary was at ease, too, for half a second, before he saw the rifle in his son's hands.

" What the hell are you doing with that thing? "

" I thought it was . . . somebody else."

Tip swallowed, a baffled look on his own face as his eyes rested on the paper knife in his father's hand.

" What . . . what are you doing with that, over there? Are you trying to . . . to find the box? "

Sprig nodded.

" Who . . . told you it was there? "

" Judge Twohey. He wrote a letter he wants put in it."

Spig O'Leary was aware suddenly that there was something essentially comic in his standing there in the corner, being catechized, as if Tip were indeed the Lord Proprietor. But there was something not at all comic about the .22 in the kid's hands.

" Don't you think you'd better put that rifle away? " he asked quietly. " Who did you expect to find here, anyway? "

" I didn't know." But it was obvious he did know even before he said, " Mr. Dunning hasn't any right coming over here all the time." He went across the room and set the rifle in the corner.

" Is the safety catch on? "

" Yes, sir."

" All right. Now listen to me, Tip. We'll see about Dunning. But we leave guns out of it. Strictly out. Do you understand that? "

Tip's jaw was like his father's. " I understand," he said. His voice had nothing in it to suggest pliant amenability to reason, sweet or otherwise.

" Okay, then. Remember it."

The whole new deal of Tip had Spig O'Leary in an untracked wilderness, with no experience to go on, least of all his own. A summary court with punishment, swift, direct and no hard feelings had been the technique of Spig O'Leary, West Point '16. but none of the eight O'Learys had faced their father with Tip's impassive assurance. He watched the kid calmly coming across the room to him.

" About this box," he asked. " How did you find it? "

" Miss Fairlie showed it to me," Tip said. " It has something of hers in it. I'm supposed to give it to you if she should die. It's a secret, but she said I could tell you if I thought I should."

He stood soberly making up his mind for a moment. Then he pointed back to the bowl of nasturtiums on the pine tap table.

" Where the blood was," he said. " There was a man killed there. He was a friend of Miss Fairlie's."

" I know." There was a certain irony in all the care the O'Learys had taken never to mention the blood you could hardly tell unless you knew it was there. " He had an accident cleaning his gun."

" No." Tip shook his head. " That's what they said, but it isn't true. Another man shot him, on purpose. Because Miss Fairlie was going to get married to him— the one that was killed."

A chill wonder moved in Spig's mind as he looked at his son, sober and completely matter-of-fact.

" He was murdered. Miss Fairlie told me so. But it doesn't matter, because the man's dead now, too. The one who did it, I mean."

In the part of the room where Spig was there was a muted silence. He was remembering Nat Twohey. *With George Sudley dead, I hoped . . . But it didn't work that way, of course.*

When he spoke at last he tried to make it sound as if

it didn't matter to him, either. "When was it Miss Fairlie told you, Tip?"

"Oh, it was a long time ago."

O'Leary swallowed, relieving the constriction in his throat.

"It was that day you and Mother wanted to take Miss Fairlie in to Judge Twohey's funeral and she wouldn't go," Tip said. "She came over here, instead. That's when she told me, and showed me how to open the box."

A long time ago. Six months is a long time when eleven years is the grand total.

"It was the same day Uncle Stan brought the men over that wanted to buy our place."

Spig brought himself sharply back to the present. "What men that . . ."

"Just some men. Kitty told them it wasn't for sale."

"Why didn't you tell me this before?"

"We tried to when you came home. But you said to just shut up and beat it. But we did tell Miss Fairlie. She——"

The sharp jangling of the telephone cut him off. Spig reached quickly over the desk to keep it from ringing a second time and waking Molly, forgetting she wasn't in the bed upstairs by the extension.

"O'Leary speaking."

There was no answer. Someone was there. He could hear the rise and fall of breathing.

"Hallo," he said impatiently.

There was still no answer, only the breath drawn longer and more audibly in his ear. He listened a moment and put the phone down.

"Who is it, Dad?" Tip asked.

"I don't know." Spig turned back to the chimney. "Now about this box."

G

" It's here." Tip pointed. As he raised himself on his
toes to reach it the phone rang again.

Spig turned and picked it up. " Hallo," he said
sharply.

" Mr. O'Leary? "

It was a man's voice, very suave and very friendly.
" Speaking."

" You wouldn't recognise my name, so I won't bother
you with it, Mr. O'Leary," the voice said pleasantly.
" But I've heard you may try to block the Ashton sale.
I wouldn't if I were you. I've heard you've even
threatened to kill Ashton. That's very stupid. I'm not
threatening you, O'Leary—I'm just telling you. Get
out and stay out. Your wife and children are perfectly
safe . . . if you mind your own business. Can you hear
me, O'Leary—or can't you? "

O'Leary started to speak, but there was no one to
speak to. He stood there, the dial tone zinging steadily
monotonous, in his ear.

CHAPTER IX

" Who is it, Daddy? "

Spig O'Leary's heart tightened sharply. The kid with the rifle in his hand a minute ago was suddenly a round-eyed boy, terribly young, a little scared, more bewildered.

" Just some clown." He put the phone casually back in the cradle. " Thinks it's Hallowe'en, I guess."

" You didn't look like you thought it was a joke."

" I didn't. But my sense of humour's shot to-night."

He turned back to the chimney breast. " Now about the box," he said. " It's time both of us were in bed."

" It's that one." Tip pointed up to one of the stones, smaller and more evenly cut than the rest. It was set in the centre of the pier, well under the jutting end of the chestnut mantel. " You push hard."

He raised himself on tiptoe and pressed one side of the stone. The whitewash fell in tiny flakes as the slab, dressed no more than a couple of inches thick, moved in. A rude iron bar, morticed upright with two iron rings around it set in the slab, formed a primitive hinge.

" It was while they didn't like Catholics here, Miss Fairlie said," Tip explained soberly. " She said one of the Edens married a Catholic and built this house for a priest she knew to live in. This is where he hid the Host—like in Holy Communion."

The opening was no more than six inches wide but the space behind it hollowed out, lined with hammered metal.

" Her letter's at the bottom. But you're not supposed to touch it now. You promise, don't you, Dad? "

" I promise." Spig took the letter out of his pocket. " And you promise not to tell anybody this is here—not even Miss Fairlie."

Tip nodded. " I promise."

Spig dropped the envelope into the hollow and pushed the stone back into place.

" You can hardly tell it unless you know it's there," Tip said.

" That's right."

Spig glanced over at the bowl of nasturtiums. The shadow under it seemed to have darkened, now that he knew the depth of the tragedy behind it . . . three lives blasted in the violent blasting of the one. George Sudley may have been the least unfortunate of the three, the old judge the most, living on so many years in the wasteland of his own heart, seeing the wasteland he'd made of Celia Fairlie's. He turned back to his son, the chill that had been with him earlier there with him again. Perhaps it was right that violence begets violence, and the murder of George Sudley there in that room was in some way responsible for the loaded rifle in a boy's hand, murder in a boy's heart. There was very little doubt in his mind that, if it had been Arthur Dunning there in the room, there could have been more blood there that night.

" Let's go get something to eat, Tip," he said. " Bring your gun."

He was acutely conscious of it standing in the corner as they divided the casserole he'd left on the kitchen counter.

" Now look, son," he said. " You remember the deal you made with your grandfather? "

It was General Dulaney who'd given Tip the gun for his tenth birthday a year ago.

Tip swallowed. " Yes, sir. I have to ask permission to use it. Or . . . or I have to call him up and ask him to keep it for me till I'm ready to . . . to respect a gun."

" All right. You think it over and let me know in the morning. Now, about Dunning."

Tip's jaw tightened. His eyes met his father's without flinching.

" I'm not going to have him over here poking around all the time," he said. " What if he found the box? "

" Is that why you don't like him? "

Tip's eyes were hot, his mouth sullen. He looked down and shifted uncomfortably. " No," he said. He shut his lips tight again.

" Okay. I won't ask you if you don't want to tell. But I want you to get this straight. Dunning's my business. He's not yours."

" He's mine when he comes out in my garden and paints his dirty pictures. That's all they are, dirty—dirty mean. And I'm not going to let him paint my mother's picture. I won't. I'll kill him."

" Now, wait a minute." Spig cut him off quietly. " That's all we're going to have of that stuff. Absolutely all—do you hear me? Dunning's my business. Not yours."

" But you're not here . . "

" I'll be here the rest of the week."

Tip's jaw relaxed. " Well, all right. If you're home."

" Thanks." There was no irony perceptible to Tip. " So that's the deal. I'm home. You leave Dunning to me. And we stack the shooting irons. Understand? "

" Yes, sir."

" All right. Now take your gun and put it away. What else do you do? "

" I unload it."

" Right."

Spig watched him go over, get the gun and take out the shells. He went with him and watched him put it on the rack in the hyphen and put the shells in the box on the shelf.

" Okay," he said. " Bed."

Tip hesitated. " Dad . . . I won't have to call Grandfather, I'll remember. I'll ask permission just like he said."

" All right."

There was a bear-hug for a moment before Tip let go, and Spig hoisted him up to the landing where the dog was waiting.

" Good night, Daddy."

The dog got up and followed him upstairs to her place outside his door.

Three minutes before the alarm was to go off at six-thirty the next morning Spig O'Leary reached automatically to turn it off.

" Wake up, Molly." He said it automatically, before the empty bed next to him brought the whole thing back to him. He kicked off the covers and got to his feet. She was already up. He could hear the house awake and alive, and see Tip and Greg out in the garden, picking peas for the Three D.

There was one unbreakable rule in the O'Leary house —they never quarrelled in front of the children. He was aware of it as he came downstairs, showered and dressed, out into the kitchen and saw her, cool and detached, the cheek she turned for him to kiss even cooler, in spite of the heat of the argument going on between Kitsy and

John Eden, still at their breakfast at the built-in nook
at the end of the counter.

" You don't even know what three o'clock is," Kitsy
was saying. " Does he, Mother? "

" That's enough, Kitsy," Molly said. " Eat your
cereal. It doesn't make the least difference to either of
you."

" What doesn't? " O'Leary poured himself some orange
juice and a cup of coffee.

" Whether Lucy got home from a movie at three o'clock,
or whether she didn't," Molly said tartly.

" But I heard her, Daddy." Kitsy was eating as
directed, but she could still talk. " The car lights woke
me up, and it was three o'clock, and she said, ' Thanks for
the movie, Uncle Art, I've had a lovely time.' And it was
too three o'clock. And Tip says there aren't any
movies———"

" That's enough, Kitsy," Molly said sharply. " Now
stop it. And clear the table if you're through. John
Eden, take Molly A. and tell Tip Daddy's down and he'll
be out in a few minutes."

She turned back to Spig. " I told them they could go
with you."

" I've got to go into town . . ."

" That's all right. They can walk back through Mr.
Sudley's pasture. It isn't too far. Helping deliver the
first batch is half the fun. You wouldn't spoil it for them,
would you? "

It was obvious from the tone that she knew nothing
would please him more.

" And Tip tells me you're taking a week off to stay at
home," she added lightly. " That's wonderful, because
now I can go to Baltimore with Arthur Dunning to-day."
She was smiling at him, but the flecks in her eyes, greener

than brown, were molten gold. "There's a Swedish exhibition at the museum out by John Hopkins. He asked me last night and I said I couldn't go. But if you're home it'll be a pleasure. And Kitsy dear . . ." She turned from him to her daughter gathering up the children's dishes. "The reason I don't want you to talk about what time Lucy gets in is that that's none of our business. Or where she went, or why. Neighbours don't spy on each other—not good neighbours."

"I wasn't spying. I just heard her, is all. Because Mädel barked and it woke me up."

O'Leary buttered a piece of toast and stayed out of it. With the Ashtons downwind, Lucy wouldn't have to speak too loud for the sound to be audible through Kitsy's open windows . . . but it would have to be louder than an ordinary "Good night and thank you, Uncle Art." Maybe she was just letting Uncle Art know his car was safely back. Or maybe it was Anita she was fooling. How Charlie Sudley had made it in was also none of the O'Leary's business—as Molly was just saying.

"What other people do is no affair of yours, Kitsy, dear. You don't want Greg to think you're an old gossip, do you? Come on, let's us go help Tippy, too. Daddy can do the dishes while I'm in Baltimore."

They went out. O'Leary pushed his cup and saucer back and got to his feet. *Well, the hell with it. If that's the way she wanted it, let her have it.* He gave the cat, rubbing affectionately against his ankle, a kick that sent her winding. "Sorry, cat," he said then as she promptly came back. He pushed her aside and went into the hall to get his coat.

Tip and Greg, Kitsy and two bushel baskets of peas and yellow wax beans were in the car, pride and happiness in addition leaving small room for O'Leary.

" Good-bye, darlings. Careful crossing the highway."
Molly laughed and waved to them with John Eden and
Molly A. beside her. O'Leary she didn't see. He could
have been a leper without his bell. But it wasn't O'Leary
who spoiled half the fun of the first delivery. It was Greg
who first saw the pile of blue glass glinting where it had
been swept up and the great jagged hole with the ripped
slats of the venetian blind dangling behind it. It was in
one of the octagonal sectors away from the road, next to
the kitchen added on to the rear of the blue glass of
Your Last Chance to Dine, Drink and Dance.

" Look . . . look! " he whispered. " They did it.
They did it anyway . . ."

Spig stopped the car next to the crates of bread and
milk still waiting to be taken inside. He looked around at
Greg.

" Who did it? " he asked quietly.

The boy's lips were pressed tight shut as he shook his
head, his face dead white.

Spig opened the car door. " You kids wait here a
minute. You too, Greg."

He pushed the service door open and went in. The
kitchen was empty. He went on through it. Inside there
was another pile of blue glass on the floor, the tables
pushed back, the floor covering marred where feet had
trampled the glass in. He crossed over to the archway
into the bar. Nick Pappas was there, sitting on one of the
blue leather stools, his face haggard, streaked where the
tears had dried.

" Who did it, Nick? "

He shook his head back and forth, trying to speak.
" Nobody. Nobody, Mr. O'Leary."

" How did it happen? "

" I don't know. I don't know."

" You mean you're scared to say."

" I don't know, I tell you! I don't know! "

" How much did they get, Nick? "

Over by the door the glass panel of the half-dollar slot machine was smashed, the back pried off.

Nick's voice rose. " I tell you, I don't know, Mr. O'Leary! "

" Have you called Yerby? "

" No! No! I don't call nobody! "

" Then I'll call him."

" No, no, no! " Nick Pappas jumped off the stool. " They ruin me if I call him! I don't call . . . you don't call, Mr. O'Leary! "

Spig turned away abruptly. " All right. The kids are out here. We've brought the vegetables. You want to go out and get them? I've got to go on in town."

" Okay."

Spig heard him running out through the dine-and-dance room and the swish of the kitchen door. He waited a moment, and went over to the slot machine. The job had been clumsy but effective. There was no way of telling how much they'd got. The sucker-bait woman had put seventy bucks into it while he was watching her.

He went back to the kitchen. The kids were helping carry the baskets in.

" They stay and have a glass of milk," Nick said.

" Okay, I'll go on."

Nick came out to the car with him. " You don't say nothing, Mr. O'Leary. Please, Mr. O'Leary."

" What time did it happen, Nick? "

" I don't know. I close up half-past one. I go home right away. I don't know what time. I got no proof, Mr. O'Leary."

" Have you got insurance? "

" No, no! They call the sheriff. I got trouble already, Mr. O'Leary."

" Okay, if that's the way you want it. I think you're crazy."

" Sure, I'm crazy. You go crazy too. Trouble . . . all the time trouble."

Spig drove on into the town. The day began early in Courthouse Square. It was a quarter to eight by the clock under the cupola, but the only empty car space was where the curb was painted a fresh new yellow too bright for him to overlook. He drove on to the side street and around to the yard in back where the cars from the sheriff's office were parked. As he pulled in beside them, he saw coming from the back door Pete Greenway, the owner, editor, copy boy and janitor of the Devon County Weekly *Times-Gazette*, a big city newsman who'd bought his Utopia and was sticking it out. He saw Spig and changed course.

CHAPTER X

" THE NEW DEPUTY, Buck tells me."

O'Leary shook his head. " That was yesterday."

" You got a minute? "

" Fifteen. I see Yerby at eight. But if it's about Ashton, no comment. I was the last to get the word."

" The hell with Ashton. That guy gives me curare darts in the seat of my chair." Greenway opened the car door and eased himself into the seat beside Spig. " This fellow Dunning. What gives with him? "

O'Leary drew in cautiously. " He's a friend of the

Ashtons. A painter. Getting ready for a New York show."

"Called ' Rural America,' " Greenway said. " Rural America—a New Look. I got a matt on him from his galleries. A noble character who's tossed aside the family riches. Prefers a dry crust in a heatless garret. After he'd bought the fancy car, naturally. How come he can afford to paint for free? Mrs. Nathan Twohey, for instance? Is she an example of the new look in rural America? "

" He's not painting Mrs. Twohey. You speak in jest," O'Leary said urbanely.

" It's the truth. I swear it. Six sittings, so far. After the fourth she gave him a tea. A ladies' tea, last week. I was invited. I went. That I wanted to see. Every time I've seen Arthur Dunning, he's been a stinker *nonpareil* . . . But there he was, charming as all hell, pouring it on, all the old Devonites lapping it up, the disembalmed I've heard about but never seen out in the three years I've been around. All bending his ear, including the old rector, the other member of the male trinity present at the party."

Spig took a cigarette from the mashed humid pack Greenway held out.

" You've got me," he said.

" Could there be a kind heart under an unlikely exterior? "

" Could be."

Greenway shrugged. " The next day, and thereafter, he comes to the *Gazette*. Devon County fascinates him, he says. He's boning up on its history, including the public prints. So will I let him see the old files? Sure, I said. But there's only one historic period he's bothered with. You couldn't guess what it is. Or could you? "

" I know nothing about the guy," Spig said patiently.

Greenway blew a sceptical feather of smoke into a series of diminishing rings.

" Well, in case you'd like to know, it's the approximate period of the George Sudley demise in the cottage on Plumtree Cove. The only scuttlebutt I ever heard about that was suicide, maybe, not accident. But I don't move among the disembalmed. Nor has Dunning, till he started painting the estimable widow of the deceased arbiter of all Devon. And every time Dunning caught my eye at this tea party, he grinned like a zany. Malevolent little bastard. Now, if you're ready for the question, this is it. Something's up . . . what's the switchblade twist? "

He backed out of the car.

" Just asking, that's all." He dropped his cigarette and wiped his foot over it. " Just asking. Wasn't it Nat Twohey and Harlan Sudley out at the blind with George, that morning it happened? "

" Not at the cottage," Spig said. " The way I've heard it. They went on across the river, oyster tonging."

" So I've been told," Pete Greenway said pleasantly. " Mrs. Sudley was at the tea, by the way. Nat was there a minute. Very unhappy, he looked to me. It was your friend Miss Fairlie that lost most blood from the velvet claws unsheathed at times. But that was a cover-up. It was the accident Dunning was trailing . . . hot scent if ever I smelled one. Well, it's your house. I thought you might have noticed him around lately."

He turned away. " So long. Your neighbours are on the rampage, by the way. Ashton sure pulled an ageing raw one on you all. I'm going to phone in some trenchant questions, next time his TV panel meets. It's not the Planned Society scares me. It's the Planners."

He lounged off across the yard to the street. O'Leary
sat there; the cigarette, a column of grey ash intact in
his hand, burned clear to the filter. It was the cupola
clock striking eight that jolted him back. As he got out
of the car he was aware of Pete Greenway on the other
side of the wall, watching him intently. Greenway
grinned at him then, waved his hand and went on across
the street to the one-story building that housed the
Gazette.

O'Leary closed the car door, the picture of Tip clear
and distinct in his mind. *I'm not going to have him poking
around here.* He hadn't asked why Tip had taken it for
granted it was Dunning he'd find downstairs at that hour
of night. He'd skipped over that far too lightly, himself
taking for granted that what the old judge said was true:
no one now alive except himself, Miss Fairlie and David
would know about the post box in the chimney breast.
If Dunning was on the trail of Nat Twohey and Harlan
Sudley, with Greenway close behind him, how long would
it take him to get to the old judge, with the efficient help
of Mrs. Twohey, getting her licks in on Miss Fairlie,
not knowing she was being rigged into an arch-betrayal?
His jaw tightened. This was disturbing. It was strange
how deeply disturbing . . . strange how much you could
care for somebody you'd known so briefly, how much you
could love someone you knew so little, the old judge and
Miss Fairlie. He'd never thought about it that way till
then, but it was the truth. It didn't matter to him what
the old judge had done, or that Miss Fairlie was bats more
than half the time. Or was it O'Leary who was bats?

He went across the yard to the back door of the Courthouse. The corridor was filled with scaffolding where
the interior face-lifting of the frowsty old building was
still going on, liquor and gambling machines licences

footing the bill—prosperity quick and easy for Devon County.

"Austin J. Yerby. Sheriff. Private," it said on the door. Spig knocked.

"Come in. Oh, it's you." Yerby grinned at him, "I was just figuring you'd forgot."

The face-lifting hadn't got to the dingy room with the creaking chair and battered desk, ruts worn in the old floor, a horsefly buzzing savagely at the rotted screen.

"I didn't forget." Spig closed the door. "But I've changed my mind."

"Why?"

"I've been sticking around. Getting the score, like you said. I'd probably have killed Ashton last night, if he hadn't been dead drunk. Also I don't like people calling me in the middle of the night, telling me to lay off or else. No danger to my wife and kids if I quit trying to block the sale. It looks like there's other stuff that disqualifies me, too."

Yerby looked at him silently for a moment. He creaked his chair forward then, opened his desk drawer and took out a typed sheet.

"This is the oath you take," he said dispassionately. "It says: 'I Blank, do swear that I will support the Constitution of the United States, and that I will be faithful and bear true allegiance to the State, and support the Constitution and Laws thereof. and that I will to the best of my skill and judgment diligently and faithfully, without partiality or prejudice, execute the office of Deputy Sheriff of Devon County according to the Constitution and Laws of the State. And I further declare my belief in the existance of God.'"

He put it down on the desk and looked back at Spig. "It doesn't say anything, any place I see, about going to confession first. A man's innocent until he's found guilty, the way they've always told me. What it says is you'll execute the office to the best of your skill and judgment, without partiality or prejudice."

" So if I kill Ashton, I arrest myself."

" Don't be a goddam fool, O'Leary. What good would it do you? Anita's a hell of a lot tougher than Ashton. Or do you plan to kill her, too? "

Spig shook his head. " No. And I don't plan to kill Ashton. I'd just like to, is all."

" What else you got that's eating you? "

" Plenty." He hesitated. It was Dunning, via Greenway, he had in mind, but he sat tight on that. " If you see something, and the guy it's happened to is scared to report it, what do you do? "

Hard ridges stood out on Yerby's jaw. " Where is it this time? " he asked evenly. " The lowdown, white-livered rats."

" Who? "

" The whole lousy bunch of 'em. The gang that does it and the suckers that take it. That's your Devon Death Strip. I hear something, I go out, and don't anybody even know what I'm talking about. This is the fourth one the last two months that I've heard of. Whose place is busted open now? "

He jerked his chair back from the desk. " You can tell me, I'll leave you out of it. It won't do them any good, they'll be scared to prosecute, but it'll do me good. I can see if it's the same gang. I'll get 'em some day. Who is it? "

" Nick at the Three D. His wall's smashed in, fifty cent slot broken open."

" Even Nick's afraid to tell me."

" He sure is."

"All right. I'll go see him. What else?" He was angry and brusque. "What else you got? I'm beginning to think you're yellow, too."

"Not yellow," Spig said peaceably. "Maybe I'm scared. I wasn't going to tell you this, but I guess I'd better. Or maybe you'd better go talk to Pete Greenway."

"I don't talk to Greenway if I can help it. His idea of news and mine don't gee. He likes a stink, I don't."

"It's a stink I'm scared about," Spig said quietly. "I'd like to ask you one question?"

"Go ahead."

"If some guy—like Dunning out at the Ashtons'—started grubbing around, deep enough, with plenty of local help, could he dig up anything . . . about George Sudley, for——"

He stopped abruptly. The anger draining out of Yerby's eyes left them old, haggard and unseeing. The rigid knots along his lean jaw slackened. He drew a long, deep breath and settled back in his chair. "Not again, for God's sake," he said, but it was to himself, not to Spig. He sat there, staring at his desk, silent for a long time. He looked up then.

"He'd have to dig mighty deep, Spig," he said slowly. "And have to dig a lot of help." He pulled his chair forward, picked up a pencil and put it down again. "Tell me about it," he said evenly. "I thought Dunning was a painter, a picture painter?"

Spig nodded. "He's also a stinker, first-class. He's getting up what he calls a gallery of rural types. People around here. Not flattering. Maybe digging up old dirt's a part of it. Greenway says he's been boning up on the George Sudley era. He's painting a portrait of Mrs. Twohey."

There was a gleam, sharp and alive in Yerby's eyes.

H

" She had a tea, Greenway says, for Dunning to meet all the old-timers."

" The damned old she-cat. Hasn't the brains——" Yerby broke off. He sat looking down at the desk again. " Look Spig," he said finally. " My father was sheriff here fifty years, right in this room. He and the old judge between them ran the county. In a place like this, you don't just die and be done with it. Sixty per cent of the people that vote for me do it because my father was a great guy. Believe me, he was. I don't want 'em to think he covered up a murder . . . just for a friend of his. George Sudley's dead. I want him to stay dead. It's not only my father. It's . . . a lot of other people. And it's not that I'm trying now to cover up for anybody. It's just wrong, Spig. Wrong to go on crucifying people, dead or alive."

He got up and picked up his hat. " Come on. The clerk's waiting. I need you. To ride herd on Dunning, if nothing else."

The clerk of the court was across the hall. Spig took the oath.

" You sign the ledger here, Mr. O'Leary."

Spig signed it.

Yerby shook hands with him and gave him his credentials, a small badge to pin in his wallet.

" I'm going out to Nick's," he said.

" I'm going to see Nat Twohey."

Yerby looked at him sharply. " Not about Dunning? "

" About Ashton."

" Maybe I'll slip across with you a minute."

They went out the front portico and down the herringbone walk to the street. There, coming towards them, was something Spig had heard about but had never with his own eyes seen. Miss Celia Fairlie was approaching them in her army jeep, painted fire-engine red, with the crystal vases of an old-fashioned electric landau attached to the windshield, pink rosebuds in one, yellow in the other. Behind the wheel, very tiny, very erect, sat Miss Fairlie, a chiffon veil tied in a knot under her chin to keep her stiff, white sailor hat from jouncing wind-blown off her head. She sounded her horn, put her hand out as far as it would go, sounded again and made a smart right turn square into the centre of the yellow painted kerb, square against the fire hydrant, ten empty feet on either side, stopped, pulled on her brake and sat there, untying her veil, preparing to descend. A fresh pair of white cotton gloves was on a straw basket in the seat beside her. She put them on, rose, slipped nimbly on to the old carriage stair that was an added accessory and on to the street, brushing her white skirt and straightening her hat.

She blinked her pale blue eyes at Yerby.

" Thank you, Austin, for saving me my place to park."

" It's a pleasure, Miss Fairlie," Yerby said blandly. " But you didn't call me. I wasn't expecting you to be in town to-day."

" Nor did I expect to be here. It's the cigarette butts he leaves around."

" Someone leaves cigarette . . ."

" The chimney sweep." Miss Fairlie blinked at him, vague again. " It's very disturbing to the child. Because he prowls."

" Do you mean someone prowls around Eden, Miss Fairlie ? " Buck Yerby asked quietly. " Day or night ? "

" Oh, at night," Miss Fairlie said. " But he couldn't be the one who's ringing my telephone, I think. It's very annoying."

" Who rings your phone ? "

" I don't know. I didn't answer it. I'm sure there's no one I wish to talk to in the middle of the night. Or in the daytime either except young Nat Twohey. But that beldame tells me he's sick to-day. I'm not sure I wish to discuss a gate with her listening at the keyhole. But I must go now."

She went. Spig O'Leary materialised from the invisibility she'd cast him into, a hard white pallor around his mouth.

" So they're calling her up too."

" Take it easy," Yerby said evenly. " You're on her line, aren't you? I'll see if they'll switch her night calls to you. Maybe we can trace them. And those cigarette butts . . . and the chimney sweep." He grinned briefly. " If any. You've got a gun, haven't you? Okay, you're a deputy sheriff. Eden's your beat. You see anybody at night doesn't belong there, you shoot. Shoot to kill. That's your instructions. I don't care who he is."

CHAPTER XI

THERE WAS a somnolent stillness out at the Ashtons'. O'Leary looked at his watch. It was ten minutes past nine, too early for them. Or for Arthur Dunning, whom he had no interest in seeing. The matchstick curtains were still drawn in the two-room studio apartment over the garage that had been Kathy's house . . . the old shack, Stan had called it. Dunning's yellow midget car was in the middle of the road where Lucy had left it. Anita's Cadillac, still alongside the bright blue convertible, where it had been when Spig made his other call, blocked the drive in front of the house. He pulled to a stop behind the midget, prepared to cool his heels.

Then he saw they were up, or somebody was. A curtain moved in one of the long windows at the bridge side of the house, and he saw a golden head, Anita's or Lucy's, he couldn't tell which, before the curtain settled into place again. Stan he did not expect to be up. In fact the whole quiet, reasonable and convincing scene he'd carefully rehearsed was based on Stan's being gigantically hung over and remorseful enough to listen to him. He took a tighter grip on himself. There was to be no violence, no anger, no recrimination, just the plain facts of Stan's obligation, chiefly to himself as a fine, upstanding spokesman whose reputation was his cakes and ale, even if Anita still supplied the bread and butter. It was all set in O'Leary's mind as he passed the yellow midget, glancing down at it, the dew shining on the red leather seat.

Something else was shining at the base of the gear shift, on the dusty, red, rubber floor mat, that he saw without seeing until he was a couple of yards along.

He stopped, frowning a little. But that was because he was fifty-cent piece conscious, as a result of the Three D. Anybody could drop a half-dollar and not see it, rolled on its side up against the small, metal dome that housed the gear shift. He wasn't conscious of turning his head to look back. It was a purely automatic response . . . as automatic as his jaw dropping, his spine stiffening, as he swung full face around, staring at the front right tyre. The sun was on it, and glinting there in the white wall was a splinter of sapphire-blue glass. It was like a minute stiletto, or a jewelled dart shot from a blowpipe, buried with real force in the side face of the tyre.

As O'Leary stood there, too startled and too shocked to believe what he knew he saw, he was suddenly aware, out of a curious mental din all around him, that he was not alone. Someone was behind him, seeing what he'd seen, knowing he'd seen it and recognised it—someone as motionless and silent and shocked by it as he was. But the silence and the immobility were only for an instant.

". . . . Oh, good morning, Uncle Spig! "

Lucy Bronson came quickly up to him, her cornflower blue eyes clear and guileless as the day. " Nobody up but me. I've been up for hours. Really, hours! "

Only the ghost of the pallor round her red lips, a ghost vanishing but not quite gone, was left to tell O'Leary he was right. She'd seen the blue glass splinter; she knew he'd seen it.

" Won't you come on in? I'll make us some coffee. And oh! Uncle Spig! Have you heard the awful thing that happened to Nick at the Three D last night? "

The blue eyes widened inquiringly.

" The most awful thing! Somebody broke a big hole in his glass wall."

She looked down then at Dunning's car.

" Oh! Oh, *look!* " Both eyes and the red mouth were wide open with astonishment. " Lookie! I must have picked up a piece when I was down there this morning! It was all over the place."

" It was in a nice, neat pile at half-past seven, Lucy," Spig said dispassionately.

" Oh, but I mean this morning last night." She laughed, but there had been a sapphire splinter of alarm behind the long, dark lashes for an instant. " It was when Uncle Art and I were coming home. We saw a light out back and drove around. That must be when we picked it up. Isn't that the oddest thing! You'd think we'd have got it on the front of the tyre, not the side . . ."

She skipped past him and tried to pull the splinter out.

" Ooh . . . that's sharp! I'll cut myself! "

She shook her fingers with a comic *moue*. " I'll run get some tweezers. I want Uncle Art to see it."

" I suppose you and Uncle Art called the sheriff's office."

" Heavens, no. Why should we? Lucy laughed again. " Nick's gooney. He'd just blame it on some of the kids. We don't go to his place any more. He lets the kids have liquor."

" I'd skip that one, Lucy."

" What do you mean, skip that one? If Nick's been saying——"

" He hasn't said a thing, Lucy." Spig looked down at her for a moment. " But it's a public place. Not as empty as you thought, last night. So don't bother to tell either me or Mr. Cameron Nick's sold you liquor. And watch it, baby. Charlie's father was down there looking for him."

He went on, aware that she was standing stock-still behind him. Then he heard her feet on the drive and glanced back. She was running to the studio, pulling the door open, and he could hear her running up the steps, banging frantically on the door of the apartment. Dunning's rôle seemed to be an oddly devious one for a friend of the family . . . if he was a friend of the family.

He went on between the two cars to the front door. His own rôle was as curious, on another level. If the oath he'd just taken meant anything, he ought to impound the car at once, with the evidence of the blue glass splinter and the fifty-cent piece still in it. He hesitated for an instant, standing there. The door was open, the screen unlocked. He listened, then went inside and down the hall to the kitchen. It was empty. He went over to the telephone on the counter and looked up the number of the Three D, keeping one eye on the yellow midget in the drive. It was Greg's high-pitched voice answering.

" Let me speak to Mr. Yerby, if he's still there, Greg. Mr. O'Leary talking." When the sheriff came on he said, " Spig, Buck. What's the deal? "

" Just like I told you," Yerby's voice was a rasp of frustrated anger. " This drunk fella backed his car in the wall, Nick tells me. A nice fella, gave Nick the cash money to pay for it. Didn't give his name and Nick didn't take his license number."

" The slot machine? "

" That old fifty-cent slot's gone to the shop. A guy hit the jackpot and the thing jammed. Like I said, O'Leary. Nothing happened. Nobody knows a g.d. thing."

He jammed the phone down just as O'Leary heard another voice, cool and bitter, in the door behind him.

" Oh. The O'Leary show."

He put the phone down and turned. Anita Ashton was poised in the swinging door from the pantry, in a tailored white terry cloth coat belted like a dress with a short, full skirt, her yellow hair sleek, her lipstick accentuating the hard, narrow line of her mouth, her dark eyes levelled on him burning with resentment.

" I'm honoured, Mr. O'Leary." She let the door swing sharply as she came forward across the kitchen. " Has your wife sent you to collect Molly Ashton's board bill she complains to Mag Cameron we haven't paid? Or have you come to check on my maid? She's quit, all right. There's her note. You may read it—if you haven't already."

She pointed to the yellow counter. Spig picked the note up.

" Mrs. Ashton—Mr. O'Leary and Mr. and Mrs. Cameron were here. The doctor said Mr. Ashton should stay in bed and not have any more to drink. I'm sorry to leave before you come home. You can let to-day's money go, unless you want Lucy to give it to my mother over at Mrs. Sudley's.—Aletha."

He put it down. " The Camerons had nothing to do with it, Anita," he said quietly. " I may have. I told her she was headed for trouble. If you'll get your daughter to tell you the truth——"

" My daughter's never told me anything but the truth." Anita was seethingly angry but controlled. " Lucy has her faults. She wouldn't be my child or her father's if she hadn't. But lying's not one of them. She's never had to lie to me. And believe me, I'm sick of all the lies the rest of you tell. Mag Cameron, and those miserable Potter girls, ugly little brats . . ."

" That's hardly their fault, is it? At least Lucy knows who her parents are. She's not adopted, the way the Potter kids all were. It's pretty lousy to take your spite out on them, Anita."

" But anybody can take their spite out on Lucy— because she's pretty and all the men are crazy about her. Like Mag Cameron. Lucy snitched a martini. Well, she did. She snitched it by request, and the alcoholic old bag she snitched it for stood right there and let Meg blast Lucy and never opened her mouth. And all the stuff about Lucy and Charlie Sudley. Lucy wouldn't be seen dead with Charlie Sudley."

" Nuts," Spig O'Leary said quietly. " If you believe that, why don't you get her in here? Ask her where she was last night? "

" Because I know where she was! She was at a movie with Arthur Dunning, and at Colby's Carnival, riding the ferris wheel while Art sketched a Devon background. I saw them leave here and I heard them come home. I'd have been with them except that Stan Ashton . . ."

Two intense spots burned suddenly in her cheeks as she yanked open the ice box, took a can of orange juice out of it and banged it shut.

"——Stan Ashton." Her voice was icy with contempt. " Stan Ashton didn't drink. That's one of the reasons I married him . . . to get away from the lushes and the liquor, down here to the pure, simple life in the country. Stan was different. Stan worked. Stan believed in something. Money wasn't important to Stan. And I believed it. I thought it was wonderful. Ha! Stan Ashton would sell his right eye for one dollar and ninety eight cents cash on the barrel head. You can buy any ideal he's got for thirty cents and get a free lecture thrown in on the cupidity of all the rest of the human race. It makes me sick . . . sick . . . sick! "

The lines of her mouth were drawn down with the bitter taste of it.

" That's the kind of stupid fool I was. I believed what he said. I believed you people in the country were different from people in New York. I wanted Lucy out of there, away from a crowd she was running with, anything to be smart, anything for a thrill. And her father . . . that's one of the reasons I divorced him— always against her, always believing the worst, never giving the kid a break. It was always her fault if she was in a mess. So I let her come down here—to what? To a lot of carping old blue-nosed bags that don't have guts enough to talk to me. Art Dunning's the one they talk to. Well, I'm sick of it. I'm through. I'm getting out. And if there's anything I can do to pay back all the hypocrisy and all the crap I've taken from you people . . ."

" And that includes selling this place to——"

" It includes anything and everything, O'Leary. You'd be surprised."

She laughed, suddenly brittle, lightly contemptuous. " It even includes watching my old and sometimes constant friend Art Dunning falling in love with your wife. You haven't a chance, O'Leary. Not when Arthur puts his mind to his wooing. He's enchanting, believe me, and this time he's playing for keeps. Molly'll never know what hit her. One third of his family pill business flows a rich and lovely green, O'Leary. All for Molly. No more cooking or washing or taxi-ing kids around. Money and charm—or vice versa. So now if you're through in my kitchen, will you kindly get out? "

" Happy to, Anita." He controlled the white-hot anger, keeping his voice cool, movements deliberate. " I came to see Stan."

" Good. He'll love it, I'm sure. Go right ahead. Whether he can talk is something else again. That's his problem. If he wants a touch of dog hair, tell him it's *kaput.* Doctor's orders. His blood pressure won't take it. Go right ahead. O'Leary. He'll probably weasel. It's unfortunate this place is in his name, not mine. If it was mine, brother, would I love it."

" I'll bet you would." He pushed the pantry door open.

" And take a look at Arthur Dunning's portrait of the Master," she said as it swung shut again. " That's Stan Ashton, the louse he is, not the philosopher king he pretends in public."

O'Leary went on into the dining-room, a gall-bitter

taste in his own mouth. He crossed the eggshell Chinese rug out into the hall, along to the double doors, closing them carefully behind him. The shattered mirror table had been taken away. In its place was a large blotch of dirty grey where the whisky and ice had dried, fading the jade-green carpet. He started to go on through into Ashton's room and stopped, moving over to the fireplace instead, not to look at the Dunning portrait but to give him time to get control of himself. He had to be calm and reasonable when he talked to Stan. But the portrait dominated the room, a living thing, the lusty gaiety of the bawdy street with a luminous vitality in its wicked contrast to the doctrinaire, superior smile of the prig getting ready to wipe it out, the bloodless puritan sanitizing the dens of the joyful unrighteous for their own good. It wasn't the portrait of a man. It was a caricature of an egoist, the truth pricked out with a rapier vicious in its subtlety, with a malicious wit as venomous as the flick of a cobra's fang.

He turned away, trying for an instant to remember the old Ashton, the one before the slow stain of the world set in, and moved his head sharply round as he heard a stealthy creak in the panelled wall next to the fireplace. The door was opening, cautiously and very quietly. Stan Ashton crept in, his eyes shifty with anxiety, fixed towards Anita's room as he closed the door as softly as he could manage with his hand shaking on the knob. He was dressed for town in a grey pin-stripe summer worsted, his hat and brief-case in his hand.

Spig watched him, his rugged face impassive. There was something revolting in the pantomime of the morning after, the careful, sneaking tread, the ghastly, grey face, razor nicked, the whole unguarded nakedness of a man who thought he was alone, unobserved, mask down, too

intent on himself and his movements to see around him.
He got the door shut, steadied himself dizzily a moment,
and set out on tip-toe across the room, towards the
steps up to the hall.

" Hallo, Stan."

The brief-case thudded to the floor, the hat rolling
under the table. Ashton staggered and caught himself,
swinging around, gripping the back of the chair by the
table to hold himself up.

" Oh . . . I . . . didn't know you were here, Spig."
He even managed a thin smile. " I hope it's nothing
important." He looked at the gold bracelet watch on his
wrist. " I'm in a good deal of a rush this morning."

Watching him intently, Spig could see the sudden
decision to face it out, the crafty glint in Ashton's eyes
as he raised his brows.

" Of course, if it's about the strip across the road that
we had some vague idea of selling the State . . ."

" It wasn't vague, Stan, and we weren't selling it."
O'Leary downed the sharp spurt of adrenalin that made
his muscles twitch for an instant. " We were going to
give it. But it's not that I'm here about. It's this side of
the road."

" Oh, well, my dear fellow . . . nothing's settled
about that. Anita's just exploring——"

" That's a lie, Stan." The wave of anger rose again,
wiping out all the sweet reasonableness he'd planned.
" It's not Anita. It's you. And it's not being explored.
It's settled—waiting for you to get out to avoid the stink.
But you're not getting out, Stan. You're staying. Right
here."

"Oh, for God's sake, Spig! " Except that he was still
holding on to the chair, Ashton had got his professional
superiority intact. "Stop being so damned Neanderthal-

lish, will you? It's so childish. And such an unmitigated bore." He managed to shrug. " That's the only reason I haven't consulted you about my plans. It's so futile to try to get you to see anything intelligently that I decided the hell with it. I get so fed up with the mores of the herd. The destructive apathy——"

" Climb down, Stan. I'm not a woman's club."

Ashton's grey face flushed, his lips tightening.

" My dear Spig . . . you barge into my house and attack me, and expect me to get down and grovel on all fours. This O'Leary superiority complex gives me an acute pain in the apse, old fellow. You're just eaten with envy. You can't forgive me for making a name for myself. You've resented every success I've ever had. Everything you can do to belittle me and undermine my influence here in Devon you've done religiously, you and all the rest of them. I've been hamstrung, pilloried . . . never the least co-operation in anything I've done here."

" Have you done anything, Stan? Except talk? "

" That's just what I'm saying." Ashton's voice rose, shaking. " All right. You've asked for it. You can have it. I am selling. Not for money. Money's nothing to me. It's the freedom . . . freedom to get out of this filthy hole, freedom to live and do my work! And you, over there, sweating like a pig to make both ends meet . . . you're a fool, Spig! A fool, do you hear? Well, I'm not. I'm cleaning up while I've got a chance. I won't have to be humiliated every time Anita doles out ten cents. I'll be rich. And for you to have the effrontery to come over to me, as if I'm accountable to you for what I do——"

" Stan," Spig said quietly. " Listen. You are accountable to me, and you damn well know it. That's why you sneaked in Nat Twohey's office and stole that letter."

" That's a lie! That's a damned lie! " Ashton's face was livid, his voice raised to a hysterical scream. " I didn't steal it! I took it so you couldn't get hold of it and change the date. You know as well as I do no court's going to uphold a phony contract you forced me to sign! That was right after my wife was killed . . . I was mad with grief, with no idea of what I was signing! You knew how much this property was worth. You were the one trying to steal. But I'll show you! I'll spread the Dulaneys and the O'Learys on the front page of every paper in the country! So sue me if you want to! You haven't got the money to sue, but go ahead. Try it. That's all you can do. There's nothing else, not one solitary other damned thing, O'Leary! "

He let go the chair, swayed a moment and broke for the steps, caught the railing and swung round.

" Do you hear me, O'Leary? Not one solitary other damned thing, you stupid, poverty-stricken fool! "

O'Leary stood, the blinding red fog swirling through his brain. Out of it he heard himself, hardly recognising his own voice, cool and deadly even.

" There's something else, Ashton. One thing. I can kill you. And if you sell this place to a gambling outfit, I'll do it. You've got twenty-four hours to change your mind. Twenty-four. If you haven't changed it by then, I'll kill you, you filthy, rotten, little swine."

He went across the room to the three steps, holding himself rigidly in control, seeing Ashton stagger away from him, his face a convulsive mask of terror, his eyes bulging with abject, cringing fright, opening his mouth to scream. O'Leary went on past him, stopped as he heard a strangled gasp, swung around and back as the doors flashed open and Anita took one step forward through them, her eyes blazing with fury and contempt, fixed past him on the abject figure of her husband. The strangled sound from Ashton's throat shattered as a cyanotic flush bloomed for one hideous instant on his face, and with it an instant's incredible horror of recognition. His jaw went slack, his hands clutched at the air as he pitched forward, the recognition still on his face as he saw death before it came.

CHAPTER XII

THE MOMENT of trauma paralysing Spig O'Leary there on the step seemed longer than it was. He sprang down and knelt, one hand on Ashton's wrist, clammy cold, no whisper of a pulse, the other ripping open his tie and collar, knowing it was useless, the way his head lolled, totally inert. He swallowed a sharp wave of nausea and closed his eyes for an instant to blot out the hideous, staring face, still contorted with terror and the incredible recognition of death as it came. The image of Anita Ashton, poised in harpy-like rigidity, was so seared on the retina of his mind that the loud, rasping sound behind him was without meaning until he heard her voice, ice-edged but crisply controlled.

" Is Dr. Parker there? Then find him at once, please. Ask him to come to the Ashtons', out by the bridge. quickly. It's an emergency. My husband's had an attack."

There was silence again, taut and waiting. Spig O'Leary got slowly to his feet.

" It's too late, Anita."

" Too late for what? " It came swift as the flick of an

adder's tongue. " He's dead . . . that's what you wanted, isn't it? "

Spig turned, shaking his head. " No. Not really."

She was standing with her hand still on the phone, her face a strange, rigid mask. Grief, sadness, pity or compassion . . . if any of them were there they were too steeped in the gall of bitterness for their light to show.

" I'll get something to put over him." He crossed the hall into Ashton's room, still darkened, the air foul with liquor-sodden sweat, turned back then and opened the cupboards along the panelled hall until he found the linen, took a sheet and came back into the living-room.

Not really. He repeated it to himself as he unfolded the sheet and laid it over the huddled figure on the floor, strangely moving to him now, the catharsis of death washing his heart of its own bitterness. It was the old Ashton he seemed to remember, not the one lying here, or the one over the mantel, still alive, still smiling down, deathless, on the ignominy of death and the empty house of clay.

The rasping sound came again.

" Sheriff Yerby, please." Anita's voice was brittle as spun glass. " It's Mrs. Stanley Ashton. You can get him a message, can't you? Tell him my husband is dead. It's possible he's been murdered. Get him out here at once, please."

The phone clicked sharply into place again.

" Which of us are you accusing, Anita? " Spig asked quietly. " It's my impression the *coup de grâce* was yours."

" But not the threat. It wasn't I who threatened to kill him, was it? " She was relaxed then, only the bitter line of her mouth left, and the bitterer embers of the fury

I

that had been in her eyes. " And how do I know you didn't strike him? There's his hat and brief-case on the floor. No, O'Leary . . . I'm afraid you didn't understand me out in the kitchen. I said if there was any way I could pay any of you people back it would be a pleasure. Even if I can't hang you I can give you a little taste of the hell I've been through. And I told you . . . if anything happened to Stan, the place was mine."

" And brother, would you love it. Let's skip the tape recording."

Her lips tightened, her eyes flashed angrily. " You're licked and you don't like it. Well, I'll tell you, O'Leary. What Stan was going to do to your road is nothing to what I'm going to do to it. You don't want a fine expensive gambling joint befouling Eden's Neck. All right. I'm happy to oblige, O'Leary."

She laughed without amusement, reached for a cigarette, lighted it and blew the smoke in a derisive feather towards the ceiling.

" Very happy to oblige. O'Leary, the evangelist of hearth and home. Beating the tom-toms. The slots. The taverns. The bars. The honkey-tonks. Okay. That's what you're going to get, O'Leary. Four solid acres of them . . . and whatever there's room for on the other side of the road. Because I don't have any contract with Stan's buyers, and I don't have any with you, O'Leary. I never signed anything. You never asked me for my word when I came down here. If you had, you'd have been all right. I keep my promises—including the one I've just now made. If you think Devon Death Strip's a shambles, you wait till I get through with you here on Eden's Neck. You just wait."

She broke off abruptly, flashing around to the long windows open on to the flagstone terrace. Lucy was

running down the steps from the upper level. She gave
one swift glance of sheer terror behind her and flew to
the screen, tearing it open, her eyes cobalt smudges in
her white face.

" Lucy! Darling! What is it? "

Lucy halted, her body as stiff and rigid as her mother's
had been a moment before.

" It wasn't me, Mother! It was Charlie! I didn't have
a thing to do with it! I didn't! Honestly, I didn't! It's
a lie! "

It came swiftly, all in one breath, from a throat dry
with panic.

" Darling . . . what are you talking about! " Anita
caught her by the shoulders, shaking her. " What's the
matter, baby? "

" The sheriff . . ."

" Oh, sweetheart! " Anita's arms went around her, her
voice suddenly warm with compassion. " Don't, darling
. . . don't be frightened. I called him. It's about . . .
Stan, darling."

Across her shoulder Spig could see Lucy's rigid little
face and blind, blue eyes. She was still taut, dry-lipped
with fear.

" It's Stan, darling. He had a heart attack. He's dead,
Lucy."

" Dead? Stan . . . dead? Oh . . ."

The relief, the unutterable relief in the girl's voice was
like a horror story read in the lonely night. Spig stared
at her, fascinated, watching her as the colour seeped back
into her face, the taut coils of fear eased.

" Oh, Mummy! Poor Mummy . . . I'm so sorry! "

" It's dreadful, darling. But you run away." Anita's
voice was gentle. " You go and tell Arthur. Stay over
there with him until they go." She led the girl back to

the window and watched her slip outside, as Spig heard heavy footsteps on the flagstones at the front door.

"That's what you people have done to my child." Anita turned back, the two bright burning spots searing her cheeks again. "That's what . . ."

She broke off, hearing the front screen door open, and came quickly across the room.

O'Leary moved quietly over in front of the fireplace, more shaken by Lucy Bronson's gifted opportunism than he had been by Ashton's death. Perhaps it was reasonable. Personal fear was a far more intense emotion than any affection she might have had for a stepfather that even her mother had come to despise. But there was the business of " It wasn't me . . . it was Charlie." Honour among thieves of all ages . . .

"Oh, Dr. Parker . . . I'm glad you've come. Close the door, will you, Buck."

They were both there, the doctor with an alarmed and bewildered look on his face as he hurried down the steps, Yerby stopping to look for a moment before he turned and closed the door. He came forward, his face darkly flushed, hard ridges along his jaws, not looking at O'Leary. When he did then, his deep-set eyes boring across the room, Spig shook his head. Yerby drew in his breath and let it go, his jaw relaxing, came down into the room and stood, watching the doctor slowly fold his stethoscope, drawing the sheet back into place.

He got heavily to his feet. "I'm sorry, Mrs. Ashton." He was a crusty, taciturn, little man, but his voice was kindly then. "I told your maid last night that he had to stay in bed, no liquor and absolute quiet. The sheriff says you think he was . . . murdered?"

"You mean it's a natural death?" Yerby's eyes were fixed on Anita.

" Cerebral hæmorrhage, almost certainly. I'll do an autopsy. But I've warned him several time the last three months."

Yerby's eyes were still fixed on Anita. Waiting. O'Leary watched her impassively, waiting too.

When she stood, silent and motionless, Yerby said, " You heard him, Anita."

" I heard him." Her voice was detached and calm. " I said it was possible my husband was murdered. It's something I should imagine an inquest would have to determine . . . whether O'Leary, knowing my husband was ill, quarrelling violently with him, threatening to kill him in twenty-four hours unless he changed his mind about selling this place—in effect frightening him to death —didn't murder him as clearly as if he'd done what he threatened to do."

" You mean you want all this brought out in a public hearing, Mrs. Ashton ? " the doctor asked sharply.

" Why not? It's the truth."

Dr. Parker picked up his bag, his face flushing angrily. " I'm the coroner in Devon County. Mrs. Ashton. I was here last night. I saw your husband in acute alcoholic shock. I'd have taken him to the hospital at once if there'd been an empty bed. If you want all that on the public record, it's your privilege. But if you had a particle of decency or any respect for the dead you'd be ashamed of yourself, Mrs. Ashton. I'm leaving. Let me know what you decide to do, Yerby. I'll prepare a certificate. You'd be well advised to accept it and be grateful, Mrs. Ashton, for your husband's sake if not your own."

He went up the steps and out, closing the door sharply behind him.

" You heard him," Yerby said again. His eyes rested steadily on hers.

" And the fact remains that Spig O'Leary threatened to kill Stan if he sold this place." Her voice was tight and bitter. " The place is mine now. I'm selling it. Is O'Leary going to barge in here and kill me? "

" Oh, for God's sake, Anita."

" All right. You don't understand. I'm charging O'Leary with assault if not battery. I demand his arrest. I know he's a friend of yours. I know that's the way things are run here in Devon County. But I doubt if the State's Attorney will be so cavalier. Will you call him? Or shall I? "

" Look, Anita," Yerby moved his hands helplessly. " You're upset. You don't know what you're saying. You're in shock and don't know it."

" It's okay, Yerby," Spig said. " If she wants me in jail, I'll be happy to go. But she knows Stan had a contract with me; she has none. She plans to wreck the road. If she wants to make what she calls a shambles of Eden's Neck, that's another one of her privileges. But she'd better check on little Lucy first, unless she wants to make a shambles of Lucy, too. She——"

" Shut up," Yerby said sharply. He caught Anita by the arms and pushed her down in her chair as she flared up into sudden incandescence. " You, too. Simmer down, both of you. Just keep your shirt on."

He turned back to O'Leary. " Go on home and stay there. I'll be over. If you want to call the State's Attorney, Anita, go ahead and call him. But I'd call a lawyer first."

" I shall." She went swiftly past him to the telephone. " I'll call my father. He'll talk to your State's Attorney. I'm not through with you, O'Leary."

" Go on, Spig. Get the hell out of here, will you? "

Spig went past him, past the supine sheet-covered heap all but forgotten on the floor. As he reached the door he heard the soft, swift scurry of feet on the other side. He opened it just as a small bare heel disappeared through the dining-room door, and he heard the sharp swish of the swinging door into the pantry. When he got to the front door little Lucy was coming out of the kitchen, saddle shoes on, very surprised to see him, the cornflower eyes said—wide and guileless until they remembered they should look worried about the trouble in the house.

" Uncle Spig, what . . . what's happening? Is Mummy all right? "

" She's just fine, Lucy. And nothing's happened you haven't already heard, my pet."

O'Leary opened the screen door.

" Uncle Spig . . ." She came forward quickly. " I found out what happened at the Three D."

" Did you, now." He stopped to look back at her.

" Yes, I did. I called him up. He told me." There was a tiny, almost complacent smile in one corner of Lucy's bright red mouth. " A man—he'd been drinking a lot, Nick said—he backed his car into the wall. That's what smashed the glass."

" Luck, wasn't it? " O'Leary said. " But I wouldn't crowd it, Lucy. Comes the time."

" Who's talking? " The smile was open and mischievous then. " But if you wouldn't mind, would you tell Art Dunning that Mrs. Twohey called him up? She wants him to call her. If he's still over at your house, I mean. I guess he thought you'd be here a lot longer, when he hurried over to see Molly just now."

" Lucy." Spig had started on. He stopped, came back

and stood looking down at her, speaking very carefully. " Those are dynamite caps you've got in your pretty little fist. And watch out for Charlie, honey child. He wouldn't like it if he knew you'd squealed on him."

" I didn't squeal."

" You damned near did . . . if your mother hadn't been too upset to hear you. Watch it, baby. Like I say."

He went on, not looking back, conscious of her standing in the door watching him, not smiling now.

The yellow midget was still in the drive. The blue glass splinter was gone. So was the fifty-cent piece on the red rubber mat. He looked back then, saw Lucy was gone, shook his head and went on to his own car, suddenly conscious that his heart was a little lighter. The yellow midget still in the drive meant that Molly hadn't gone off for the day with Dunning. He drove out the Ashtons' broad, new road through his own woods into the narrow, bumpy lane towards home, and stopped half-way. It was the pain that made him stop, the dull gnawing, no place in particular, harder for him to take because he'd been happy so long he'd forgotten what it felt like to be un-happy. It wasn't Stan or the road. Granted the situation was a mess that O'Leary had done nothing to improve and a lot to worsen, all that really mattered was Molly. And that deal he had certainly fouled up.

He could hear Anita's bitter voice. *Including my old and sometimes constant friend falling in love with your wife . . . you haven't a chance, my friend, when Art puts his mind to his wooing. He's an enchanting guy* . . . It was crazy, of course. Always some guy had been in love with her. It was all right during the war, because he hadn't known anything about it, and he hadn't minded it the last seven years. He'd got a kick out of it, as a matter of fact, knowing it was him she belonged to. So what was different about

Dunning? He certainly wasn't afraid that that little black-bearded rat would take his girl. Or was he?

And instead of sitting there groaning at the misery in the seat of his emotional pants, it would be smarter to get the hell home and do a little wooing of his own . . . try to refurbish some of O'Leary's bedraggled enchantment . . . if any. A wry grin creaked along one side of his thin mouth. He started the car, thumping into a pothole he'd planned to fill every time he thumped into it, and grinned again. It was possible it wasn't his enchantment that needed refurbishing. Perhaps just a little attention to minor details like the well pit, various leaks, various other domestic sins of happy omission, was all he needed to restore him to grace again. And maybe quit treating her like a plough horse, if that's what anybody thought he was doing.

Because I love you, Molly. I couldn't live without you, girl.

CHAPTER XIII

HE SAID that just as he came out into the open drive, just as the first faint chill of emptiness touched him, when no children came running from the garden, even before he saw her car was gone. It wasn't in the circle and her space in the garage was empty.

He drove on around, parked, got out and stood listening to the suddenly desolate silence around him. He went into the house and listened again. It was so still he could hear the hum of the ice box out in the kitchen. Not even the cat came to purr and rub affectionately against his ankles. He went back outside and looked around. Then he saw the dog, sitting at Miss Fairlie's end of the little white bridge across the marsh at the head of the Cove. That meant the kids were over at Eden. Miss Fairlie didn't like dogs. There was nobody else in sight, except John Eden's tame crow, hunched dejectedly between a couple of cedars along the drive. Then he saw the gnarled, stooped figure of David's cousin, old Currier, out hoeing the corn in the O'Leary's garden, not as tall as it was.

He went across the field. The old man straightened up and pushed his hat to the back of his grizzled head.

" 'Mornin', Mr. O'Leary."

" Good morning, Currier. I guess the kids are over at Eden."

" That's right. Mis' O'Leary fix a picnic lunch for 'em to take with 'em, 'fore she an' that artist fella lef' for Bawpmur."

" Thanks."

He was a little sore until he got back to the empty house, felt the hollow, also empty, in the pit of his stomach, and realised suddenly he hadn't even bothered to tell old Currier that Ashton was dead. He stood there in the hall in a moment of unbiased self-scrutiny, slightly grim and wholly sardonic. How long ago—not more than half an hour—was it he'd been appalled at little Lucy when the facts of Stan's death relieved her from the pressure of the sheriff's arrival? That was bad. Callous. So what about O'Leary's lightened heart when he thought the yellow midget still in the drive meant that Stan's death had relieved him of the pressure of Dunning and his day with Molly? Now the pressure was on again he hadn't even paid old Stan the common civility of telling his maid's uncle he was dead. So what was the difference between him and Lucy except that he was old enough to know better? He went out and stood there in the drive, looking down at the white bridge that the dog was guarding till the children came back. John Eden's crow was still there with her, perched on the hand rail now, like a raven, a moulting symbol of doom, or of the dead end O'Leary had come to. He'd never been at a total dead end before. It was a strange feeling, like trying to chew a mouthful of old and bitter ashes. It wasn't despair, or hopelessness, or even anger, just a total dead end. And he had one job left to do.

Now that Anita was in charge, all the sweet reasonableness he'd rehearsed before he talked to Stan and never uttered a word of was clearly as useless as it no doubt would have been with Stan himself. The gambling outfit Stan had had in his mind would have been less of a menace, or a menace to fewer people, than the honkytonk shambles Anita had in hers. For that O'Leary could blame nobody but O'Leary, and the bitter part was the necessity he could no longer avoid of going to Eden and telling Miss Fairlie. Telling her he'd failed her, failed the old judge, failed everybody. It was probably what the Greeks had called hybris. The O'Leary's pride in their unbounded good fortune that had made them toss their gift of the ten velvet acres to the Ashtons had probably offended one of the lesser gods; this was the result. And O'Leary's pride and general arrogance in sounding off to all and sundry, making Devon County fit for human habitation. It was all part of the bitter taste of the dead ashes that went with him across the circle down the path to the bridge to the Gardens of Eden.

The borders, fragrant masses of phlox, white and brilliant pink, backed with regal lilies and foxglove, edged with spice pinks, were alive with bees, gay with butterflies. The brick wall was a shower of roses, pink

Van Fleets, the silver moons, pale gold between the pleached apricots and peaches. The turf was blue-green, soft as foam rubber under his feet. This was the Eden he'd promised would never be threatened in Miss Fairlie's lifetime.

He came out of the borders into the old carriage drive. The fireman's red jeep with the vases of rosebuds attached was on the other side of the picket gate where Mrs. Twohey had once hung suspended by her corset, pelted with rotten pears. It stood in front of the little Greek Revival office with its porch and white pillars, where Miss Fairlie had lived her five dark years, David and the old judge her fortress against the world.

We may have been monstrously culpable in many ways, but my faith in the ultimate Court of Appeals is such that I'm sure we will be judged with mercy as with wisdom.

Spig stopped, looking down at the house. A few late, long, graceful pinnacles, still hung from the century-old wistaria that made a heavy canopy over the porch. The double wings of the front door were open, but the louvred doors behind it closed. He'd imagined the central hall, but he'd never seen inside, or into the rooms on each side of it where the windows were open but the carved inside shutters folded forward to let in the summer air but still close the rooms to view. The rest of the house, the dormered windows upstairs, the two single-story wings connected with the main house by the bricked-in passageways known as hyphens, was as tightly shuttered as the day the old judge waded through the floating ice on the river to find the house locked, barred and deserted. Only now the forty-year added growth of ivy and Virginia creeper had sealed the windows, obliterating them with a sable pall. The six great chimneys, one at the end of each hyphen, two at each end of the house itself, were clothed with ivy, too, no sign of the brick beneath it.

The only sign of life itself, except for the partially open windows downstairs, was old David's wife washing clothes in a pair of wooden tubs on a bench beside the pump at the end of the kitchen wing, facing the O'Learys', where Spig had been admitted the morning the old judge died. But he waited. Miss Fairlie had an eerie way of suddenly appearing, from the house or from behind the boxwood or a border, sometimes seeming to materialise out of the air itself.

He couldn't see the children, but he could hear enough noise to wake the dead—or the sleeping child—down behind the bamboo screen bordering the duck pond. He went over through the borders across the boxwood circle to tell them to stop their racket. As he got to the giant weeping willow at the lower end of the pond there was a sudden silence, and out of it a peal of laughter as gay and crystal-clear as a dancing fountain, before the children joined in it and somebody retrieved Miss Fairlie's sailor hat from a maurauding gander. Spig knew she laughed with David and the children, but he'd never heard her. It was rippling, infectious and silver-light. He went through the willow branches and watched them for a moment. The boys, Tip and John Eden and David's grandsons, were cutting bamboo for fishing poles, Kitsy and David's granddaughter were laying out their lunch. Miss Fairlie, bareheaded, was with Molly A., feeding a welter of baby ducks. If anybody was worried about a sleeping child it was not apparent and unless it was an eccentricity to like other people's young of assorted colours, there was no evidence of that, either.

A forgotten picture came suddenly to Spig's mind . . . the rabbit warren in Washington, the grass patch with the Keep Off sign, Tippy's paper box of leaves in the garbage can, the crowded little room with Molly knocking over the laundry rack. All this around him was what the mad woman of Eden had given O'Learys to take its place, and given it on faith.

He went silently back and headed home, not the way he'd come but down through the rose arbour, where primroses and sweet herbs bordered the shady path, to the summer house, a small open Greek temple like the office, overlooking the river. No one ever came there now, not even the children, because along the other side of it, in front of the cryptomeria that hid it from the house, was the old Eden graveyard. At each corner of the rusted iron paling that enclosed it was a yew tree, neatly clipped, four dark guardian sentinels. He stopped, looking at it an instant. The stones were old, chipped and weather-scaled, all but one that was still legible. On it was chiselled: " Celia Eden Fairlie, aged twenty-four. Beloved wife of Ammon Fairlie." Below that was " Ammon Eden Fairlie, aged one day." It was Miss Fairlie's mother and the child she'd died in bearing. Beside this was another grave, the one they'd had to boil the snow to thaw the ground for, that had been covered with fresh pine boughs the day the old judge came. There was ivy on it now, but no headstone.

" The judge say some day we put one," David had told Spig when he'd passed there once, when the judge was still alive and David was clipping the ivy and yews. " But it jus' seem like that day don' never come. Firs' when her mind was sick it didn' seem right to call attention. Now, looks like she jus' forgot. Bes' she forget. Ain' nobody need his name writ down for the good Lord to fin' him. Nor the Devil neither. Tha's what I tell the judge and he agree."

O'Leary went on. The dog lying on the bridge waiting for the children wagged her tail, the crow cawed and stumped along the railing to follow him to the house that was still empty. He was crossing the circle when he heard the car in the lane and stopped, his pulse quickening. But it wasn't Molly. It was Joe Malotti, one of the neighbours, with two acres on the corner next to Sudley's place across from Miss Fairlie's gate on the old road. Spig went over to meet him.

"Hi, Spig. I thought I'd better come and tell you. I'm the first rat off the sinking ship."

It was what O'Leary had been waiting for, not knowing he was waiting.

"I hate like hell to do it, Spig," Joe said. "But . . if Sudley's going to put up a factory, it's no place for my kids. I've got a chance to sell. A service station-motel arrangement. I feel like a skunk, but we can get out whole if we get out first."

"I know."

"It's different with you people. You're lucky. You've got fifty acres. Nobody's going to hurt you."

Spig glanced across the field at the Ashton house, seeing in his mind's eye the neon glow of Anita's honky-tonk, hearing the sonic attack of the jukes a lot more clearly than Kitsy had heard Lucy's " Good-bye, Uncle Art " downwind that morning.

"If we coulda got a zoning law . . ." Malotti went on. "But that's the way it goes. Everybody that can's going to run for cover. It's the ones off the road out in back I feel sorry for. They're stuck. But you can't blame the rest of us, can you? "

Spig shook his head. Then he said, " Ashton's dead. Or have you heard? "

" Just now, on the radio. But my tears have dried.

Pete Greenway told me there was a rumour about Ashton's selling out and I asked him. He said nothing was settled but we didn't have to worry about the highway. He'd fixed that when he bought a right-of-way for his entrance through your woods."

" He didn't buy it. We gave it to him."

" That's what I suggested. He said he regarded the protection of the highway as in effect a purchase price. Smug as hell. I damn' near socked him. But there's not likely to be a change . . . with Anita in the driver's seat ? "

Spig shook his head. " We'll try to do anything we can."

" So if we all held off . . . ? "

" I wouldn't ask you to."

" Well," Malotti got back in his car. " I just wanted you to know where we stand. I'm sorry. But we just don't have the dough to take a chance."

Nobody had, of course, except the Camerons and the Potters, and they were out at the end of Eden's Neck with three hundred acres apiece, safer than anybody else.

O'Leary went out into the kitchen and got a glass of milk and the devilled eggs and sandwiches Molly had set aside from the children's picnic, at least remembering him to that extent before she skylarked off to Baltimore. It didn't make the house any less empty or fill the emptier hollow somewhere inside him. He was thinking that when he heard another car and went out. It was Yerby this time.

He got out of his car and took off his uniform hat to wipe the sweat from it.

" Boy, has she sure got it in for you. And for Devon County. Her father's flying down. She's gone to meet him now."

" I take it she still wants me in jail."

Yerby shook his head. " Not in jail, in the pen. But she didn't call the State's Attorney. She's waiting for her father. She tells me he's a smart operator. Maybe she'll cool down, I don't know. I came to tell you to sit tight for a while. I don't want her to tell the papers I'm playing any favourites and she can't get a square deal here in Devon County. It's lucky Doc and I were both just leaving Sudley's when my office got me. If you'd got a couple of deputies there, you'd have been in the can for sure."

He opened the car door. " If she gets us out on a limb and we have to hold an inquest, and she charges you with scaring Stan to death . . . But maybe her father's got some sense if she hasn't."

He started to get in the car and stopped. " One other thing. You have something on your mind when you called me at Nick's? "

As Spig hesitated his dark eyes smouldered with sudden anger.

" What's the trouble, O'Leary? You turning yellow, too? "

He slammed the car door shut and came back. " If you know any more about what happened at the Three D last night, I want it."

" I might want to know what you were doing at Sudley's, first? " Spig said.

Yerby stared at him. " What I was doing at Sudley's is no business of yours. But I'll be glad to tell you. I was checking if they heard any noise last night. They didn't." His face darkened with anger. " And I don't like what you're saying or the way you're saying it, O'Leary. I've heard it too many times. You took an oath this morning. ' Diligently and faithfully, without partiality or pre-

K

judice . . .' I took the same oath. Now if you know anything about that job at Nick's I want it. I don't care if it was the Governor. I'm waiting, O'Leary."

" All right," Spig said. " When I called you, I'd just seen a car with a splinter of blue glass shot into the side of a white wall tyre."

He saw Yerby's face relax into a wary stillness. " Go ahead."

" There was a fifty-cent piece rolled up against the base of the gear shift. I called you——"

" Then what happened? " Yerby asked quietly.

" Nothing. The glass and the half-dollar were gone when I saw the car a little later."

Yerby's eyes were still steadily on his. " The people that own this car . . . they friends of yours? "

" I know them."

" I followed you out from town this morning, as far as Nick's," Yerby said slowly. " You hadn't seen this car then. You were headed for Ashton's. Was this car a yellow midget? "

Sprig nodded.

Yerby was silent for a moment. " You're dead sure? "

" Dead sure."

" Okay. That's enough." His face looked like old shoe leather. " One of my boys saw that car parked out past the Old Mill round half-past one. He's got kids of his own. He told those two to move on, it wasn't safe if some sex psycho was on the prowl. He told me about it, just in case it backfired."

He turned his hat slowly around in his lean, brown hands. " This sort of knocks me. I knew it was amateur. But . . . this boy's father's done a lot for me. One of the best friends I've ever had."

He got in his car. " I don't know what to do, Spig.

You try to figure it as if they were your own kids. I can't get it. They've got everything, those two . . . everything they want. Did you tell Anita? Is that why she——"

Spig shook his head. " I didn't tell her. Lucy did— or started to. She knows I saw the tyre. She thought that's why you were coming this morning, before she knew Stan was dead."

Yerby nodded slowly. " I saw her run when we drove in, but I never thought a thing about it." He was silent for a moment, and started his car. " I'll talk to the kids first. Before they get a chance to get together. If Lucy was that scared. When I get through this, I'm going back to the automobile business. This makes me want to vomit."

He shot his car forward, the tyres digging into the gravel.

CHAPTER XIV

O'LEARY SMOOTHED the ruts over with the side of his shoe, and went back to the house. It had been a great day for the great O'Leary. A great day. The only fitting end to it would be to find himself in the local jailhouse accused of frightening a hungover former friend to death. Plus ratting on a couple of teen-aged kids. Plus having a wife he was supposed to treat like a plough horse. It would make a fine story by the time it got the rounds.

John Eden's moulting crow stumping along behind him, croaking and blinking its jaundiced rimmed eyelids, seemed equally fitting.

" Cah," it said.

" Get out," O'Leary said. " Beat it, will you? " He went on inside. If there was just something brilliant and dynamic he'd done, it wouldn't have been so depressing. Or if there was something dynamic he could do. Instead, he got a washer and fixed the leaking faucet in the bathroom. That was the great O'Leary's speed. Then there was the loose rubber tile in the kitchen, the cellar window that creaked, and finally the loose plank down on the pier.

The crow followed him down. " Cah, cah! "

Spig looked around. It was headed down the sea wall towards the blue heron soberly fishing the bank. They'd tangled before, the lost feathers black, not grey, the home champion game but over-matched. He picked up a nail to throw and stopped. The Ashtons' back windows were in full view from the end of the pier. One of them was open, and running out of it was a black-haired boy as tall as a man. He dashed down the lawn and over the bank, ducking as he waded out of sight around the retaining wall under the great chestnut oak. It was just in time. Charlie Sudley had barely disappeared when Buck Yerby came around the side of the house. The window was closed then. Yerby stood a moment and went back along the house to the living-room windows on the terrace, also closed. If he was knocking, he was not admitted. When he left then, the bedroom window opened again and the fair-haired child slipped out. But only for a moment, and when Yerby came in sight again it was too late. Lucy was back inside, the windows tightly shut. Spig grinned, cheered a little to find Yerby's efforts as non-dynamic as his own.

Which was why there was something essentially comic,

in spite of everything, about Joe Cameron's barging
around the house just as he came up from the pier.

"For God's sake, Spig! I got here as quick as I could."
He was in his city clothes, sweating, his brown ox eyes
and ruddy face stricken with dismay. "I went to the
jail. Thank God you're out. I told you to watch it, Spig.
I just happened to call up, to talk to Stan, and Lucy
told me what happened."

O'Leary took a long breath. "Look, Joe. I don't know
what little Lucy told you, but let's get it straight. I didn't
kill Ashton, if that's what you've got in mind."

Cameron let himself down into a chair and wiped his
forehead.

"And I'd like to know what little Lucy did tell you."

Cameron's face reddened. "It doesn't matter," he
said defensively. "She was just upset, I guess. All alone
there. You'd think her mother'd have more sense. Anita's
not fit to have a kid."

"Yeah," Spig said. "Poor Anita."

Joe Cameron looked at him doubtfully. "Well, I
better call Mag." He got up and made a bumbling
embarrassed move towards the door. "I called her
from the office. She wanted to come right over. But
. . . well, Lucy told me about Molly and Dunning,
Spig."

"She did? She tell you they're in Baltimore for lunch
and a Swedish art exhibition of some kind?" Cameron's
distress suddenly gave a little perspective of O'Leary's
own. "I don't know what Lucy made of it, Joe, but that's
the way it is."

"Nobody around here's threatened to kill Dunning?"

"It wasn't me and it wasn't about Molly," Spig said.
"It was about a painting. You remember last night
over at the Ashtons'? You said if Dunning painted you

the way he did Stan, you'd kill him? Let's call it a manner of speaking, shall we? "

He said it casually, trying not to think of the loaded rifle in Tip's hand.

" It wasn't any manner of speaking." Joe Cameron's face reddened again. " I said it and I meant it, by God."

" Then don't tell Lucy. And watch it yourself. You're probably right in there, in his gallery of rural types— along with all the rest of us."

He turned, listening. " If you're going to call Mag, better do it. The kids are coming back. I don't want them to hear any more of this than they have to."

" Okay." When he came back he'd taken off his coat and was rolling up his sleeves. " Mag says why not let me bring the kids over to our place? Sorta out of the way a while. Ours'd love to have 'em."

" Thanks, Joe. That'd be a break." About the only break so far, that day.

" I'll collect 'em. We've got everything they need, Mag says." He started through the house and turned back. " And Spig . . . if you get in a jam . . . I mean, if you need any quick dough, for a first-rate lawyer, or anything . . ."

" Thanks. May do. I'll let you know, Joe."

He watched Cameron go with a lift of one ginger eyebrow. Or was it O'Leary who'd better be more worried then he was. He'd told Anita the *coup de grâce* in Ashton's final collapse was hers rather than his, but he hadn't told it to Yerby or the doctor or to Cameron. Maybe that was a mistake, too. He sat down and took out a cigarette.

" Daddy."

" Oh, hallo, Tip. I thought you'd gone with——"

" No." Tip came on around. " I've got work to do."
He looked bewildered and not very happy. " Could . . .
could I talk to you a minute, Daddy? "

" Of course. Why don't you sit down a while? "

Tip sat tentatively on the edge of a chair, poking at
the edge of a flagstone with his foot, not looking at his
father.

" What is it, son? "

" Why . . . why did Mother go away with Mr.
Dunning, Daddy? "

O'Leary drew a deep inner breath. " Maybe we didn't
handle things very well, Tip," he said. " She's got a
right to have her own friends."

" Not Mr. Dunning, Daddy. He's . . . he's a bad
man. Miss Fairlie says so."

" I don't know how she'd know that, Tip."

" Because when Kitsy told her about Lucy and the
movie she said Mr. Dunning wasn't at any movie with
Lucy. He was over at her house then."

Spig sat forward abruptly. " At Eden? "

Tip nodded. " Outside the office, painting. He had his
stool and everything."

" *Painting?* In the dark? "

" It isn't so dark. The moon's up late, and the river
makes it sort of light, with the stars all out. And those
glasses he carries around, they're like the ones they used
in the war for night patrol. I told Miss Fairlie he was
over here to see Mother, but she said it was later when
he came to Eden—one o'clock. And he stayed till after
three, she said. She was watching him all the time."

O'Leary felt a chill prickle at the base of his spine.

" I don't like that very much," he said.

" I don't like it at all. He's not going to paint Miss
Fairlie. I'll ki——"

" Wait a minute," Spig said. " That's plenty of that. We're not talking about killing anybody. Not any more."

The child's eyes were hot, his face sullen.

" Look, Tip. It's wrong to say that sort of thing. I'm not going to preach at you—I'm just going to tell you what happened to me to-day. I lost my head and told your Uncle Stan I was going to kill him. He had an attack and died. Now Anita's trying to have me arrested. She says I killed him. I said that because he was going to sell the place over there and I was trying to stop him. I couldn't have gone about it in a stupider way. Now he's dead Anita's going to sell to an even worse crowd, as far as Eden's Neck's concerned. So it didn't get me any place, along with the rest of it. It just doesn't work, Tip."

" But . . . Uncle Stan couldn't sell the place, Dad. He promised he wouldn't, when we gave it to them."

" He wasn't keeping his promise. People forget. That's what Judge Twohey told me a long time ago."

" But we wouldn't, Dad. Not when Miss Fairlie's been so——"

" No. We wouldn't. Or I don't think we would. But maybe if we didn't like it here and somebody offered us a lot of money . . ."

Tip shook his head. " That would be wrong, Dad."

" I know it would. I'm just telling you, that's all. In a pinch people can always find a lot of reasons for making wrong look right. Like your saying you'll kill Dunning. It's wrong, no matter how right you think your reasons are."

Tip contemplated that for a moment before he got up. " Well," he said. " I guess there's one thing. We don't have to worry about Molly A., do we, any more? "

Spig looked at him inquiringly. He hadn't even thought of the child in terms of her father's death.

" I mean, Kitsy thinks we ought to adopt her, like the Potters' girls," Tip said. " To make sure she belongs to us. Can you adopt children that are your own relations, Daddy? "

" We'll see. I don't think we have to worry about it."

" Not unless Lucy thinks we want her. That's why none of the kids like Lucy. She's sort of mean. Like Ginny Potter was going steady with Charlie Sudley, and that's why Lucy . . . The kids say she doesn't want anything she can't get away from somebody else. Nobody trusts her. She tells awful lies. Like the time . . ."

He broke off, listening. " There's a car. Maybe it's Mother! " His face lighted.

" All right. Scoot. But mind your manners, Tip."

And you mind your own, O'Leary.

He waited, listening a moment before he followed through the hyphen. She was there getting out of the car, laughing, Dunning holding the door. (How long since O'Leary had bothered even to reach over and open it for her?) He saw her go to Tip quickly and bend down to kiss him. As she straightened up, her arm still around his shoulders, Spig caught his breath. She was always lovely, but in her dark green silk suit and small, green hat and white gloves, not just Molly in blue jeans or a sweater and skirt dressed for Plumtree Cove but a lady dressed for town, slender as a spear of goldenrod, her hair as bright and shining in the sun, she seemed suddenly remote, urban, chic and sophisticated, of a different world, no well pits to pump, dishes to wash, grimy kids to feed. As Anita said. He forgot it was the way she always impressed him, a part of her infinite variety that custom could not stale, and that his heart always stood still an instant when he saw her after he'd been away from her for a day. And there was Dunning, not in his paint-spotted denims but immaculately tailored, goat's beard trimmed, even distinguished-looking in a casual way O'Leary was forced reluctantly to admit—O'Leary, still trailing cobwebs from the cellar window, not even having bothered to shower and put on a pair of fresh shorts.

" Hi, Spig! " Dunning's bright eyes dissected him, missing nothing, as he came towards them on the drive, trying to look as amiable as possible. " We've had a wonderful time. Missed you, except you'd have been bored to death, we both decided."

" Hi, darling." Cool and remote was Mrs. O'Leary. She'd been laughing up to then.

" Will you come in and have a drink? There's some Scotch around some place, I think? "

O'Leary, also casual, was fooling the Tattoo Artist not at all.

" I much prefer rum." Dunning's black eyes above the black beard sparkled with mischief. " But a rain check, if I may. I'll leave you dear people to yourselves a while. Thanks again, Molly. See you soon. Don't forget— to-morrow at ten."

He glanced at Tip, headed stolidly for his garden. " Shall I go the long way? Or will the Lord Proprietor give me royal leave to pass? Still, what's a clod or two when the weather's dry? Good-bye . . . good-bye, my loves."

He set out between the cedars across the field to the trail through the woods.

" Tip tells me you've sent the other kids to the Camerons'," Molly said. " Thoughtful of you. But I've had a lovely day. I don't want a row even if they aren't around to hear it. So if you'll excuse me, I'll go take off my one good dress."

She went coolly past him, treading carefully not to scar the heels of her one good pair of shoes in the gravel.

O'Leary flushed. *Okay. The hell with it.*

" Dad."

He hadn't heard Tip come back.

" I guess I'll go over to Miss Fairlie's. I'll stay to supper. She'll be glad to have me."

" Okay, Tip."

" And Daddy . . . don't be mad." He ran then, calling the dog.

O'Leary took a deep breath, relaxing a little before he went along to the house, waiting outside till he heard Molly coming down the stairs.

" Molly."

She stopped, taut, her hand on the banister, eyes green, the flecks in them molten gold.

" Molly, I'm sorry. I was a damned fool."

" That's quite all right. Let's skip it, shall we? "

" We can skip that, if you want to. But there's something else we can't. I've got some bad news. It's pretty lousy, Molly. Maybe we'd better go and sit down and both of us try to keep our temper. Tip's gone to Miss Fairlie's."

He opened the door of the old cottage and waited till she came across the hall. She was walking rigidly, wooden as a doll.

" It's not Molly A.? Nobody's taking——"

" No."

She sat down at the far end of the long sofa against the wall, looking straight ahead of her. " I can stand anything but that," she said tightly. " What is it? "

" It's the Ashtons. Stan's dead, Molly."

" Stan . . ." She stared at him. " Stan Ashton? Why
. . . Why didn't you tell Art? Why——"

" Because he knew it already. This morning. Before
he came for you."

Her eyes were blank, drained grey-green.

" No . . . he didn't. He couldn't have . . ."

" Lucy told him."

The gold flecks flared hot again. " Who says so?
Lucy? Lucy wouldn't tell the truth to save her own soul.
Just because you loathe Art Dunning——"

" Stop it! "

O'Leary caught himself sharply. " I'm sorry. Maybe
she didn't tell him. Her mother told her to, but I guess
she didn't. She was sticking too close to the living-room
door. I should have thought of that. I guess I was just
too sore at his taking my girl to give him a break."

He was sitting hunched forward, his hands between
his knees, and didn't see her face start to soften.

" If he had one coming," he added, and she stiffened
abruptly again, waiting.

" But I guess I'd better give it to you straight. It isn't
easy."

It was harder than he'd thought, with her sitting there
like a rocket ready to flare up. He hunched forward
again, looking at his hands.

" I met Sudley coming home yesterday. He told me
Ashton was selling."

" *Selling?* "

" Selling the place to a gambling outfit. Dunning
does know that. I heard him talking to Mag Cameron
on my way through here to your party yesterday. But
we'll skip that. I don't want to quarrel about him any
more. Anita says he's fallen in love with you and he's
playing for keeps. She also says I haven't a chance, and

maybe she's right. As a lover I guess I'm pretty much of a failure—the same as I've been in the rest of this deal. Anita's trying to get Yerby to arrest me for Stan's murder."

" Stan's murder . . . ? " It was a dry, incredulous whisper coming to his ears.

" That's what I'm trying to tell you." He went steadily on. " I was over there last night. He was dead drunk. I went back this morning. I was going to try to make him see he couldn't let us down without hurting his own reputation. Anita was in the kitchen, sore as hell at him and everybody else. I went in. He was supposed to stay in bed, but he was up and on his way out. I didn't say any of the things I was going to say, because he started a lot of stuff that made me blow up, too. I told him I'd kill him if he sold the place. I started to leave. He thought I was going to kill him then. Anita barged in, and that finished him. He had cerebral hæmorrhage, Parker says. Anyway, he's dead, and I'm under some kind of unstated technical arrest till the State's Attorney makes up his mind."

He rubbed both hands through his ginger stubble, kneading his scalp; his rôle in the morning's fiasco more ignominious with each new telling.

" Anyway, Anita's out for blood. She's not going to sell to the gamblers. She's going out to chop the place up into another honky-tonk like Devon Death Strip. Anything to get even. She hated Stan, she hates us and everybody and everything else around here. And Sudley's selling out, to get even with Stan. Joe Malotti's clearing out—selling to a service station-motel arrangement. So this whole end of the road's going to be shot to hell. Instead of helping, I've made a stinking mess a lot worse. So anything you want to say, go ahead and say it. You can't say anything I haven't thought. I've really fouled things up for everybody."

She was silent so long that he straightened up at last and turned to look over at her. She was sitting stiffly erect, her hands folded in her lap, her face pale, her eyes wide, staring into nothing.

Then she shook her head quickly. " What is there for me to say? It's my fault. It was my sister. It was me that wanted to give her . . ."

He saw her eyes swimming with tears, blind as she tried to keep her voice from breaking.

" No, it wasn't, Molly. It was both of us."

What happened then wasn't too clear. All he knew was that she was in his arms, and when he heard himself finally all he was saying was, " My girl . . . you're my girl, Molly. I love you so much. I've been bats without you . . ." saying it over and over, no epic prose or tender music, but it healed the empty ache in his heart, and her lips were warm and sweet on his. " . . . You do love me still . . . don't you? "

" Stupid . . . don't be so stupid . . ." She batted back the tears. " I was just furious at you. How do you think I could ever love anybody but you, and Tippy and the other kids, and this place, and all the things we've worked for together . . . just because somebody else comes along and paints a ceiling for me? You're so stupid."

" I know I am."

" You're not, either. Don't be silly. And I really had a miserable time to-day. I hated it. And then you came out looking like Jove with his nose out of joint and Tippy like a thundercloud. I won't have it. Tip's got to learn he can't have everything his own way. He'll end up like Lucy and Charlie Sudley, spoiled rotten."

" No, he won't."

" He will unless he learns. But I can't bear this. I was so proud we could help Kathy."

" So was I."

She drew away from him, sitting erect again, wiping her eyes. " It's what can we do? We've got to do something, Spig. Miss Fairlie's done so terribly much for us. We promised we'd take care of Eden as long as——"

She broke off as the telephone rang. " It's probably Mag about the children." She went across the room and picked it up.

" Hallo. Oh . . . why, hallo, Anita. I'm so terribly sorry about Stan."

Spig saw her face smooth out abruptly, blank and pale.

" Why, of course . . . we'll come, as soon as we can. Very anxious, of course. You know that, Anita."

He saw her swallow then and moisten her lips.

" She's fine, thank you. Yes. We'll be right over."

She put her hand on the receiver bar, pressing it down, the phone still in her hand. She put it down then, turning slowly.

" . . . Anita. Her father's over there. They . . . they want to talk to us. She says if we . . . if we want the place they'll be happy to let us have it. But—it's the way she sounded . . . like a trap. The way Arthur Dunning sounds when he's being malicious, laughing at people."

Spig got up. " I'll go over. You stay here."

" No. I'm coming with you." She pushed her hair back quickly and moistened her lips again. " I'm frightened, Spig," she whispered. " She . . . she asked me about Molly A.—for the first time. She's never mentioned the child before."

CHAPTER XV

As SPIG and Molly came out of the trail through the woods into the Ashtons' grounds the telephone was ringing in Dunning's studio apartment. It stopped and started up again as they crossed the lawn. Anita's father was on the lower level of the terrace outside the living-room, with the others, seated casually at ease, Anita and Lucy laughing at a story Dunning was telling them—a pleasant gathering at the end of a pleasant day.

Molly's hand closed for an instant on Spig's arm. " Careful, darling . . . let's be just as smooth as they are."

Smooth was not quite the word for Anita's father, coming across the lawn now to meet them, a large handsome man with a glistening white mane and an impressive paunch, benign in his cordial warmth.

" It's a pleasure to see you young people again." He shook their hands. " Even under circumstances distressing to us all."

Distress most admirably concealed, O'Leary thought as they followed him down the flagstone steps towards the others, Anita calmly watching them, her pencilled brows raised a little, a slight smile of neither warmth nor friendliness on her lips.

" Good evening," she said. " Shall we go inside? Art's telephone drives me mad. If you don't want to answer it you could at least close your windows, darling."

Dunning got to his feet, grinning at her. He had changed back into his denims, not the paint-spotted faded ones but a fresh pair, navy blue.

" Would you like me to go answer it for you, Uncle Art? " Lucy was the demure and well-bred little lady, her blue eyes clear and innocent as an angel's.

" She'll give up," Dunning said easily. He crossed the terrace to open the screen door, holding it for Molly, his eyes lighting as she went through. Spig waited for Anita and her father and Lucy, aware that Dunning, watching him, was suddenly grinning.

" Don't worry . . . the remains are gone."

It was *sotto voce* at O'Leary's elbow, startling in the unerring accuracy with which Dunning sensed his distaste and his surprise at Anita's casual use of the room. The image of Ashton's body, huddled, horribly staring, in there on the floor was still in his mind. He'd have thought it would be in hers, until he went in, a strange eerie sensation prickling along his spine. It was as if Death had been the transient in the house.

Ashton was still there, vividly alive in the portrait dominating the room . . . the supercilious smile, the spidery hands, the spirit more tenacious than the flesh in the painted eyes that followed Spig. He turned away uncomfortably, flushing as he was aware of Dunning still watching him, a bright satanic grin on his bearded face —the Tattoo Artist enjoying a malicious triumph in the immortality he had bestowed.

" Sit down, won't you? " Anita's father took his place at the centre table where his brief-case was open, several piles of papers beside it. " I'd like a brandy and soda, Anita. Arthur, I expect you and Lucy know what brand of poison the O'Learys prefer. If you'll——"

He stopped as the phone rang and Lucy flew across the room to answer it.

" Hallo." She flashed her bright gold head around inquiringly to Dunning, and back. " I'm sorry. He isn't

L

here." Her blue eyes danced mischievously. "No, he hasn't been home all day," she said earnestly. "We're terribly worried about him. We'll call the State police if he isn't here by morning. Oh, that's quite all right. We're concerned ourselves. It really isn't like him, you're absolutely right about that. He's never disappeared like this before. Good-bye . . . we'll let you know if we hear."

She put the phone down, laughing with delight. "Mrs. Twohey. Uncle Art had a date he didn't keep."

Anita laughed. "Lucy . . . you wicked child."

"Tell the old cat I've gone to New York, when she calls again," Dunning said, bringing the tray around. "But don't do that . . . there's one more visit I'd like to make."

Spig looked at him casually, alert to the sudden venom in his voice. He glanced at Molly then. If she had heard it there was no indication. She was sitting there retired behind a familiar mask, cool, serene, completely opaque even to him.

Anita's father sipped the drink and put it down. "Now, if you're through with pixie diversions . . ." he said, smiling with affectionate amusement at his blue-eyed grandchild. "Shall we get down to business? Fortunately, it's very simple."

He turned to Spig. "The first thing is, I've talked to your State's Attorney. I assured him of our entire co-operation. We wish to have this matter on the most friendly basis. He has the coroner's report, the autopsy will reveal the cause of death, and there'll be no question in anyone's mind . . . least of all my daughter's. Anita realises she acted badly this morning. It's understandable, I think. She was under considerable emotional strain."

It seemed to O'Leary that she still was, as if his physical

presence had destroyed the polite urbanity her father had brought with him. Or Molly's presence. He didn't know. But her mouth had thinned, her dark eyes were smouldering. He wondered again then as he saw the flint-edged glance she shot across the room at Dunning. The Tattoo Artist was standing, leaning casually against the bar, looking at Molly, not grinning but intently grave, his face curiously pale, an almost rapt expression in his black eyes, unaware of any of the rest of them in the room.

" Now, then." Anita's father took a pair of horn-rimmed pince-nez out of his breast pocket. " I have a copy of Stanley's will. I won't read it now, as he goes into several ethical theories of his at considerable length. The gist of it is this. He names Anita and me as co-executors of his estate, which he divides equally between her and his daughter, Mary Margaret Ashton."

He riffled through the pages, and stopped, looking over at Spig and Molly. " He has named you two her guardians during her minority . . . unless Anita would be interested in taking the child."

Even before Spig had seen her relax, smiling, her brows lifted again, he felt the sickening premonitory wave through the pit of his stomach. Her father's slight pause, the quality of his voice, had spelled it out. Spig kept his eyes carefully on the centre table, not daring to look at Molly.

" . . . But of course, I'd be more than interested, Father," Anita said. " I'd adore having her. The O'Leary's friends have been complaining about my failure as a stepmother. I'm delighted to relieve their minds—and the O'Learys' budget."

" Oh, Mother! Do you mean it? We can have Molly A.? Oh, what fun! "

Lucy danced across the room and threw her arms around her mother's neck. " How wonderful, Mother! I've always wanted a sister! When can we get her? "

Anita's eyes rested coolly on Spig, her lips tightening. " As soon as I get a maid . . . and a nurse to look after her."

" Oh, good! " Lucy danced over to the table and kissed her grandfather, laughing then as she wiped the lipstick off his cheek.

He smiled, indulgently pleased. " Sisters aren't all skittles and beer, Lucy," he said with mock severity. " But of course, I heartily approve. It'll be an excellent thing for you. An only child needs a companion."

He smiled at Molly and Spig and turned back to pick up a single typed sheet. " So all that we have to settle now is the matter of the property, and the agreement that Stanley made with you young people after the death of his first wife, to whom you gave the property at the time of their marriage."

O'Leary saw Anita Ashton relax back into her chair, a half-smile on her lips, her eyes alight with cynical amusement. He glanced at Molly. Her brown throat moving as she swallowed was the only sign of what he knew was in her heart. Her face was serene, her hands quiet in her lap.

" And let me say at the very outset, that my daughter and I, as co-executor for her and the little girl, have no intention in the world of not honouring Stanley's agreement with you. My daughter hadn't . . . realised the extent that public feeling here has been roused, until several people who have homes in the area called her up this evening. It seems they are pretty generally aware of the fact that Stanley had made a commitment that puts the responsibility of . . . shall I say, retaining the rural character of the neighbourhood jointly on Anita and on you people. Anita wants to do her part, and therefore of course she is more than happy to carry out the terms of Stanley's agreement with you."

He looked around expectantly at Anita.

" Indeed, yes, Father," she said pleasantly. " I wouldn't for the world want the people of Eden's Neck to think I didn't give them a chance to keep Sudley from bringing in a factory here. I'm happy to let the O'Learys have the place just as Stan promised them. You've got his records there. I'd be happy to let the O'Learys have the place for nothing, except that you and I have a legal responsibility to Molly Ashton."

She smiled at Spig, her foot moving like the tail of a cat, waiting. Her father was judiciously examining the papers in his hand.

" As a matter of fact," he said, " there's every indication that Stanley always intended to honour his agreement with you. Until fairly recently, at any rate . . . when I think there's no doubt he'd become a sick man. I say that because I have in these papers an almost minute record he'd kept of his expenditures on this place. For example." He picked up a piece of brown paper apparently torn from a grocery bag. " Here's an item of three azalea plants he bought at a roadside market. Three dollars and six cents. The six cents is the sales tax, I presume. Ten dollars for a load of cow manure from Mr. Sudley. Five dollars a bale of peat moss. Three hooks for screen doors, forty-five cents. I mention these to show you that he kept very complete records. An item, for instance, here for forty-eight dollars and eighty-three cents for trimming and feeding a chestnut oak tree. Of course, all this material will be at your attorney's disposal. Here's——"

" I'm sure the O'Leary's aren't interested in Stan's passion for financial detail, darling," Anita murmured.

Her father smiled benignly at her, and turned back to the O'Learys.

" Roughly, this is the amount that has been laid out on this place. I've lumped the smaller items into general categories. For the original survey and workmen's insurance, $350. Clearing, $500. For the original lane and additional gravel, $500. For the original house, $7,500, and $10,750 for converting it into a studio and apartment with two baths, its own well and water conditioning system. For the pier, five hundred feet of sea wall and landscaping, $5,000. For the new road, $6,500, and $150 for the preparation of the deed and the survey. Miscellaneous items, taxes, insurance, $8,500. For this house, $55,000. Totalling roughly, $99,750."

He put the papers down and took off his glasses. " Now, I should add that my daughter has not included numerous items she has personally contributed since she's been here, and further, that she feels you should not have to pay for the survey and drawing of the deed for the right-of-way you kindly gave them through your woods. The amount of $150 is therefore to be deducted, the total being, consequently, $99,600. The offer Stanley had, by the way, and that's still open, is somewhat beyond that figure, due to the property's peculiar location in terms of their special needs. So that's the story, my friends."

He smiled at them with benevolent kindliness, and picked up his glass. " May I have a touch of ice, please, Lucy? "

" Yes, sir."

Lucy sprang foward obediently. Except for her, the

motionless silence in the room was long-drawn and rigid.

"How much time are we allowed, Mr. Waltham? And what are the terms of sale?"

It was the Sea King's daughter who asked—cool, crystalline and innocent of irony.

Anita's voice was a steel trap biting shut. "The terms are cash. The time, three days."

"I thought a week," her father said mildly.

"I've changed my mind. It's Tuesday. They can have till Friday."

"Thank you, Anita . . . Mr. Waltham." Molly rose calmly. "Good night. Good night, Anita."

Spig followed her across the room. The only flaw in her complete composure was that her eyes were fixed ahead of her, oblivious to Dunning or Lucy off in the corner by the bar. Spig looked over to nod to them. But Dunning was not aware of him, nor was Lucy. Dunning's black eyes were fixed on Molly, no glitter, no grin or gleam of malice, nothing but absorption intense and devouring, his own soul naked in them. Lucy watching him, was like a bird fascinated, her lips parted, blue eyes blank until they darted from him to Molly and back to him, widening brightly, her whole body quickening with understanding and excitement. There was something so tangible, so like a physical beam, shooting towards Molly that Spig moved sharply to intercept it, shielding her from it, his arm in hers as she pushed the screen open and stepped out on to the terrace. He could feel the tremor, the spasm of taut nerves, as he touched her. He tightened his hand on her arm then, aware that they were not alone.

"I'll walk a piece with you." Anita's father moved

into step beside them. " I'm pleased with Anita's decision about the child."

Molly's arm was rigid in Spig's hand.

" It means a great deal to Lucy." He was blandly unaware—or was he?—of the taut silence of the O'Learys. " She's been rather spoiled in some ways, always being the centre of attraction. Being unusually bright, it didn't take her too long to discover it was a big help to keep her father and mother at odds. I expect that had a lot to do with their divorce, in fact."

It was a fact he seemed to find more amusing than otherwise.

" But I'm enormously pleased with the way she's turned out. There have been times when she was somewhat of a problem. A born poltergeist, Dunning's always called her. Having a younger child to share things with is going to be a real blessing to her."

He stopped on the edge of the drive. " I have to be in court in the morning, so I'm going back to-night. I'll be here Friday, for whatever arrangements Anita makes about Ashton. Now, if I can be of service to you——"

A car coming out of the O'Leary woods on the Ashton road stopped him. It was a khaki-coloured car, the sun setting over beyond the bridge lighting up the round red disc on the front bumper.

" Who is that? "

" That's the sheriff."

" But I understood everything was settled . . ."

The car stopped. Spig saw Yerby's long rangy figure back itself out. He closed the door and stood, wiping the inside of his uniform felt hat, a determined set to his jaw, his eyes fixed on the yellow midget still in front of the garage.

" Excuse us, will you? " O'Leary said dryly.

There was a certain comic relief in seeing Anita's father, impressively confident, set off across the drive to meet the sheriff. It was the second comic touch. The first had been Anita's sudden switch to three days for the O'Learys to raise the $99,600 cash, as if the week she'd agreed on with her father had somehow seemed suddenly not as academic as she'd thought it. Academic meaning totally preposterous . . . as Anita and her father both knew so well it was highly admirable of them to conceal it as well as they did.

CHAPTER XVI

HE'D LET GO of Molly's arm as they came to the trail, not realising how blindly she was walking until she stumbled and he reached quickly forward, catching her before she fell.

" Watch it. Easy, girl."

" I can't bear it, Spig. I just can't bear it! We'll buy the place . . . if it ruins us, if we're in debt the rest of our lives, we'll buy it! But she can't take Molly A.! She can't! Oh, I hate her! "

She broke away from him and ran wildly along the trail. He started after her and stopped, letting her go on alone. Her voice had been so passionately like Tip's, threatening Dunning in his garden, that the old question, " I know who his father is but who's his mother? " was startlingly answered. And no laughing matter, as he'd once thought it was . . . the passionate anger and the golden tiger in her green eyes as she tore away from him frightening him more than the loaded rifle in Tippy's hands had done. He quickened his pace through the dusk in the leafy woods, a chill at the base of his spine, aware of the intensity of her devotion to the child that even before Kathy had died had been almost as close to her as one of her own. And what a four-year-old's life would be with Lucy, and with Anita hating Stan with the virulence he'd seen . . . But it wasn't either of them he was seeing, materialising strangely out of the twilight there. It was Dunning's bearded face, his black eyes suddenly absorbed, intense and devouring. It wasn't jealousy any longer. It was something else, deeper and more ominous.

She'd better get out of here. Take the kids and go to her father.

It seemed surprising to him he hadn't thought of that quicker. It was the obvious solution, for Molly A. and Tip as well as Molly . . . the only intelligent thing he'd thought of so far. It seemed that simple for an O'Leary to tell a Dulaney what to do.

Or it seemed so until he came into the children's hyphen and the devastating solution—and the only one— to the whole problem suddenly struck him. Whether it was something of the quality of Molly's voice in the old cottage living-room talking on the telephone, or the simple revolt of his own unconscious, refusing to let self-interest blind him any longer, he couldn't have said. He stopped and stood there, absorbing the blow, quietly facing the inevitable reality that he knew she'd already seen and faced He heard her put the phone down and heard the long silence before he moved on across the hyphen to the cottage door.

She was still by the desk, her hand still on the phone. The small windows and satiny panelled walls made the old room a place of dusty twilight when the outside world still glowed amethyst and rose through the gold of the setting sun. Her face was pale silver-gilt under her shining hair framed motionless against the window. Spig came slowly across the room to the fireplace and stood there, his back to her, neither of them speaking for a long time.

" That was Joe Malotti," she said finally. " The Home Owners are having a meeting. They saw Mr. Sudley this afternoon. He told them to see Mrs. Ashton. Some of them talked to her. They're delighted. She told them it was entirely up to us. She was . . . willing to sacrifice the place at cost to let us . . . practice what we preach."

He came over and put his arms around her, but she stepped quickly away from him. " She didn't tell them how much the cost was. They say she couldn't have been nicer. So everything's divine. Mr. Sudley tells them if we get past this, he'll see there's a zoning law. No more threats to this end of the county. It . . . it just seems so . . . so horrible."

" Don't, Molly. Please, don't."

He thought she was going to cry, and she cried so seldom it was heartbreaking when she did. " You take the kids and——"

" No. I won't—I know what you're thinking. You think if I get Molly A. to Daddy, she'll be all right. But I won't do it. Not even for Molly A. I'm not going to put him in the middle of any custody fight. It wouldn't be fair, now he's getting ready to retire, with a wonderful job. Anita fights dirty. She told me how she got her divorce. I'm not going to give her a chance at Daddy. He's probably sworn at enlisted men . . . you know what they can do to people."

Her voice caught and she turned quickly away. " It's my fault. I should never have——"

" It's not your fault. Quit saying that."

" But it is. That's the trouble. Nobody'll ever admit they're to blame for anything. Everything's always somebody else's fault. Like Art Dunning. It's not his fault everybody hates him. It's because he's a pigmy. His brothers are great stupid louts like you and Joe Cameron, buried like maggots in the family pill business. But if they weren't, he'd have to work for a living. He couldn't refuse to sell his pictures to the moronic rich. He couldn't go around insulting people all the time . . . He can't put on a bathing suit and go swimming because you people laugh at him."

" That isn't true, Molly."

" Of course it isn't, but he thinks it is. He's just eaten alive with an inferiority complex. That's the reason for his beard and all his malice. You tell him he's got gifts and talents that make him a giant of another sort and you ought to see his ego bloom. He's witty and amusing then . . . really sweet, when he wants to be."

"Okay, he's a wonderful guy, and I'm an s.o.b. because I don't see it. But that show Tip put on in the garden wasn't any business of being possessive and having everything his own way. It was about a picture Dunning painted."

She looked around at him quickly. " That's silly. I was out there when he was doing it."

" Mean . . . dirty mean, was what Tip called it. And you know Tip. He's the only rational peaceable person in this house. If he gets to the point of wanting to kill somebody, and comes in here at midnight with his rifle loaded, ready to shoot, because he thinks Dunning——"

" *Tippy?* "

" Tippy, last night. Right in this room. That's when

he told me about the picture. That's the reason he's so
hell-bent on keeping Dunning away from you . . . so
he can't paint you. And now it's Miss Fairlie he's upset
about."

The incredulous disbelief was still on her face, but at
least she was listening.

"Dunning was over there, at Eden, last night. Not
at any movie with Lucy, or sketching Colby's Carnival,
the way Anita says he was. He was outside Miss Fairlie's
picket gate between one and three . . . painting Eden
by moonlight. And you're not going to like this, but
Yerby's made me one of his deputies. My instructions
are to shoot to kill if I see anybody at night on Eden
that doesn't belong there."

She shook her head slowly. "I . . . don't understand.
It's very strange."

She went back to the desk and turned on the lamp,
looking at her watch. "I wish Tip would come home.
He's never been over there as late as this."

"Tip's all right."

"I know. It's just . . ." She glanced uneasily out
of the window. The river was still shining with the
afterglow of sunset, but the trees were casting longer
denser shadows with the creeping in of night. "I wish
she had a dog over there. I asked David why she didn't
. . . he said it was because of her father's dog. An old
Gordon setter. He howled so pitifully during the . . . the
time of sorrow, David called it. When George Sudley
killed himself."

"He didn't." It came out abruptly, before he thought.

"Oh . . ." She looked over at the bowl of nasturtiums,
and back at him.

"He was murdered," Spig said shortly. "It doesn't
matter. It was forty years ago."

"But if Art Dunning . . ."

"That's right. If he goes digging around, just for the fun of it . . ."

"It wasn't Harlan Sudley . . . was it?" Molly asked abruptly. "Because Art's been over there a lot lately. You know the way he sees all the things people try to hide . . . like that horrible thing of Stan Ashton. To-night, all the time we were over there, I kept feeling he was right in the room—gloating because we . . ."

She caught her lip in her teeth and turned quickly away, her shoulders quivering.

"Don't, Molly." He took her in his arms and held her tightly. "Don't. We'll manage. We can start again"

She pressed her forehead hard against his breast.

"It's Tip. It's Tip I've . . . betrayed, giving away what was his. It wasn't ours to give. It's just so awful. It breaks my heart. But . . . it's the only way we can get the money. This place is the only thing we've got. We couldn't keep it, and go on living here, with everybody hating us, knowing Anita's given us a chance to save them, and Eden's Neck. And . . . Miss Fairlie. We've got to sell this place, Spig. It's like selling a piece of your own heart, but it's the only way we can do it. It's the only way we can possibly raise the money."

"I know." He kissed the top of her head gently, holding her until she was quiet again. "It's just something I never thought about . . . until now when I came in. It just seemed cockeyed, over there, when he reeled off the list of how much they'd put in the place. I never thought about this place being ours to sell. It's been more like a . . . a trusteeship. I don't know what I thought, barging in Nat Twohey's office and demanding the stipulation. But I guess that's why Ashton took it.

He'd probably figured just how much this place would bring—we might be able to do him out of his extra profit."

" And that's what scared Anita over there," Molly said. " She and her father hadn't figured we could possibly raise that much money, so they were going to give us a week. I could just see her all of a sudden thinking we might, and cutting the time down so we wouldn't possibly have a chance."

She went across to the telephone and stood there a moment, then raised it and picked up the receiver. The dial rasped under her fingers.

" Mrs. Cameron, please. Oh, Martha—tell her Mrs. O'Leary called."

She put the phone down. " They've taken the kids out on the boat. They're going to sleep out to-night."

She came back and sat down beside Spig. " Those friends of theirs. This place is just what they've been looking for. Miss Fairlie'll approve of them. They've got five children. If they paid us fifteen hundred an acre, that's seventy-five thousand, and something for the house . . . we could borrow the rest. We'd have the Ashton place. We wouldn't dare sell it . . . but we could give both sides of the road to the State for our park . . . for Kathy. You . . . you'll have to go and see Miss Fairlie, first thing in the morning. And just wait till Anita and her father find out they haven't beaten us! She'll be furious. And I guess . . . I will send Molly A. to Daddy. Her and John Eden."

Spig nodded. " That makes sense."

" Because Anita doesn't really want her. She's just doing it to hurt us. I'll call Daddy in the morning. She won't have a maid and a nurse that quick and she wouldn't want her if she had to look after her herself.

By the time we get the thing to court she'll decide she doesn't want her anyway."

She raised her head, listening to the dog's quick happy bark down at the little bridge. " There he comes. Oh, Spig . . . let's not tell him, not to-night! "

Spig got slowly to his feet. " It's his place, Molly. We have to . . ."

" But not to-night! "

They heard him coming, running with the dog, throwing her ball for her.

" I can't bear it! I can't even bear it to see him! "

She ran, suddenly blind, to the door, and Spig heard her stumble on the stairs, running again, and the bedroom door slam shut behind her. He stood there a long moment, and went out through the hyphen to meet his son.

" Hi, Dad. Where's Mother? "

" She's gone to bed. She doesn't feel very well. We've had some pretty rugged news to-night. Do you think you can take it? It's really rugged."

Tip motioned the dog to sit. His face was a pale blur in the shadow of the night. But there are things you don't have to see to know.

" Is it . . . about the place? "

" That's right. Anita will sell us hers. The only way we've got to raise the money is to sell our own . . . if Miss Fairlie will let us. To those people the Camerons had over here a few weeks ago."

Tip was silent a moment. "Miss Fairlie liked their children," he said then, gravely. " We took them over to see her. She said it would be nice if they could live down here."

" We'll get in touch with them in the morning."

There was an aching hollow where Spig's throat was. Tip put his hand out, touching his father's.

" It's all right, Daddy. Don't feel so bad. We don't need this big a place. We promised Miss Fairlie. She doesn't like people who go back on their word. Is there anything we could get to eat? I'm hungry."

CHAPTER XVII

IT WAS twelve-thirty when Spig left Molly asleep and went quietly downstairs and out into the night. He would have taken the dog, in spite of Miss Fairlie, but she was in Tip's bed where she was not allowed, wagging her tail, alert with a special knowledge that to-night was different. Tip asleep with his arm around her shaggy ruff. He didn't take a gun.

Once he had been at Eden in the dark of a winter's dawn, but he'd never been there at night before. The late moon through the ragged cumulus cast a filtered glow, bright as hoar frost on the open lawns, intensifying the darkness crouching under the trees, as he left the white bridge at the head of the Cove and came up the turf into the gardens.

Death is a flower that blooms at night. It came into his mind, as if he were in some way himself on death's business, as his rubber soles trod the springy turf as silent as death in the sudden cessation of sound—all the tiny voices, the cicadas and tree frogs and the myriad things singing in the night, pausing as he came, singing again when he had passed. But the borders themselves were intensely alive, the nicotiana, dreary during the day, waxen fresh, star bright as a milky way though the sleeping beds, its delicate fragrance mingled with the tube

M

rose and night-scented stock. The trimmed yews, black silent sentinels at the four corners of the graveyard, hid the river. Next to them were the taller, blacker forms of the cryptomeria. The small Greek temple between them and the arbour emerged touched with moonlight, its slender white columns as tenuously intangible as smoke rising from the altar of the oracle in some far-off Aegean land.

He came to the boxwood circle, black and billowing, its sheen as elusive as its fragrance, and moved on up to the picket gate, stopping to whistle softly. " I told her you would, Dad. So she'd know it's you." He whistled again and looked down at the big house, dark, sealed and shuttered, its six ivy-clad chimneys broad, black planes magnified against the slate roof shining with its silver frost. It was the way it must have looked the day Judge Twohey came and found it locked, barred and deserted. Except that Spig felt a sense of life about it. It seemed poised and waiting, watching, as somewhere in the silent rooms he'd never seen she was watching, as she'd watched the night before. He waited, half expecting to see her materialise out from under the canopy of the wistaria over the porch, through the door hidden in its depths. But there was no sign of her, outwardly or visibly, only the whispering fragrance of her gardens and the lonely quack of a duck disturbed down in the pond behind the pallid silver screen of the bamboo and the weeping grace of the old willow.

He turned to unlatch the picket gate, listening. Dunning must have come on foot the night before. To-night, with Lucy presumably housebound by the presence of her grandfather, or Yerby, or her own discretion, he'd have the midget car. He opened the gate and went through, and stood, listening again. There was nothing he could hear except the tree frogs and cicadas, the leaves whispering, and the lonely disembodied call of the chuck-will's-widow off in the woods. He closed the gate, startled at the metallic click of the latch, loud in the sea of foam-rubber silence around him. He was at the end of the lane where they'd parked, leaving the children in the car, the day they came to Eden. Ahead of him on the left, shadowy in the light filtering through the leafy arabesques of the dogwoods, was the little Greek Revival office, where Mrs. Twohey, Cerberus with a cigar box guarding the portals, had been that day, and where Miss Fairlie had lived the five dark years. It was easy to imagine that it as well as the big house was haunted, the white columns strangely insubstantial, like slender ghosts, pale against the sable shadow of the porch under the pediment.

The soft scrunch of the gravel under his feet was the only sound he heard. He moved off on to the grass. Almost to the office porch he stopped. It was something he could feel, not hear, that stopped him, the cold sweat coming out, prickling sharp along his spine. He could hear it then, a soft slurring sound, as the door in the dense shadow of the porch seemed to open, a vague white blur that grew there, the musty odour of old books, in a closed-in room, strange incense, seeping like a formless ghost around it.

" He may not come to-night."

The faraway, childish voice didn't shatter the illusion, but for an instant heightened it.

" What the hell are you doing out here? "

O'Leary reacted sharply then, aware that it was no way to speak to Miss Fairlie of Eden. He reached down to pick up the flashlight he'd dropped, and started to apologise. But she hadn't seemed to notice.

" I was looking for the man with the broom."

" Broom ? "

Maybe he was crazy himself, but " broom " was what he thought he heard.

" Like a witch," Miss Fairlie said.

She came on, her slippered feet whispering on the boards of the porch until she emerged into the filtering light, still not solidly real in her long white wrapper, until Spig saw the white straw sailor hat on her head, a fantastic touch that set her firmly back into reality . . . as firmly as she was ever in it.

" Or like a chimney sweep," she said. " All black."

She came down the two steps to the ground.

" It's very peculiar. No one sweeps chimneys any more. Not with a broom. Vacuum bags are much cleaner."

O'Leary drew a deep breath. " I'm sure they are, Miss Fairlie," he said gently. " But don't you think you'd better go on in? Let me talk to him when he comes."

" He seldom comes two nights in succession. Sometimes not for a week or more."

He came closer to her, looking intently at her in the moonlight.

" You mean he's been here before, Miss Fairlie? Before last night? "

" A number of times," she said. He couldn't see her face clearly under the stiff white brim of her hat, but he sensed the blinking faraway look in her faded blue eyes, the way she stood, erect, hands primly folded in front of her. " I expect it was that woman sent him. Very irritating. It disturbs the child. Privacy is repugnant to Mrs. Twohey. It's surprising to me that Nathan retained what sanity he did. I must go now."

She started past him towards the gate.

" Here. Let me give you a light."

" There's a light," she said. " If you know the dark, you find it has a light of its own to let you see."

She went a few steps farther and stopped without turning.

" You're disturbed," she said. " Don't be. Everyone dies. Mr. Ashton was his own dark angel. Baal, I expect, was made of gold. The people who worshipped it were the ones devoured."

" Then you knew he planned——"

" But surely." She seemed even surprised, in a vague way, that he should have thought to ask her. " A niece of David's worked there. Mrs. Ashton was against it, at first. But she hasn't been happy here. I expect she'll be glad to get away. But don't let it disturb you."

She came back to him and stood, scarcely coming above his elbow, her hands fluttering in a brief gesture.

" It doesn't matter. Eden has had strange tenants before these. And gamblers. There never was an Eden who wasn't a gambler."

" You gambled on us, Miss Fairlie." He wasn't sure she was listening to him, there seemed something so elusive about her, as if she were already moving away again. " We promised Judge Twohey you'd never regret it . . . we'd see that Eden was safe, never threatened because you gambled. And that's what's happening. Not only to Eden but to everybody else out here. I was coming to talk to you to-morrow morning. Anita's agreed to stand by the promise that Ashton made us. We can buy the place for the cash they've got in it. We can raise the money—if we can sell the Plumtree Cove . . ."

" In which case you'll stand by your own promise. Or so I assume."

There was nothing vague, nothing elusive about Miss Fairlie of Eden then. He couldn't see the blue eyes, but he could feel them, as direct and unblinking as her voice was tart, far more effective than any physical blow she could have delivered him.

" Of course, Miss Fairlie. There's no question——"

" Then tell Nat Twohey to prepare a deed," she said curtly. " I'll take your property back. It's clearly evident you've lost your mind. I'm going now."

O'Leary stood stupidly where he was, staring after her. Half-way to the gate she stopped and came back again.

" My dear child." She put her hand out. It rested, light as a moth but definitely firm, on his. " You don't have to save Eden. Eden will manage. And don't be impatient. I'm as responsible for the Ashtons as you are. I knew the bridge was coming. I was curious to see how you would act when your wedding present to Kathy became so valuable. You acted very well. It was Mr. Ashton who acted badly. Very grasping. But that place isn't worth what they put in it. It was a sinful waste of money. Don't worry. It's not important."

" But . . . it is important, when Mr. Sudley——"

" Blackmail." She cut him off astringently, her hands dropping as her shoulders stiffened. " Nothing but blackmail. As I told him this morning. He was dead set against any form of property restriction. Now his own's involved, he doesn't like it. He was mistaken, he says. Very well. But you're not going to impoverish yourselves to pay for his mistakes. Or assume his responsibilities for the people on Eden's Neck. He sold them their homes, you didn't. He'll support a zoning law. What kind? And what will his support be worth? People may easily resent his changing his mind . . . knowing his reasons. And the Eden's Neck people. What assurance have you that one of them won't sell before a law is passed, if it passes? The Edens are gamblers, Tipton, not suicidal maniacs, I'm glad to say. If you wish to sell, you may sell to me. But you're not going to pauperise yourself and your family with any quixotic nonsense about saving Eden or anybody else. I'm astonished at you. I thought you had a little sense."

O'Leary stood there, on what little ground there was left for him to stand on, all the turmoil and heartache of the last few hours reduced to specious absurdity by the practical realism of a presumed eccentric. But without changing any of the basic problems . . .

" Still, Miss Fairlie——"

" Do you want to sell the place or don't you? "

" No, of course not. But——"

" Then don't talk any more."

There was no use talking. He felt she was no longer there, except in the literal sense of the words. The rest of her was gone, dissolved, evanescent as smoke, back into her own remote and cloudy land.

" I must go away now," she murmured. " It's the spiders. They worry me."

She moved vaguely off over to the gate, opened it, went through and closed it softly, disappearing then around the billowing sea of boxwood. She appeared again, a frail indistinct blur on the steps for a moment before she vanished into the darkness under the wistaria. An invisible door opened, and closed. Spig O'Leary was alone again in the eerie silence, eerier suddenly with the haunting lament of the owl down in the marsh, the hunter crying in the lonely night.

He went over and sat down on the office steps, with a feeling of sardonic but intense footlessness, and tensed abruptly, listening. It was not sound that alerted him but the absence of sound. The host of tiny sentinels of the night were suddenly mute.

He got quietly to his feet and moved out to the edge of the lane, waiting for a light or the scrunch of tyres on the gravel . . . of the scrunch of a footstep along the road. But there was none of them. Only the tree frogs. He turned quickly, realising his mistake. The song of the night wasn't in the woods or along the lane. It was across the wall over in the garden, the way he'd come, where he'd met with the same muting of voices, the same renewal when he was safely past. He moved along the grass silently, back to the picket fence, keeping inside the shadow of the wall, waiting for a footstep to reach the drive. And wondering. If it was Dunning coming up the garden, he would have to cross the O'Leary's field to the bridge, and the dog would have barked. It could be Miss Fairlie coming back. He searched the dark perimeter of the boxwood for the frail blur of her white wrapper, listening for the soft sound of her tread. Then abruptly he heard the restless chirp of a bird in a sudden well of silence centred down towards the arbour, and a faint rasp that could have been a footstep retreating. Again he heard a restless chirp, but along the arbour, away from the house towards the little Greek temple down by the yews. A distant tree frog muted its song, one closer to the gate renewed his.

He moved over to the gate, unlatched it, slipped through and closed it softly. The moonlight on the borders and the roses of the arbour, made graceful corridors of snow above the darker paths of the turf and the dense black cluster of the cryptomeria, spangled with fireflies, concealing the columns of the summer house. It was that way Dunning, if it was Dunning, was headed, his progress marked by the cicadas, silent, and the birds, restless.

Spig went out on the grass again, aware of small wells

of silence he himself created as he crouched a little to keep
below the massed lilies and foxglove and made his way
down to circle back up around the river path, the way
he'd taken home that morning past the graveyard.
What Dunning would possibly be doing there was nothing
but a formless uneasiness in his mind. It was anger he
felt chiefly. Dunning wouldn't be here at all if he didn't
know there were neither guns nor dogs on Eden. He'd
been careful to avoid the lane where he would have to
pass David's house near the gate out on the old road. In
here he was safe, with nothing to disturb him but one frail
little old woman in a sealed up house.

He stopped, straightening up warily. He was at the
end of the borders, where the river path joined the path
down to the bridge across the Cove. He looked over the
frosted lawns. The cryptomeria were a dense screen
hiding the house, hiding the arbour. Behind them, where
he was seeing now, the moon was bright on the rigid
guardians, the clipped yews. Between them he could
make out the shadowy grey forms of the stones in the
hollow square they watched, and catch, beyond them, the
tenuously shining columns of the temple against the
silver sheen of the river showing through them. There
were other forms, or shadows so tangible they seemed
forms, the whole scene alive with the pale ascending glow
of the fireflies. Then he saw one light, close to the ground,
ruddier than the rest, as intermittent as the fireflies but
glowing as it fell, not as it rose.

He tensed again, watching its casual arc, waiting. But
it didn't move then, except to glow bright an instant
before it faded in its downward arc. The smoker,
stationary and at ease, was seated, not standing.

He moved then, quickly, his rubber soles noiseless on
the familiar path skirting the bank above the cover,

circled around it to the river-front, and stopped abruptly.

Dunning was in front of him, in the open lawn half-way between the temple and the graveyard. He knew it was Dunning by the easel set up, a square of white canvas on it, and the binoculars raised to his eyes. And because it was Dunning he had come to find. He would not have known otherwise. The man was solid black, or appeared so in the silver patch of moonlight there, his white hands holding the binoculars, the white strip of his fore-head above his bearded face, the only parts of him not black.

The black hair, the black beard, the navy-blue denims that looked black at night. Like a chimney sweep. Like a chimney sweep . . . or a devil from hell, perched there on his stool, his binoculars fixed on the graveyard, wrong end to, to throw it into distant minute perspective —like the bawdy street in the Ashton portrait. Like a devil, not like a witch. There was no broom there, only the palette case on the grass beside him; and it was not the blackness, or his perching there, outside the graveyard, that was devilish. It was some quality of almost obscene excitement, in the way he was perched, in the quick darting turns of his head, the binoculars first on the graves, then on the temple, the avidity of his absorption so intense that he wasn't conscious of O'Leary full in the path, not twenty feet from him. As he laughed suddenly, O'Leary's flesh crawled. Obscene. There was no other word.

He went deliberately up to him. " On your way, Dunning."

Dunning flashed around. He was startled, but it was surprise only, not fear. He relaxed at once.

" Why, bless me, it's O'Leary."

He put the binoculars on the turf and crossed his leg,

clasping his hands around his knees, leaning back, rocking, grinning complacently.

"I'm a ghoul, O'Leary. I love opening graves in the dark of the moon. So run along. I've got some work to do. It's only the pure in heart who're safe to prowl the sepulchres by night. What the hell are you doing here, anyway, if you'll permit me to inquire?"

"I'm telling you to pack up and clear out."

"By whose authority?" Dunning asked pleasantly.

"Look, Dunning. I don't need any authority. But I've got it, if you'd like to see it."

He took his wallet out of his pocket, opened it, turned the white ball of his flashlight on the badge pinned inside, held it out for Dunning to see.

"Oh, my God!"

Dunning uncrossed his knee, laughing, doubling himself up with mirth.

"How humourless can you get, O'Leary? Really, Spig. No wonder your wife finds you lethally a bore. You——"

"That's enough, Dunning." O'Leary put his wallet back in his pocket, watching him impassively. "You've got three minutes. Get going."

"Oh, don't be such an ass, O'Leary," Dunning said impatiently. "I'm just painting a picture of a grave by the light of the moon. It's not hurting a soul. Not a soul."

He laughed, the way he'd laughed when he thought he was alone. O'Leary felt the cold chill again.

"I'm not joking," he said quietly. "I gave you three minutes. You've got two left."

Dunning sat forward, grinning. "Two minutes before what, O'Leary? Before you hit me? Before you knock all my teeth out?—Neanderthal man, as Ashton called

you. Or are you trying to scare me to death, too? Hit
me if you dare, my friend."

" I'm not going to hit you. I'm going to take you in
to town to jail."

Dunning looked sharply at him. " Of all the
stupid——"

" Jail, Dunning. One minute."

Dunning's foot shot out, kicking his easel and canvas,
cursing as he grabbed the easel up and grabbed his stool,
his face livid, the saliva spraying from his mouth, his
voice choking with rage.

" Hit me! I'm cursing you, O'Leary! Hit me! You
wouldn't take it if I were your size! You wouldn't . . ."

" I wouldn't," O'Leary said. He kept his hands
rigidly at his sides, fighting back the red fog around him.
" Time's up."

" I'm going, blast you! Can't you see I'm going! I've
got a boat! "

He caught up the palette case. " I'm going . . . but
you wait, O'Leary! I'll crucify you! You'll see! You
and all the rest of them. And Miss Crazy Fairlie! Wait
till I get through with——"

Spig took a quick step forward. Dunning dodged and
ran, screaming, invective pouring out of him like a river
of pitch. Spig stood where he was. If he caught him
he'd kill him. He stood there, the gutter swill and filth
of a language he hadn't heard since the war and had
forgotten even existed burning into his brain. His hands
were shaking violently when he heard the rattle of oar-
locks and saw the dark form of the Ashton's dinghy shoot
out into the silver surface of the river, the Tattoo Artist
sobbing with fury.

O'Leary waited a moment and walked back along
the bank towards the big house, stopping to watch the

boat as long as he could see it. The floodlight went on above the Ashtons' pier. He turned then and saw another light, in Miss Fairlie's kitchen. He saw the door open. She stood there, in her white wrapper, her white sailor hat still on.

" He's gone, Miss Fairlie." The assumption was she wouldn't have understood any of Dunning's valedictory or he'd have been more embarrassed then he was. " He was painting the graveyard. I don't think he will come again."

" I'm out of whisky," Miss Fairlie said. " Would you like some brandy? "

" Why . . . yes, I mean, thanks. I'd like some very much."

She didn't ask him in, but she left the door open. She came back almost at once. He took the glass she handed him. She stood there blinking absently while he drank it, smooth as cream, clean as golden fire, to burn the taste of Dunning out of his mouth.

He gave her back the glass. " That was wonderful. Thank you."

" It's very old," she said. " It's the black widow spider. Very dangerous. But they only attack when they're provoked. Mr. Dunning's a very stupid man, I'm afraid."

CHAPTER XVIII

It was around two o'clock when Spig went home. The moon was clouded over, and a light rain starting to fall made it certain Dunning wouldn't come back to Eden again that night.

He went quietly upstairs, taking off his jacket and shirt as he went.

" Who was that screaming over there? "

He turned on the light. Molly was over by the windows, partly dressed, tense, blue shadows under her eyes. " I was coming over. I was beginning to worry."

" Just your friend Dunning."

He sounded brutal where he'd meant to sound casual —the macabre picture of the Tattoo Artist, the black figure midway between the graves and the white shining temple, the devilish excitement and glee the more sinister the more he thought about it.

" He was over there with his paints. He was sore when I made him clear out."

Her body stiffened.

" Look. Let's not start this again," he said. " If you think it's all right for him to be over there at night——"

" I don't think it's all right," she said sharply. " I think it's horrible. It's . . . frightening. But it would make more sense to find out what he's doing."

" I know what he's doing," Spig said shortly. " Out of his own mouth. In his own words. He's crucifying Miss Crazy Fairlie. Also me. And everybody else around here."

" But . . . I thought you said it was George Sudley. That he was trying to find out——"

" For the same reason. Pure malice. But let's skip it. I don't pretend to know how his mind works, what reasons he gives himself—or you. But he's damn well going to stay away from Eden, and stay away from here from now on. This is where Sudley was killed. He's not poking around here any more. And this date he said you had with him—call him up and break it. If you don't, I will."

" Those are orders, I take it. Sergeant O'Leary to the troops. In triplicate."

" And another thing. We're not buying the Ashton place."

He saw the colour rise in her cheeks. " Who says so? "

" Miss Fairlie says so."

She looked at him blankly. " Miss Fairlie? You mean she won't . . ."

" That's right. She won't." It wasn't the way he'd planned to tell her. No tender scene, just a couple of snapping turtles again. " She says we're halfwits. If we sell, she buys. Which is probably just what Anita and her father thought. They must have figured if Miss Fairlie wanted the place she'd have done something about it. But that's the story."

" Well," Molly said. " Dear me." She reached down and pulled up the cotton blanket. " I guess we were just born lucky. Not everybody's got a mad woman for a guardian. But it doesn't change our obligation. We've got to do something."

" I just wondered what I'd do about my contract," was all Tip said when O'Leary came out in the morning. The vegetables were already in the car.

" You coming with me? I have to go on into town."

Tip shook his head. " I'm going to stay home." He stood there, his hand on the car window. " Dad . . . what do I do if Mr. Dunning comes? "

" He won't," Spig said evenly. " But if he should, you don't do anything. I won't be long. Just forget about him."

He hadn't forgotten him himself, or the dream that had dogged him through the night, the black figure stealthily recurring, twitching with horrible excitement, his laughter always an echo even when he'd waked. But he'd had sense enough not to say anything about him at the breakfast table. No more orders to the troops.

" Take it easy, Tip. I want to see the sheriff and Nat Twohey and I'll be right back."

He saw the first of the " For Sale " signs of the Eden's Neck people where the old road past Miss Fairlie's gate entered the highway. It was on the white fence of the house next to Joe Malotti's. The Home Owners weren't waiting to see what, if anything, the O'Learys could do —not even giving them the three days Anita had given them. Miss Fairlie's prognosis coming true quicker than she'd thought. He drove on between Sudley's mile-long white fences, turned into the crossway on the other side of Bill's Live Bait, Blood Worms and Peelers, and waited for a truck to pass to get across to the Three D side. As he did he saw Anita Ashton over there in the air-conditioned Cadillac, her blonde head greenish through the tinted glass. When the truck passed she shot out from the gravelled space in front of Nick's around the truck, burning the road towards home. It was twenty-four minutes to eight, early for Mrs. Ashton.

The hole in the blue glass wall was patched with plywood.

" The man's coming to-day." Nick Pappas was very
busy with the garbage cans and cases of milk and bread.
It was cool, but he had tiny beads of sweat on his fish-
belly brow. " It's like I told Buck Yerby, Mr. O'Leary.
Just an accident. I got the money. Right in my pocket."
He patted his rear end where his wallet was, avoiding
Spig's eyes.

" You mean Mrs. Ashton's paid up."

O'Leary opened his door and hoisted the baskets of
wax beans and beets on to the ground.

Nick mopped his face with his apron. " You shouldn'a
told, Mr. O'Leary. It just makes trouble. All the time
trouble. Yerby got his cars up and down, all night.
Korvac at the Breezy Inn, he calls me up. ' What the hell
you doin', Nick—monkey-wrenchin' my business? You
got a piece of busted glass, so you gotta squeal, huh?
Monkey-wrenchin' the whole Strip.' You tell Yerby.
Tell him I got my money. I bring it in and show him
with his own eyes." He slapped his pocket again. " Right
here I got it."

" When you get it cashed, you mean." O'Leary got
back in his car. " Okay, I'll tell him, Nick—if you want
to go on being pushed around."

Buck Yerby's secretary smiled apologetically at the
half dozen people waiting in the outer office when Spig
got there. " The sheriff's been trying to get you, Mr.
O'Leary. Go right in, will you? "

" I thought you were on the job at Eden, O'Leary."
There was a calm in Yerby's voice not matching the
gleam under his black brows.

" 'Mornin', Mr. O'Leary."

That was old David, sitting in the chair by Yerby's
desk, his Sunday panama on his knees, an old man late

N

in his seventies, grizzled and shrunken not much bigger than Miss Fairlie.

"I was tellin' Mr. Buck. Somebody been messin' roun' my graves. Smokin' cigarettes. That artis' fella is the one I had in my mind. I foun' that this mornin'."

He nodded at a small tube of paint on Yerby's desk. "I ain' tol' Miss Fairlie. But we don' like strangers we don' know foolin' aroun', daytime or dark."

"I guess he dropped it when I chased him out," Spig said. "Miss Fairlie knows it, David. She was up when he was there."

"I expec' so," David said complacently. "She ain' scared of th' devil hisself if'n he was to come. But I jus' thought I'd let you know. She need her res' at night."

"We'll see she gets it." Yerby pushed his chair back and went over to the door with him, a compliment he seldom paid. "Mr. O'Leary will be around. We'll look after her."

His face was grim as he came back. "Orders were, shoot to kill."

"I was smart," Spig said. "I left my gun at home."

"What time was he there?"

"Round one. He was all set to paint the graveyard by moonlight."

"Then it wasn't him in his yellow car at Foggy Bottom at one-ten, going ninety. My man damned near smashed up trying to catch him. There was a girl in the car, too."

O'Leary said nothing.

Yerby shrugged. "According to Dunning, he was with Lucy the night before. Not Charlie. Charlie just stopped to say hallo to them outside the Three D on the way over to his aunt's. That's what Lucy and Dunning

told me at the Ashtons' last night, Anita and her father
both present. Anybody that says any different is lying
for reasons best known to himself. That's you, O'Leary.
That's the——"

He broke off and reached for the phone. " Yerby
speaking." Spig saw him draw in his breath and half close
his eyes. He leaned back, listening patiently.

" All right," he said at last. " We'll certainly check.
We sure will. Thanks for calling."

He put the phone down and sat there staring at it,
swearing softly under his breath. " That . . . that
dame's going to drive me psycho. I swear to God she is."
The muscles of his jaw worked savagely.

O'Leary looked his question.

" Mrs. Twohey—Dunning's missing. She's been trying
to phone him. She can't get him. Nobody out at the
Ashtons' has seen him for two days."

" Why didn't you tell her——"

" Look." Yerby glared at him his face flushed. " The
guy's a s.o.b. So what? He doesn't show up to paint
that old she-cougar's picture. That's no g.d. business of
mine. If he was a polecat I wouldn't tell her where to
find him."

" Someday you'll break a blood vessel," Spig said.

" If it gets that old witch out of my craw it'll be
first-rate with me. If one of her neighbours is three
minutes late getting in the milk bottle, she's smelling gas
and yelling for a deputy. And she'd have sent Nat
out to hunt for Dunning, but Nat's home with his
heart to-day. Look . . . if Nat Twohey had the guts to
move out and leave that old hellion, he wouldn't have a
heart."

He relaxed suddenly, grinning. " Ah, well, the poor
old girl. That's all she's got to do, I guess. But the less

she sees of Dunning, the better I like it. Or *vice versa,* is what I mean."

" Unless he's seen her all he needs to."

" What do you mean by that? "

Spig shook his head. " Just an idea." He remembered suddenly what Dunning had said to Lucy the night before *There's one more visit I want to make*—and the look on his face as he'd said it.

" He hasn't been digging around your place, has he? " Yerby asked abruptly.

" I didn't know there was anything to dig. Do you mean physically dig? "

Yerby shook his head. " No, no. It's just that that was the place. The duck blind was about where the bridge is now. You've still got the table, haven't you? " He was silent for a moment. " The position of that stain, he said then slowly. " It's funny—nobody ever got rid of that table. Of course the place was locked up. Shutters nailed, my father said. David did that. But it's a funny thing."

He was silent again, frowning. " I was thinking about it the other night. They say all kinds of people get away with murder. I doubt it. Most murderers convict themselves. Or another thing. Say you killed somebody, in the heat of passion. Maybe you'd want it known some time. To explain. Or to justify yourself, maybe. Or just to get it off your conscience. Or maybe there's something else, out of your control. Like this fellow Dunning coming along, for instance. Something you'd never expect. George Sudley's been dead and dust for forty years, and he comes along . . . You take my father. He was plenty tough. But he couldn't go to his grave without telling somebody. You wouldn't like to set fire to that table, would you? "

He said it so without changing tempo that it took
Spig O'Leary a moment to understand what he was
saying. If that was what he was saying.

" It's Miss Fairlie's table," he said then. " I guess I'm
not suspicious, Buck. We've lived with that stain for
seven years . . ."

" Well," Yerby examined the back of his hand carefully. " George Sudley knew guns. Gone gunning all his
life. But suppose he hadn't. If he was sitting there at the
table with a blanket around him, his clothes drying in
front of the fire . . . if he was sitting there, cleaning his
gun—a loaded gun with the muzzle towards him—and
the gun went off and blasted his heart out, he'd have
slumped right down in his chair, wouldn't he? Hard to
see how he'd get up and fall out in the middle of the
table. But let's forget it—if we can."

He leaned forward, straightening the blotter on his
desk. " I was going to have a talk with Dunning.
But when he sat there last night backing up Lucy and
Charlie's story, word for word—well, I figured a liar's a
liar."

He shrugged, but the angry glint was back in his eye.
" Just the way Mrs. Sudley and her sister backed up
Charlie's end of it, tooth and nail. That's five of 'em
against you—you and one regular deputy used to be a
farmer before Sudley's bank foreclosed."

" And Miss Fairlie."

" That's right. Everybody *knows* she's crazy."

" There's a cheque in Nick's pants pocket," O'Leary
said evenly. " Anita took it to him this morning, at
seven-thirty."

" For the new Greek church, I bet it says," Yerby
remarked dryly. " But I'll get 'em, don't you forget it.
Every man I've got's out——"

" Monkey-wrenching the Strip. That's the beef Nick's getting."

" That's right. I'll monkey-wrench 'em right out of . . ."

He reached a long arm for the phone. " Yerby speaking."

It was not the second Mrs. Twohey again. He straightened up and brought his chair forward abruptly. " Where? " He listened soberly. " I'll be right over."

He put the phone down and sat there a moment. " Ramey," he said. " The old teller over at the bank. Blew his brains out."

He pushed his chair back and reached for his hat. " Come on. Back way—just across the street. Nice old fellow . . . just one of the nicest old fellows I ever knew."

They went out and across the parking square. A small crowd was already gathered, gaping around the door set in the wall next to a grocery store. They went on through. Yerby turned at the door. " Why don't you move off a-way's, folks? He's dead. Let him have a little peace. What do you say? "

They moved back soberly, a little ashamed. The two went on through a long narrow hall, up sagging stairs to the second floor. At the end of the upstairs hall a deputy and half a dozen people were outside an open door. A dark-haired girl was sitting in the window, her eyes red. Spig had seen her in the bank. Beside her was a coloured girl with a blue checked apron over her cotton dress, her face putty-grey.

The deputy came towards them. " You'll want to see them two," he said. "And this is the landlady." He nodded at the middle-aged woman there.

" He lost his job, was why he did it." The landlady

had been crying too. " Been here fourteen years, and
never a speck of trouble. I'd never have thought——"

" All right, Mrs. Rogers," Yerby said. " You go downstairs. Take the rest of these people. I'll be down."

They went on into the room. Dr. Parker was already
there. It was bare, with a white iron bed neatly made, an
oak dresser, mirror and morris chair. Between the two
windows was an oak table thickly covered with newspapers. Seated in a straight chair in front of it, his coat
hung on the back of the chair, was the old teller from
the Sudley bank, his body forward, his grey head lying
on the papers, a small revolver still in his hand. Except
for his eyes staring blindly he looked alive, his face tired
and sad.

" Didn't want to make a mess for anybody," the doctor
said, pointing down at the newspapers.

Yerby nodded. " He leave any note? "

" Maybe under the papers. We haven't moved anything."

There were heavy steps outside.

" The boys are here, if you're ready, Buck," the deputy
said.

" Put the two girls in the next room or some place till
he's out."

Yerby came over to Spig, looking at the framed en-
largements of the bank's outings on the wall. There were
two dark rectangles in the faded paper where pictures had
been. When he heard the slow laborious steps going down
the stairs, Yerby turned back to the table. There were
still very little blood on the papers covering it, but there
was some. Yerby folded the papers carefully and put
them in the metal waste basket. He stood with Spig and
Dr. Parker looking down at what they had covered.
There were two picture frames, face down. Yerby

picked the first one up. It was a photograph inscribed across the bottom corner, " With warm personal regards to James Ramey, from Harland Sudley." The second was a framed memorial with an engraving of the bank at the top. " To James Ramey in appreciation of twenty-five years of faithful service to the Farmers' National Bank of Devonport." It was signed by the officers and board of the bank, dated in 1948.

Beneath one was a note, written in ink on a sheet of ruled tablet paper. Yerby read it and handed it to Spig. It said, " I swear before Almighty God I did not know the money was stolen. I never made a dollar or kept a dollar of it. My account in the Drovers' Bank in Baltimore is from stock market transactions from my savings. I leave it to my sister Mrs. Ethel R. Allen, 9 Elm Street, Barber's Point, Pa. Every penny of it was honestly earned. I am entirely innocent. I did not know the money was stolen. The balance of it is in the bottom bureau drawer.—James V. Ramey."

Yerby went over to the bureau and opened the drawer. In it was a tin box with the key in the lock. He took the box out and put it on the table to open it. There were six fifty-cent pieces loose on top of a small pile of paper used to roll silver coins in. Beside it were ten rolls, made up, marked: " 10——50c."

Yerby stood looking down at them for an instant. " Get those girls in," he said quietly. He stood at the window looking down into the yard until the two of them came in. " You found him, Alice? "

The girl nodded. " It's my fault he lost his job. You know how Mr. Sudley is about slot machines. Nobody in the bank's allowed to play them. Three or four times I noticed Mr. Ramey with more silver than he's supposed to have. I asked him. He said it was slot machine money he was changing, a friend had won a couple of jackpots. I told my boy friend and he told Mr. Sudley. I didn't even know it. Or that they were watching him. Yesterday they caught him, and Mr. Sudley fired him. I was sick about it. I came by to tell him it was my fault and I was sorry. He didn't answer when I knocked, but there was a sort of funny smell, and I opened the door. It's all my fault. And I just don't believe what Marie says." She nodded at the coloured girl. " I mean, I don't believe he was a thief."

" I never said he was." The girl shook her head quickly. " I just told her he was all right when I came. I brought him up his coffee and the papers. I didn't know he wasn't at the bank any more. I told him— Brother works for the Acme, and last night they had another slot machine broken open. Nobody knows who did it and the mechanics don't want to get blamed, so Brother told me to ask Mr. Ramey to watch and see if anybody brought a lot of half-dollars to the bank, just on a chance. I asked him this morning. He asked me when was the last one and I told him at the Three D night before last. He looked like he was going to faint but didn't pay any attention."

" All right—thanks," Yerby said. " You can go on. Don't talk about it any more than you can help."

He waited until they had gone and looked at Spig, his face expressionless. As if O'Leary were somebody he'd never seen before.

Then he said, " Just get the hell out, will you? "

" Sure."

" Anything I can do, Buck? " the deputy asked.

Yerby was silent a moment. " Yeah," he said. " Phone Sudley. Tell him I want him. Here. Right now."

CHAPTER XIX

OUTSIDE IN the street Spig saw the long lanky figure of Pete Greenway headed over from the *Times-Gazette* building, and turned into a side street to avoid him and get to the Twoheys'. Actually there was no real reason for him to go there except the off-chance that the old judge was right about his son's not being totally devoid of imagination and legal resources, and that, slow but sure, Nat Twohey might come up with something that would keep another honky-tonk version of Devon Death Strip off the Ashton place and the bridge approach. And it was hardly that so much as some inner feeling that he'd better check with Nat even if he was laid up with his heart and the second Mrs. Twohey was a necessary hazard. She could be marketing . . . or hunting Dunning.

O'Leary grinned without conviction as he came up the walk to the porch and rang the bell, his heart sinking only slightly when he heard the brisk efficient scurry of high heels coming to answer it. But prepared as he was, his preparation was wholly inadequate.

The second Mrs. Twohey, beaming with welcome, was in panoply. She had on a pink satin evening gown with rhinestone shoulder straps, her full bosom and vigorous bare shoulders swathed in a cloud of misty pink tulle, a pink velvet rose in her hair that was dyed a handsome chestnut, and upswept into a coronet of curls, with earrings and bracelets, eyebrows pencilled, rouge, powder, lipstick, the works, including a wide open pink feather fan.

O'Leary took a backward step as Mrs. Twohey's bright expectancy, the toothy smile, bursting cordiality and delighted voice passed into instant *rigor mortis* in mid-air.

"Oh . . . I . . . I thought you were Arthur . . .'

The speed of her recovery alone would have showed how stout the stuff she was made of, without any decolletage to aid it. She managed a brisk and efficient smile. "I'm expecting him. He's coming to paint. I didn't want to waste a minute of his precious time. It's such a privilege. But do come in."

"You found him, then." O'Leary recovered more slowly.

"Oh, no, but that sweet child Lucy called me." She closed the fan. "He's got me down in his book for nine-thirty," she said. "But he's always a little late."

A pixie diversion, no doubt, O'Leary thought. It was striking ten when he crossed the square.

"But I expect it's Nat you've come to see," she said cheerfully. "He had a little attack yesterday morning. The doctor said for him to rest in bed."

"Then I'd better get along."

Mrs. Twohey tapped his arm playfully with the fan. "Before you go, I'm going to let you have just a little peek. Arthur says I mustn't show it before he's finished, but there are a few people I just can't resist. Now, you wait. It's right in here"

She went over to the living-room door. It was closed, as was the library door directly across the hall from it . . . fortunately, Spig thought, if any conscious part of the old judge were still lingering in its shabby precincts.

"Now, close your eyes! Don't open them till I tell you. And I want you to be honest. Brutally honest."

She's pleased with it. But Ashton was pleased with that thing of him.

" Now! "

Spig opened his eyes, and opened them wider. The lady in pink smiling at him from the unfinished canvas was Mrs. Twohey as Mrs. Twohey might, in her fondest dreams, have longed to look somewhere back in her middle thirties—wistful, ethereally lovely, graceful and gentle as a summer cloud. He stared at it, keeping his eyes resolutely away from the robust figure of its original, posing with pride and happiness beside it.

" I tell him he's idealised me." She paused for him to contradict her if he could.

The poor damned woman . . . she believes it. It was the first twinge of sympathy he'd ever felt for the late judge's second wife. He looked at her then. Beside the clear and lovely rose-petal pink on the canvas there she looked as if she and all her finery had been steeped in stale coffee, old, brazen and of the earth earthy, without any of the earth's kindliness to save her. *The switchblade twist.* In itself this was one—the woman who made the picture a caricature, more cruel than if it had been the other way round.

He remembered suddenly what its purpose had really been.

" It's . . . beautiful," he said. " Did you talk much while he was painting you? "

" Oh, yes. Arthur says painting a portrait is just like going to a psychiatrist. Of course, you don't discuss sex. I don't mean that. You talk about your hopes and fears . . . the things that have meant the most to you. Arthur says it's that way the artist sees the true image, the psyche behind the stultifying mask of environment. It's the soul the artist paints. Arthur is a deeply spiritual man, you know."

" I'm afraid I didn't "

She moved the portrait back to the map stand by the window and closed the door, almost reverently. "And he's been such a joy to me. He's the only sympathetic person I've met in all my years in Devon County. Bitter years, many of them, Mr. O'Leary."

"Oh, come, Mrs. Twohey." It was the touch of drama that made it suddenly too much for O'Leary. "You've had a pretty good life, here in Devon."

"That's what you think, Mr. O'Leary."

There was no drama in this. Her lips tightened. "It took Arthur to see the truth. He's heard the stories. He knows what it means to a woman to be told her husband only married her because he needed a housekeeper. He understands what I've suffered, being constantly told it's that crazy woman out at Eden my husband was in love with . . . the humiliation I've gone through."

"Nuts," O'Leary said. "I'll bet you never thought about it until——"

"He's certainly the one who made me see it in true perspective, Mr. O'Leary," she retorted. "And opened my eye to people who've pretended to be my friends when all the time it was their own precious hides they were saving. Instead of slaving, second fiddle, in this house all these years, I should have demanded my husband put that crazy woman where she belonged. But you wait!"

She snapped her jaws together, her eyes gleaming. "Just you wait! This town's put up with her crazy didos long enough. And with Harlan Sudley's. The time has come for a real accounting."

"Accounting?" Spig asked quietly.

"An accounting, Mr. O'Leary. Why do you think Harlan Sudley slaves for a mad woman, ploughing her fields, selling her tobacco for her, taking care of her farm machinery, giving her discounts she doesn't need? What hold has she got over him, Mr. O'Leary? Ask yourself that, if you haven't already done so. What hold does a crazy woman have over——"

" What do you mean? "

" Exactly what I say."

Her bare bosom had angry splotches under the filmy pink tulle, her eyes snapped angrily.

" *Hold !* " The strident pitch of her voice filled the hall. " Do you think it was any accident that gave Harlan Sudley his brother's fine, big farm? Do you think for one minute that that crazy woman doesn't know what hap——"

" *Eloise!* "

Mrs. Twohey clapped her hand over her mouth, dismay in her startled eyes. They were like darts thrown at the library door, held there, waiting. Behind it Spig could hear Nat Twohey's slow unsteady tread coming from his bedroom behind it. Mrs. Twohey's eyes were fixed rigidly. Without moving she seemed to have shrunk, her pink finery standing out around her like something that was no part of her. The door opened and Nat Twohey stood there, leaning against the frame, grey-faced, his lips blue, only his eyes intensely and cogently alive, in them a kaleidoscope of emotions, anger and disgust the chief, but so varied it was hard to follow them.

" Come in, Spig." He stepped aside for O'Leary without looking at him, his eyes fixed on the speechless old woman across the hall. Spig felt his second twinge of sympathy in seven years.

" Listen to me, Eloise," he said, with a frigid dignity that was worse than unbridled rage. " Harlan Sudley had nothing whatever to do with his brother's death. There are penalties for slander. Just keep your mouth shut hereafter. And go take off those ridiculous clothes. Or if you can't do that, have the decency to stay away from the front door. You're the laughing stock of the whole street."

He closed the door after Spig and stood there steadying himself against it.

" The woman's mad," he said bitterly. " This house has been a nightmare ever since that fellow started coming here."

He went over to the worn leather chair in front of the old judge's desk and sat down. His hands, bloodless except for the blue shadows dyeing his nails, were trembling.

" I should have seen from that outrageous picture that there was something behind it. But what's his motive? I was . . . shocked when I . . . Yesterday morning at breakfast, Eloise asked how you proceeded with an order for exhumation. Then it came out. She's never been able to keep anything to herself. Just like a child. But she didn't say it was Harlan Sudley this man Dunning's after. Good God! Harlan Sudley was on the other side of the river all day. I was with him. We didn't start back until time for him to milk. His brother had been dead for hours, his body brought into town, the cottage nailed up. No question it wasn't an accident. No question of any kind or description."

Except for a heart attack when you heard it's being questioned now . . . Neon letters, ten feet high . . . Spig O'Leary sat down, studing the worn carpet between his feet, his own heart cold. This was the compulsion nagging him to come and see Nat Twohey. He recognised it then, without knowing whether he'd come hoping Nat would some-how relieve him of his own fears about the old judge or whether it was a confirmation of them he was hunting before he went on—if he was going on—to stop Dunning . . . if there was any way of stopping him.

He put his hand in his pocket and got out a cigarette. It was an odd thing. It wasn't till that moment that he was conscious that was what he was going to do, or conscious of the reason. Or perhaps it was Mrs. Twohey's "But you wait! Just you wait!" that had focused the picture already in his mind.

"Look here, Nat," he said deliberately. "What's behind this deal? Where did it start?"

"I don't know," Nat Twohey said curtly. "But it's mischief. I know that. Mischief and malice."

"Behind Mrs. Twohey's part in it."

"She's always resented the Sudleys. They were Father's and my best friends."

"I'm not talking about Sudley. She didn't start with him. She started with Miss Fairlie."

"My father was in love with Miss Fairlie. She's never forgiven either of them for it."

He took a small cotton-covered cartridge out of his dressing-gown pocket, crushed it in his handkerchief, held it to his nose, breathing in laboured gasps until the tension in his chest relaxed.

"I'd better go." Spig got abruptly to his feet.

"No, sit down. If you've got any explanation, I want to hear it. It's important to me . . . desperately important."

The poor devil, Spig thought. He sat down again. Whether it was actual knowledge that his father had killed George Sudley, or the fear he had, long held, long hidden, more harrowing than knowledge, the hideous irony of having his father's widow the unconscious harpy, hell-bent on tearing it all wide open, he didn't know.

One or the other was the switchblade giving an almost lethal twist.

"I don't know it's the explanation," Spig said slowly. "But I think Dunning just came here to paint Mrs. Twohey for his so-called gallery of rural types, until she got started going to town on Miss Fairlie. He never came here to do that candy-box top in there. Or maybe his curiosity about Miss Fairlie sparked the thing. Mrs. Twohey didn't start out to do in Sudley. It's Miss Fairlie she was down on. I'll bet you anything I own that Dunning's promised to help her put Miss Fairlie behind the bars in the looney-bin and that's the whole reason behind it. It was George Sudley's . . . murder that put her off in the first place. Dig it all up, she can go off again. God knows she's border-line enough right now."

He got up and moved back and forth across the free space in the room, to the black marble fireplace, back to the leather chair where he'd been sitting. When was it he became conscious that that had been where the old judge had always sat to read under the goose-neck lamp with the green glass shade? And when conscious that the worn horsehair carpet wasn't worn except in the line from the chair to the black marble fireplace . . . the track he was pacing, worn deep in the tough red-and-blue dyed horsehair fibre? He stopped, a sharp sense of psychic identification prickling ice-cold down his spine . . . the old judge's feet and his own pacing the same line, with the same anxiety, the same fear?

"Did your father kill George Sudley, Nat?"

The words were there, spoken aloud, words that came out of his mouth and that he'd no intention of speaking, that he'd had every intention not to speak . . . *as if he hadn't spoken them . . . as if the old judge . . .*

"It's strange how much like my father you sounded

o

then," Nat Twohey said simply, without tension of any kind. He hesitated only a brief instant. " I believe so. I've always known it, in fact. Harlan and I both know it." He stopped again. " We weren't across the river, Spig. It was too damned cold. We rowed up here. Our orchard went down to the water then, before they put the street through behind us. We came in here the back way. The house was empty. We looked. At the inquest my father said he was here, writing a brief at this desk."

He looked calmly down at the desk he was sitting at, his voice low and perfectly even.

" Not answering the phone he said. It rang, but we didn't answer it, either. The sheriff, Buck Yerby's father, said he picked my father up here and took him out to Eden, the rector and the doctor a little behind them. The rector's memory of it now is that he went out with them. My father had an old tweed overcoat he used to wear out in the country. He promised it to an old man who used to work around here. Gus. Gus found a piece of it in the furnace the next morning. It hadn't all burned."

He paused again, a long, slow, silent time.

" My father gave him a black chesterfield to take its place. It had a velvet collar. He was terribly proud of it. He told the story all over town. It used to frighten me till I nearly died. But nobody . . . nobody doubted my father's word, or Yerby's. Not then. Gus is dead. His son's seventy now. Gus was a preacher on Sundays. His son asked me about a month or so ago if I remembered the coat my father gave his father, that he used to wear when he preached. He had a sermon about it, showing how the Lord takes something from you and returns it a hundred-fold. The son remembers it almost verbatim."

He closed his eyes for an instant. " If Dunning hasn't

heard it I'm sure he will. Gus's son sometimes preaches that sermon at parties where they bring in a group to sing spirituals. I heard it at the Ashtons' when Anita first came down here. Folk art, I believe she called it."

When he stopped then, Spig waited a long time to ask the question that had been forgotten, or omitted.

" Sudley, Nat. Harland Sudley. You said he knew."

" Yes. He knew," Nat Twohey said quietly. " His getting the farm had nothing at all to do with it. I'll ask you to take my word for that, Spig. He loved his brother. It's true he loved Celia Fairlie, too." He smiled a little. " He still does, or he'd never have put up with her all these years."

He drew his chair closer to the old desk and lifted the blotting pad. " I have this for you."

O'Leary looked at the cheque in his hand.

" It's for five hundred. Miss Fairlie wants an option to buy the Plumtree Cove tract under the terms of your agreement with her."

Spig looked at him blankly.

" She called me this morning. She doesn't think you'll sell the place against her wishes, but she's afraid you might try to raise money on it, to buy Anita out, and land yourselves head over heels in debt. The option will stop that."

" We don't have to give it to her, do we," Spig said quietly. " It's the only security we've got. We promised your father——"

" She told me you said that. Are you sure you under-stood what he meant, Spig? He had a way of saying things for you to figure out later. I've been thinking about what you said just a minute ago. That could be the threat to Eden my father had in mind—not the physical threat. I don't know. You think it over."

The phone rang as Spig was starting out. Nat Twohey answered it. "He's right here. Just a second, Tip."

"Daddy." Tip's voice was not too steady. "I had to call you. Mother's gone . . . over to Mr. Dunning's. We've got to stop her. Please, Daddy."

"I'll be right out, son."

"Okay, Daddy."

The dial tone zinged. Spig held on a moment. There was hardly any sound as Mrs. Twohey put the extension softly down.

CHAPTER XX

IT TOOK him forty minutes to get out. There were two accidents on Death Strip, a woman with an armload of groceries from the supermarket and a car going sixty in a twenty-mile zone; another car ploughing into the rear of a sedan waiting behind three other cars for a light to change. Then Joe Cameron came out of the bank.

"Hi, I took your youngsters home. At their request. Miss Fairlie's taking them on safari to the Elm Tree Field. To hunt a rabbit. A red rabbit."

He boomed it out, laughing. O'Leary looked quickly around. There were only half a dozen of Mrs. Twohey's friends in earshot, none of them deaf.

Then when he came off the highway around the bend in his own road where he'd braked to keep from running head-on into Harlan Sudley's green truck, when Charlie Sudley was disking the field, he braked sharply again, to keep from running down the county surveyor with his transit and stakes in the middle of the road.

" What's the idea? "

" Ask Miss Fairlie. It's hers. She says your road's way over on her property. Plenty tough when she gets that little back of hers up."

Spig flushed. " I know my road's on her property. So does she. She told me to put it there so I wouldn't have to cut those beeches." He pointed to the silver trunks of the trees. " I'd have had to cut them or run into the marsh if I didn't. It was her own idea."

" Take it up with her, brother. I'm just a hired hand. She asked me to come check her line and I'm checking it."

Spig went on, started in to the Ashtons, and slowed down when he saw the yellow midget flying towards him out of the oyster shell road through the woods. But Dunning wasn't driving it. It was little Miss Lucy, in a hurry. She put on her brakes and stopped beside him.

" You're not hunting for Molly, are you, Uncle Spig? "

She was clear-eyed and bright, with none of the strained taut look her mother had had through the tinted glass of her car window leaving the Three D after her deal with Nick.

" Because she's gone home. I just saw her."

Lucy's face clouded with innocent concern. " I guess she didn't know how crazy Uncle Art can get. She's all right, but she looked awful, really she did. Running out of there with her blouse all torn. She was a mess. But for golly's sake don't let him know I told you. He'd be wild. 'Bye now."

She was off, the yellow car bouncing through the gate out towards the highway. O'Leary's car shot forward, the red fog building up, blinding him, until through it there focused a redder light flicking a warning so sharp that he jammed his foot on the brake and dug to a stop on the oyster shell surface.

Lucy. Lucy the born poltergeist. Lucy with the dynamite caps. A face too bright, too suddenly clouded.

He started his stalled engine and put it in reverse. *You'll damn' well check this time, O'Leary. See if it is the truth . . . not another pixie diversion—at your expense.* He was backing into the fork when another idea flashed up into his mind. At his expense? Or was this one at Dunning's? Was the blue-eyed child egging him on for her own amusement, or was it just possible she'd like to see Dunning with a broken jaw? So he couldn't talk, perhaps? He shifted into forward and went into his own lane, his grey eyes flat.

Molly's car was in the drive. He saw it first, then Tip, running out of the house.

" Didn't . . . didn't you get her, Daddy? "

" Isn't she home? "

It was nothing he'd needed to ask. He got out of the car. " Where are the other kids? "

" Gone to Miss Fairlie's. I was just . . . just waiting."

" You get along with them" He tried to keep his voice casual. " I'll go over and meet your mother. She went through the trail, didn't she? "

Tip nodded. " A long time ago. Right after the kids came home. She . . . she didn't know I waited."

" Okay. Trot along. I'll wander over. Have a good time. Find the rabbit."

" Okay, Daddy."

Spig waited until he saw him running across the bridge up the bank to the garden, out of sight. Then he started across the field, wary again. It could be Lucy's story was all made up—Molly running, looking awful, the torn blouse. A pixie diversion, to have him barge into Dunning's studio to find them both . . . in what state little Lucy's mind might imagine was neither here nor there except as it could be a product of her intense and excited awareness of Dunning's naked passion as he'd watched Molly leaving the Ashtons'. But trying to sift what could be true from what might be false out of the little blue-eyewitnesses's story was like sifting the sands of the wide blue sea.

He slowed down as he got across the field almost to the woods. Ten to one Lucy had him cast in the rôle of out-raged husband, and the thing for O'Leary to do was be suave and casual . . . *casual and suave as all hell, O'Leary.* He suddenly remembered the row they'd had last night, or this morning, when he'd got back from Eden. He'd forgotten that, and Molly's ten o'clock date with Dunning that if she didn't cancel O'Leary would. Sergeant O'Leary, orders to the troops, in triplicate. The general's daughter showing the sergeant just what he could do with all three copies. He grinned a little, feeling slightly more rational. It was probably all false, none of it true, just the product of two disordered imaginations.

He went along the trail through the dogwood and oaks, the sweet gums and tulip trees, whistling, relieved a little, and halted abruptly, swinging sharply to the side.

" Spig! *Oh, Spig!* Here I am . . . here! "

He saw her then, behind the old chestnut stump, pulling herself up from where she'd been crouching. He saw her bright hair first, then her face, white with circles smudged indigo-blue under her eyes, stricken pale. Then her white blouse, ripped and torn, pushed under her bra straps to hold it in place to cover her. He sprang through the holly beside the stump and caught her as she stumbled towards him, burying her head in his breast, clinging to him.

" Oh, *darling!* I was hiding . . . I was afraid you

were Tippy! He's been down here. I was so afraid
Mädel would show him where I was! I couldn't go home
as long as he was there. Oh, darling, hold me tight!
He's horrible, Spig! He's evil . . . evil! Oh, Spig,
we've got to stop him! "

She caught hold of his arms, shaking him, the way he'd
shaken her coming from the Ashtons', to break the rage
she could feel in him.

" Listen, darling! Listen to me. I'm all right. It
isn't me. Listen, darling . . . please! "

There was the red fog then, no light flicking redder
through it to warn him.

" You're sure you're all right? "

" Oh, yes. It's just my blouse. It's nothing—I just
didn't want to go home when Tippy's there. I could see
him. I thought he'd gone to Elm Tree Field with Miss
Fairlie and the others. I just didn't want him to see my
blouse torn. It's not me . . . it's the pictures, Spig.
The gallery. They're horrible. He can't show them.
We've got to stop him. They're cruel . . . horrible.
That's why I went, Spig. That's what our date was for.
He hasn't let anybody see them. But he wanted me to.
He thought I hated everybody. He thought I was in
love with him the way he is with me. He showed them
to me. He . . . he'd said he would but I wasn't going
till you . . . you said there was something about the one
of Tip's garden. That's why I went. And it is horrible. I
don't blame Tippy. Just slugs, and everything eaten and
foul, and Tip too . . . the Lord Proprietor. It's dreadful.
It's obscene. I . . . I couldn't bear it. Everybody. Mag
and Joe Cameron, the Potters, Mr. Sudley, Charlie, Anita
. . . everybody."

She put her head down, pressing her forehead against
him, shaking convulsively.

" But I'm all right. He just frightened me. He was mad—crazy mad—when I wouldn't let him kiss me."

Spig held her arms hard against her, steadying her till she stopped shaking.

" Can you get home? "

He hardly recognised his voice.

She nodded, her eyes closed. " Stop him, Spig. Some way. Stop him. I don't care how you do it, but we've got to."

" I'll stop him. You go on. I'll wait till you get inside."

" No, I'm all right. See if you can't talk to him. He might sell them to us . . . I don't know. There must be some way! "

He watched her run through the woods, up towards the garden, out of sight of the fishermen trolling close to the river bank. The red fog had turned to a cold white rage, still no warning light flickering through. He cut back into the trail into the Ashtons' grounds, moving deliberately. No one seeing him cross the drive to the studio entrance would have known it wasn't a casual visit unless they'd seen his face. He looked aside once, at Anita's house, closed, her big car not in the drive, the blue car back in the garage. He went to the door at the foot of the stairs to the studio apartment, opened it and went up the stairs. He knocked, waited and knocked again, opened the door and stepped inside, and stood motionless.

In front of him on an easel facing the door was a canvas slashed to ribbons. He saw it not first but at the same time he saw the ruinous havoc of the rest of the room, the living-room, not the skylighted workroom that was on through the door to the left. The room was torn apart in a frenzy of rage, the matchstick curtain in tatters, chairs upended, lamps smashed on the floor, a shambles of rage, a cursing screaming rage like the one he'd seen at the Eden graves. But it was the slashed portrait his eyes were riveted on across the wreckage. The hair, the one eye that was left, the line of one cheek and one shoulder, the yellow and brown plaid shirt, the old blue jeans . . . they were all Molly's. And over and above them, through the slashes, apart from any one feature or detail, there was a glowing lovely thing that was Molly herself. Slashed with a sadistic fury that froze O'Leary's feet, a symbolic act of murder so real it clutched at his throat.

He went on in. " Dunning," he said. He knew before he spoke that Dunning had gone. The studio was empty. It had an empty feel and an empty sound, the muted hollowness of a spent passion.

He stepped over a shattered crystal bowl. The yellow roses that had been in it were trampled, mud-stained from the water they were lying in. He stepped over cushions and a broken chair to the other end of the room to the studio door, and knocked on it.

" Dunning! "

The reverberation of his voice was all that came back to him. This was the studio room with the skylight. The slashed portrait of Molly was the only painting in the living-room. The rest of them would be in here. He put his hand on the knob and turned it. The door was locked, a Yale lock in the solid frame. He put his shoulder to the door. There was not a quiver to answer his thrust. He stepped back, looking around, and remembered an extension ladder Ashton had borrowed from him and never returned. It would be in the tool room under the studio at the end of the garage. If the studio windows were locked, too, he could break one of them in easier than he could break down the door. He started back across the room and stopped.

A car was coming. Anita possibly. He waited, listening for it to go on past the garage to the Ashton house. It stopped then, at the garage. He heard a door open and slam shut and steps, heavier than Anita's, on the stairs. Then a knock . . . a determined knock. The living-room door opened.

For a moment as speechless for O'Leary as it was for the woman who stood there, her face mottling an angry red, the two of them were motionless. It was the second Mrs. Twohey who first recovered, but not to smile.

"Where is Arthur, Mr. O'Leary?" she demanded sharply.

Spig moved a step to relax. "I don't know, Mrs. Twohey, where he is."

Her jaws snapped together. "Yes, you do. He was here when you came. Lucy told me so. I met her on my way out. She asked me to hurry. She said you were blood-mad and she feared for Arthur. Where is he, Mr. O'Leary?"

"I don't know," Spig said quietly. "He wasn't here when I came."

"That's a lie, Mr. O'Leary."

The angry red faded slowly out of Mrs. Twohey's face as she caught her breath suddenly, her eyes on the slashed canvas, riveted to it as Spig's had been, but with a fantastic difference.

"You . . . did that!"

It was not a whisper but a hoarse gasp, incredulous at first, strengthening into a sudden shattering conviction that drained the last colour from her face.

"You did that! You . . . you've murdered Arthur! You have, I know it! You've murdered Arthur . . . and now . . . you'll murder me!"

Mrs. Twohey clutched at her bosom and screamed. It was a ghastly scream. *And God knows she means it*, O'Leary thought with a shattering incredulity of his own as Mrs. Twohey seemed to dissolve, slipping down slowly in a dead faint, green hat and dyed hair among the trampled yellow roses and broken crystal shattered on the floor.

CHAPTER XXI

MRS. TWOHEY was prone among the trampled roses, a faint trickle of crimson where her hand had struck a piece of the shattered crystal. Spig O'Leary stood there letting his breath out slowly. Miss Fairlie's comment on the blasted woman was the truth if ever truth was uttered. *It's surprising that Nathan retained what sanity he did.*

The telephone was on the window ledge over behind the easel. He picked it up. Yerby was out.

" Get him by radio, will you? Tell him I'm at Dunning's studio out at the Ashton place. Ask him to step on it."

He pressed the bar down, released it and dialled Nat Twohey. As he waited for an answer, his eyes moved to the slashed canvas. Through one of the rents in it he saw the blood on Mrs. Twohey's hand. He knew it was her hand and her blood, that a painted hand has no blood, but the illusion was so intense and so frightening that he snapped the bar down and dialled his own number, waiting, his throat tight. When Molly answered, casually herself, his relief made his voice grate harshly.

" Listen, Molly. He's out of here. He's gone berserk.

Lock the doors and stay inside. Get Tip's rifle. If he comes, let him have it. Legs, any place—just show him you mean business. I've got to stay here."

A gasping sound made him turn. Mrs. Twohey was floundering to her feet. She looked ghastly, her face as green as her green print dress, her mouth opening and closing, as she gasped for air like a fish.

" You're all right," O'Leary said. " You just fainted. Yerby's coming. You stay here. I'm going downstairs and wait."

He let her get away from the door before he crossed the room. Her eyes fell on the roses and she saw the blood, mixed with the water and looking more than it was. The scene of the crime. Mrs. Twohey clutched her throat, backing away, as he went past her and down the stairs. It wasn't surprising the old judge had retained his sanity; it was miraculous. O'Leary took another long deep breath, turning then as he heard a car coming through the woods. He saw the red disc on the bumper.

" You made it quick."

" Yeah. I was just back there with Harlan talking to the surveyor. Your road's trespassing on Miss Fairlie's property."

" Thanks." Spig said dryly. " You tell Harlan I'll be happy to build another road." Having always been the beneficiary of Miss Fairlie's eccentricities, it was a peculiar sensation suddenly becoming a victim. " Mrs. Twohey's upstairs. Dunning's living-room's a wreck. She thinks I did it and murdered him while I was at it. She'll show you the spot. She's all yours—I'm going home."

" Where's Dunning? "

" No idea." Spig moved back to where he could see the pier. " The boats are down there. Lucy's got his car. He's on foot. I told Molly to shoot if he came over to our place."

Yerby glanced at the Ashton house. "Anita's in town. At the courthouse. Looking for Judge Banks. You better see if Dunning's at Eden."

He took a long breath and crossed the drive to the studio door.

Spig was around the corner of the garage when he heard the shots. There were two, in quick succession. He dashed through the woods, slowing down at the edge of the field, everything quiet ahead of him, no sign of commotion. Somebody shooting crows, probably. Except for his own fears he wouldn't have thought twice about a couple of stray shots in the middle of the day. He relaxed a little, moving on towards the kitchen door. It wasn't locked, and Molly was in there, the ironing board down, pressing a dress of Molly A.'s. On the counter were two piles of clothes, hers and John Eden's. Spig stopped, looking at them.

" Daddy said if we'd put the two kids on the four o'clock plane he'd meet them, and Anita can sue till hell breeds polar bears. We should have shipped them last night, he said."

It was probably that that had upset her. He could see the sharp white line around her lips.

" It'll be all right, sweetie," he said gently.

" I'm sure it will. John Eden's been by plane before. He'll love it."

She pulled the cord out of the iron and set it aside. " And your father wants you to call him. The Fuller brothers are in town. He can handle it but he needs the dope."

" Okay. Then I've got to see if Dunning's over at Eden."

" I'm sure he's not. Why don't you let him alone? "
Her voice was taut as she pushed the ironing board back
into the wall. Spig watched her picking up the children's
clothes, the wooden-doll rigidity of her movements
sobering his face.

" Molly . . . you didn't fire those shots, did you? "
he asked quietly.

" What shots? Listen—I've been busy trying to get
the kids packed. I haven't even finished our beds.
You're making a great big mountain without even a
molehill to start with."

" You didn't see what he did to your portrait. It's
slashed to bits."

" So what? It was his. If you're going to call your
father you'd better hurry."

He listened to her go into Molly A.'s room and stop,
standing still a long time. A slow dread was creeping
around in the pit of his stomach. He looked at the clock.
It was ten minutes to twelve. The call to his father would
take him some time. He went out and stopped at the
hyphen stairs.

" Molly. Buck Yerby's going to be over."

There was a long pause before she answered. " Okay."

Yerby was there when he came downstairs. It was
twenty-five minutes past twelve and they were out in the
kitchen, Yerby with a roast beef sandwich and a bottle
of beer, sitting in the dining nook, Molly across from him.
She'd put on fresh lipstick, but she hadn't been able to
get rid of the taut lines and faint blue circles under her
eyes. Spig saw Yerby looking at the torn white blouse
on the table.

"—Pretty harrowing," she was saying. " I'm still a
wreck. But he's probably all cooled off by now. And
the studio's Anita's problem, isn't it. If he'd gone to

Eden he'd have come through here. It's over a mile and a half by the road."

" You didn't tell him Miss Fairlie and the kids were away? "

" I'm sure I didn't." She avoided Spig's eyes.

" We'd better check anyway," Yerby said. " I want to find him before Mrs. Twohey raises any more hell. She's got it all three ways. He's disappeared because he's dead. Spig killed him this morning and his body's in the locked room. And Harland just now shot him to keep from being exposed as his brother George's murderer. And Miss Fairlie doesn't allow guns on Eden."

It seemed irrelevant only for a moment.

" You tell me Tip's got a rifle. Where is it? "

" In his locker."

O'Leary put his glass down and started to get up.

" Let Buck get it . . . you clean up your dishes." Molly spoke sharply. " I'm in a hurry. Right out by the stairs, Buck."

Yerby went out into the hyphen. Spig watched Molly, his throat dry. He could only see the side of her face, but her knuckles were white where she was gripping the faucet, holding her breath, waiting. He heard Yerby open the locked door, take the gun out of the rack, examine it, put it back and close the door. Molly turned the faucet, releasing her breath slowly.

Yerby came back. " If you're ready, let's go, Spig. Mind if I use your phone first? I want to check in."

" Go ahead."

Spig heard him go into the old cottage and close the door.

" Molly."

" What, darling? "

He turned and went abruptly towards the door into the hyphen

"Spig!" she whispered. "Stop it! Don't!"

He went on quietly, and quietly opened the door of Tip's locker. There was a rifle there, but it wasn't Tip's. It was Molly's—stored in the attic the last time Spig had seen it. He stood there for a kind of small eternity, pushed the door to and went back into the kitchen. She was out on the porch.

"Molly." He took her by the shoulders, trying to make her turn around to face him, but she stood rigidly, holding to the rail.

"Let me alone!" She broke away and ran down the steps. Spig heard Yerby open the cottage door. He went back in quickly. Yerby was standing by the pine taproom table, looking down at it. He lifted the bowl of nasturtiums aside and pulled the painted chair over from the desk.

"George Sudley was about my size," he said. "If I was sitting here with my gun . . ." He sat down. "And I had a blanket around me . . ."

"For God's sake," Spig said, "we all know he was murdered."

"I'm just trying," Yerby said deliberately, "to find out how Dunning knew it." He looked up at Spig. "They had a post box. In the fireplace there. Harlan told me. Sometimes he'd deliver or collect a letter for George. And Nat tells me his father left you a letter. Said he gave it to you when this Ashton business came up. Nat's been thinking. He thinks maybe it wasn't the Ashton business . . ."

"He wrote me a letter," Spig said. "It's sealed. I'm not to open it till Miss Fairlie's ill, or dead, or David dies. Some kind of crisis at Eden."

P

Buck Yerby's eyes rested steadily on his. "The crisis is here. This is it."

"What is?"

"Dunning. And the murder of George Sudley. And Mrs. Twohey. Someone told her this morning that Miss Fairlie sees red rabbits. The red rabbits set her off. She told me Dunning's got all the evidence they need. To put Miss Fairlie away for good and all. That's one of the reasons she's trying to find him—and one of the reasons she thinks he's been killed. It's another reason I want him."

The determined virgins, married and single, male and female, of this community may decide Miss Fairlie should be sent away when I am no longer here to prevent it. Open the letter.

Point Four of the old judge's letter moved with sudden clarity through Spig O'Leary's mind. And point Six.

With the rapidly changing scene in Devon unforeseeable situations may arise. Your own discretion will direct you.

He hadn't moved. Nor had Yerby, his eyes, sombrely burning, fixed on him across the shadow of the blood deep in the fibre of the satin pine, signature indelible, the echo of the shot still reverberating, sound indelible, blood that flowed in a crimson gush from one man's heart by another man's hand.

"I know it's time to open it," Spig said. "I don't want to. Not if there's any other way."

Yerby looked at him a long time. "Miss Fairlie's our job. The rest are dead."

"All right."

He went over to the side of the fireplace, aware that several times in the less than forty-eight hours since he'd put the letter there the impulse to get it and open it had been in his mind, and he'd denied it because he loved

the old judge and he loved Miss Fairlie. He put out his
hand to the stone and turned back to Yerby.

" I thought you knew all about it."

" I know who killed George Sudley. I don't know why.
My father said the judge knew and promised him he
wouldn't die without telling it. For Celia Fairlie's sake.

Spig pressed the stone and put his hand down in the
hollowed cavity. The cold sweat broke out suddenly on
his forehead as his fingernails scratched the solid rock.

He turned his head. " It's gone, Buck."

Yerby got to his feet, the blood draining out of his face,
surging back into it. " You should have told me," he
said harshly. " A hell of a place to keep anything."

" The judge said——"

" The judge forgot what men in love tell their girls.
Harlan was engaged to Martha when George was killed.
Martha Sudley's one of the Dunning crowd."

O'Leary pushed the stone back into place. As he did
the phone rang. He stood there as Yerby answered it.

" Speaking." He listened silently. " Okay. Tell His
Honour I'll be right in." He jammed the phone down.
" That damned woman . . . Get Nat, tell him to get
over to my office if he comes on a stretcher. Then go
find Dunning. I want him here, dead or alive, when I
get back."

Spig dialled the Twohey house. He heard the signal
ring ten times, put the phone down and went out into
the kitchen. " Molly! " He looked out the back door,
then dashed up to the children's room. She wasn't there.
The suitcases for John Eden and Molly A. were packed,
out in the hall, ready for him to carry down. He went
quickly down the stairs and outside. Across the circle
he turned into the path to the bridge, went over it, the
German shepherd and the crow on guard at the Eden

end, and went up the bank. His heart jolted then as, suddenly, through the trees he caught a flash of Molly's red-gold hair. She was over by the graves. Then for one almost sickening moment he saw Dunning's blue denim figure and black face through the rusted iron palings, and breathed again as he saw it wasn't Dunning but old David. And in Molly's hand was Tip's rifle, the sun glinting on the barrel. She was moving around apparently hunting something on the ground, and moved abruptly away then, towards the little Greek temple. But when he got up there she was hurrying through the arbour towards the house, nothing in her hand.

" Mis' O'Leary said tell you she was goin' to see if Miss Fairlie and the children was comin'. It's gettin' late, they promise to be back in time to get the little ones ready."

Old David was on his knees on Ammon Fairlie's grave without a stone. *The Lord knows where to fin' him, the Devil too.* On the grass beside the grave was a strip of brown tarpaulin with clumps of ivy he had dug up there and clumps of myrtle in deep spadesful of earth he was putting in their place. " That fella near 'bout ruin my ivy. But I been fixin' to move it. Mr. Ammon never liked ivy. Seem like Miss Fairlie never get away long enough to get much done. No use remindin' her of what she bes' forget."

He reached for a clump of myrtle and set it in place. Under it was a print of the heel of his work shoe, sunk deep in fresh-dug earth. The ivy had been level with the ground. The myrtle clumps were raised. *So when the soft earth settles* . . . O'Leary stood there, his heart beating not as if it belonged to him. He'd already seen what Molly had been hunting for. It was the brass jacket of a used shell, glinting under the dark leaves of the myrtle growing around the outside of the iron paling, a sombre ribbon tying the clipped yews together. He turned, strangely slow motion, and looked across the Cove. The upstairs windows of their bedroom, where Molly had left one bed half made, were in full and open view. He let his breath out carefully. When his voice came he was surprised how normal it sounded.

" Did you happen to see Mr. Dunning over here this morning, David ? "

" The artist fella." David put the last two clumps of myrtle in place. He got up then and came out through the rusty gate, looking back. " I get it cleaned up, it'll look like it growed there itself," he remarked with satisfaction. " Mis' O'Leary was tellin' me you all was huntin' the fella. I expec' he'll show up in his own good time, as they say. I ain' bother about him long as he leaves us alone. Them children sure done Miss Fairlie a world of good. Don' want him gettin' her all upset and sick again."

He gathered up the tarpaulin with the ivy on it, took his spade and trudged off across the garden. Spig stood there a long time. He picked up the shell case then and went over to the temple. It took him a moment to find the rifle. It was tucked down under the ivy that grew, a thick mat, around the stone foundation.

When he crossed the bridge he could hear the phone ringing. It was ringing still when he was half-way to the house, but when he got inside and picked it up the dial tone was all he heard. He put the rifle in Tip's rack, took Molly's upstairs and slipped it through the trap-door into the attic. Then he went past the unmade bed to the window and looked back across the Cove. David was coming out from behind the temple, moving slowly around, as Molly had done. On the floor at Spig's feet

was a cigarette with a tint of lipstick on the end, burned
to the filter tip before it went out, almost its entire ash
still intact, the paper burned into the floor board. She
must have just lighted it as she stopped there and saw
. . . whatever it was she'd seen. He looked back at
David then, still crawling around, poking in the myrtle
where the shell case had been, until suddenly he got
up and disappeared quickly into the arbour.

It was the jeep coming. Spig heard it before he saw it,
heard the children shouting and laughing, saw it then
come bounding down between the borders, Miss Fairlie
at the wheel, Molly beside her, hanging on for dear life,
the children bouncing around in the back, the dog barking
on the bridge, the crow cawing. He held his breath as
Miss Fairlie bounced them down the bank and swerved
to a stop at the bridge, all still intact, jumping out then,
trooping noisily across the bridge, waving back at Miss
Fairlie, John Eden running back to say good-bye again.
Miss Fairlie drove the jeep back up the bank, through the
borders towards the picket gate.

Without partiality or prejudice, faithfully to perform . . .
The words of the oath he'd taken slipped quietly into
his mind as he stood there listening to Molly and the
children, laughing, hurrying towards the kitchen hyphen.

" You get the bags down, Tip," Molly was saying.
" And Kitsy, you help Molly A. John Eden, wash those
ears again. I have to get dressed."

She'd be coming up in a minute. Spig went quickly
out and down the stairs into the living-room. He couldn't
face her then without her seeing his dismay—if that was
what it was—and there was no time to go into anything
before she started the drive to the airport. He heard
her come out of the old cottage, run lightly up the stairs,
go across to the window and stand there several moments.

He could hear her steps overhead then and trace each move, the dressing-table to the closet again, the rap of high heels to the dressing-table, and down the stairs.

" I don't know where Daddy is," he heard her say, and saw Tip lugging the bags over to her car.

CHAPTER XXII

HE WENT OUT. Molly and Molly A., dark curls shining, and John Eden all spit and polish, freckles glowing, were coming from the hyphen. Yerby was back. O'Leary saw his face as he pulled up, at the same moment he saw Anita Ashton's big car coming out of the lane. Yerby got out, slamming his door shut.

" It's a court order, Spig. For the Ashton kid. She went to Judge Banks. It restrains you from moving the child. I tried to call you."

Spig held the paper Buck thrust at him, too numb to read it. He turned back to where Molly had stopped, her face drained very white, her feet frozen to the ground. It was like a horrible game of statues, with Tip and Kitsy and John Eden turned to marble where they were, and Molly A., the four-year-old, holding Molly's hand, suddenly clinging tightly to it. Anita came across the drive, her lips thinned to a smile.

" Just in time, aren't we." She turned to Molly. " Sorry to interrupt your trip, darling, but I'm glad the child is all packed. Get her, will you, Buck? "

" Daddy! " It was John Eden. " He's not going to take Molly A.! Don't let him, Daddy! "

" Sorry, fella," Yerby said. He took a step forward and

John Eden rushed at him, kicking, his fists hitting at Yerby's long legs, tears of rage blinding him. Spig caught the dog's collar, handed her to Tip and went back for his son.

" It's okay," Yerby said. " It's how I feel myself."

Spig pinioned the two small arms to John Eden's side and lifted him, still kicking, out of Yerby's way.

Then the Sea King's daughter smiled and stooped down to Molly A.

" Darling . . . Mrs. Ashton's come to take you to her house. You'll have a lovely time, and go see Grandfather some other day. It's over where Daddy lived . . . you remember. It's the blue bag, Tip—will you bring it? "

She took Molly A. by the hand and led her across to Anita. " You remember Mrs. Ashton."

The child held out a frightened hand.

" Hallo, darling." Anita Ashton took it, two crimson spots burning in her cheeks.

Molly lifted her then and carried her over to the car. " You're going to have a lovely time, baby."

" I tried to phone you," Yerby said again.

" It's okay." O'Leary was still holding on to John Eden, trying savagely to get away and over to Anita's car where Tip was—the dog, hackles up, snarling, held in one hand, Molly A.'s blue bag in the other. " 'Bye, Molly A. We'll come see you."

" I think she'll be happier if there's a clean break," Anita said curtly. " We shan't be here long. You still have till Friday if you're buying the place. Otherwise I've decided to sell it to Stan's friends. There are some technical problems he knew that I didn't. Good-bye."

The big car backed and shot into the lane. The stricken child's face through the tinted glass stayed with them all.

It was a nightmare day. A dragging nightmare of

Molly's wooden face, eyes washed grey-green, the gold flecks silver-pale, Tip and Kitsy in stricken silence, John Eden's stormy tear-stained face and quivering shoulders passionately rejecting any comfort, and always the picture of Molly A. through the tinted glass. It was why Spig went around the house and collected every shell in it, took them down to the river and threw them in, and why he couldn't talk to Molly or speak to Tip about the rifle and the stolen letters. But by the end of the day—an end he thought would never come, and hadn't come, in fact —he knew what he had to do. He had to find Dunning, and not on Eden. When he called Yerby in the morning, Dunning's body was going to be as far from the Eden graveyard as he could get it.

It was quarter to twelve when he let himself out of the house. It had taken that long for the sleep of sheer exhaustion to settle Molly, the children, already worn out, sound asleep. He crossed the circle down to the bridge where he stowed a tarpaulin with a spade and flashlight wrapped in it, under the honeysuckle on the bank. He got it and crossed the bridge silently, up and around the path to the graveyard. The moon was brighter than it had been the night before when he came on Dunning sitting there, laughing. He stopped to listen. The peacock-hoarse cry of the blue heron, disturbed, up the river, was the only sound, except for the velvet lap of the river and all the myriad tiny songs of the night, ceasing, beginning again, as he went by, the moonbeams on the water and the fireflies in the dark screen of cryptomeria that hid the house from him and him from the house, the only visible movement in the perfumed night.

He opened the iron gate, stepped inside and laid the tarpaulin down as David had laid his, on the grass beside Ammon Fairlie's grave. He took up the spade.

The myrtle had been watered, but the square clumps of heavy clay soil were still intact, easy to lift out. He put them on the far edge of the tarpaulin, to leave room, as David had done, for the earth from under them. He worked quickly. Then he stiffened suddenly, alert, as a sound seemed to come from across the garden. He put the spade down quietly and slipped behind the cryptomeria. There was nothing he could see across the moon shining on the lilies and foxglove and the white waxen stars of the nicotiana. He stood there, every nerve intent, listening. But there was nothing.

Silent as the grave. He thought it with a quiver along his spine as he went back and picked up the spade again. The clay under the myrtle was as soft to the touch, as newly dug, as he'd believed watching David lay the clumps neatly on top of it. He worked carefully, lifting it off in layers, laying it on the tarpaulin. Suddenly the taut nerves of his hand and fingers sensed through the steel and wood the touch of a different substance, soft as it caught and stayed the blade, not deeper than six inches under the heavy clumps of the myrtle on top. He knelt down and took his flashlight, holding it low and close so as not to show. It was burlap his spade had touched. Light new burlap. He took up his spade and lifted off more of the earth. What it struck then was not soft. He put it down again and pulled the burlap aside, his hands freezing motionless then, cold sweat drenching his back, the silence thundering in his ears.

It was not Dunning. He knelt there motionless for a stunned moment, the white skeletal bones of a man's hand shining in the ball of light he was too numbed to turn off. When he did, the hand still shone, pale, luminescent in the moonlight slanting through the clipped yews. And besides the fleshless bones of the hand were other bones, half hidden by the dark patches of cloth that had rotted but still clung to them.

He thrust the burlap back into place then and worked, faster than he had worked in his life, putting back the earth and the clumps of myrtle above it, his heart pounding, his ears hearing a thousand sounds, all of them Dunning, waiting to hear the quiet hideous laughter . . . the sound he'd heard over in the borders real to him again as he pressed the squares of myrtle together, covering the grave, too numb to think, in too desparate a hurry to try to reason.

He folded the spade in the tarpaulin, closed the rusted gate and went fast back towards the bridge, halting sharply as he saw two gleaming balls of fire in front of him there, like a wolf's eyes, or a devil's, until he realised it was the dog Mädel. He hadn't known she was outside to follow him. But if Dunning had crossed there, she'd have barked. He stopped short, thinking rationally again. If the sound he'd heard had been Dunning, waiting there, biding his time . . . Dunning not dead but alive. . . He put the tarpaulin and spade on the ground, went quietly back to the borders, and stopped again, his heart sinking. Miss Fairlie's kitchen light was on. He could see it like a spangle of tiny candles through the chinks in the shutters of the door and windows.

Could she have heard . . . seen him in the graveyard, the moon glinting on the spade . . . ? A cold hand tightened on his heart. He moved quickly along the turf towards the kitchen, stopping to whistle softly, as he'd done the night before, and waiting then. He saw a long sliver of light grow down the centre of the shutters at the door, as one wing opened a little. Then she was there, peering out.

" It's me, Miss Fairlie. O'Leary."

She opened the shutter a little wider and slipped out, drawing it shut behind her, blinking at him, the moon on her long white wrapper and bare head as he came over to her.

" Were you out in the garden just now, Miss Fairlie? "

She didn't answer.

" I thought I heard somebody. I was looking for Dunning."

It was the truth, a kind of horrible truth.

" Go away now," she said softly. It was hardly more than a whisper. " The chimney sweep . . . he hasn't been here. But the child . . . the child's asleep now. Go away. I'm not afraid. It's just the spiders. The spiders worry me. But the child's asleep. I must go now."

She stepped back inside and closed the shutter. He heard the bar come down and the door behind it close quickly, the bolt slip home.

Dear God, he thought wretchedly, the saliva flooding his mouth. Then he stiffened, tensing abruptly, as he saw the floodlight leap on at the Ashton pier and then in an instant the floodlight on his own house, the one at the corner of the children's wing that threw a white blanket over the field and garden. He dashed back down between the borders to the bridge, no dog guarding it now, and up across the circle. He saw Tip and Kitsy in pyjamas out in the floodlit field up towards Tip's garden. " Molly A.! Molly A.! " they were calling, before Tip set off running across the field to the woods with Kitsy still calling, and Molly came around the back of the house in her dressing-gown, her face a white blur.

She ran towards him. " She's gone, Spig! Oh, the poor baby! Trying to get home! Hurry, go find her! Don't frighten her. Anita called. Hurry! Here's a flashlight—give it to Tip."

She thrust another flashlight into his hand. The floodlights behind the Ashtons' went on. He caught up with Tip on the edge of the woods.

" Molly A.! It's Tip! " he was calling.

Spig gave him the light. The dog was with him, dashing in and out, barking.

" There's places we hide, Daddy . . . I'll look in them. Molly A.! It's Tippy, Molly A.! Find her, Mädel—find Molly A.! "

Spig ran on through the trail, the lights from both houses casting shadows heavy as blackened tree trunks across the path, out into the Ashtons' drive. Yerby's car was there, the light still blinking.

". . . the hell were you leaving the kid alone for? " he was demanding angrily.

" I had to go meet my father." Anita's voice was like a strip of parachute silk being ripped apart. " She was asleep. Lucy was supposed to stay with her. But Arthur Dunning called—she had to take his car to him. She left a note. She hasn't been gone but a few minutes. The time's on the note—12.32."

She flashed around to Spig. " I thought the child was at your house. I thought Molly . . . till I called her."

" What room was she in? "

They followed Anita into the house. It was the second door across from the dining-room, next to the room Spig had seen Lucy looking out of the morning of the blue glass splinter. The bed was torn up, the pillow still wet where a child had cried herself to sleep. Her clothes were there, except her shoes.

" She took her toothbrush," Anita said, her voice choking.

The light was on, the window open. There was a chair she'd pulled up to climb on to unlatch the screen.

Yerby and Spig went out through it and turned their lights on the grass. There were faint tracks in the dew, around towards the front of the house.

"—We find her, she stays with you," Yerby said curtly. "That note of Lucy's. I don't believe a damned word of it. She wouldn't have got mixed up and headed for these woods instead of yours, would she? The baby, I mean?"

Spig had halted suddenly. "Wait a minute, Buck. I know. Get Anita out front. Where's her father?"

"He's out looking on the woods road."

They went back inside. "Come out here, will you, Anita?" Yerby said. She followed him out. Spig went on to the kitchen phone.

"Not yet," he said to Molly's taut questioning voice. "Where's John Eden?"

"Asleep. He didn't wake up. I don't want to——"

"Take another look at him. Mädel was out—down at the bridge when I was at Eden. Call me back here."

He stood there. Anita's father had joined the two outside, the benign confidence missing from his voice coming to Spig through the window.

". . . told you it was a mistake to take the child unless you have a staff of servants here. How far would Lucy have to go for Dunning?"

Then he heard Yerby speaking monotonously. "All cars. That yellow midget convertible. Bring 'em in. Contact——"

The phone rang. "He wasn't asleep, Spig! He's just pretending. His shoes are damp and there's a grass stain on his pyjama legs. He had Tippy's alarm clock under his pillow, set for eleven o'clock. He won't say anything . . . but he knows, Spig!"

"So do I. Don't worry."

He put the phone down and went outside. " The kid's okay," he said curtly. " But it wasn't any 12.32 that Lucy left here, Anita. It was before 11.15, anyway." He hadn't been at the graveyard long when he heard the sound in the borders. It wouldn't have taken John Eden much time alone, but it would be a slow job with Molly A. " If I were you I'd worry about my own kid, right now. You can pay Nick off——"

" That's a lie. It wasn't Lucy at the Three D. It was Art Dunning. He ran into the window. He gave me the money to pay Nick. It was after that that somebody got in and broke the slot machine . . ."

As if there were some kind of design in the universe, functioning to save or to destroy, to prove the truth or to confound the lie, the radio in the sheriff's car started its hollow crackle as they heard the metallic voice out of the crash of static droning its report.

" Joe Anders, Yerby. Foggy Bottom. Chasing the yellow midget. Foggy Bottom road west to Strip. We're going eighty. Light in back room My Hideaway. Caught 'em prying back off a slot——"

There was a crash of static, and another crash. The whine of tyres, the crash still reverberating, a confusion of voices scrambling the short wave, and Anders, panting, coming clear again.

" They were thrown out before they hit, Buck. I don't know whether they're alive or dead. Get the ambulance quick . . ."

Anita stood motionless, as if in some way she had herself died, her face a terrible mask, raddled, great circles spreading under her eyes like india ink spreading in the snow. She swayed a little, holding to the car window.

" They'll . . . take them to the hospital, won't they? Come, Father . . ."

" Do you want me to drive you over, Anita? " O'Leary asked.

" Oh! Why should you, after all I've . . . I've done to you? " Her eyes suddenly flooded with tears. As suddenly, she moved towards him, her arms around him, her blonde head pressed an instant against him. " Oh, forgive me, Spig—I've been a beast! "

" I'll take them in." Yerby pushed the seat forward. " You get in with her," he said to her father, whose whole handsome façade had suddenly crumpled. Then he reached in the compartment, took out a gun and handed it to Spig. " Take a look in the studio. I think there's somebody up there. I'll be back—either here or your place."

Spig stood in the lighted drive looking at the gun in his hand, then at the blinking red light disappearing out the Ashtons' road. He kept his eyes on the studio door and called Tip, his voice echoing sharply back to him. In a moment he heard him and Mädel scrambling out of the woods. Tip's pyjamas were ripped and his face and legs torn with thorns.

" John Eden took her over to Eden, Tip."

" Oh . . ." Tip's eyes widened. " I'd better go see about it."

Spig nodded. " And look. Our post box——"

" I know it," Tip said. " I got worried if Mother's still a friend of his. I moved them to a safer place. Come on, Mädel."

If individual initiative in the young is desirable, the young O'Learys were doing all right. The ironic glint in their father's eyes faded as he went over to the apartment door, switched on the light and went upstairs. He knocked and waited an instant before he opened the door and reached around to switch on the light there. The slashed portrait of Molly was gone, the only change in the room, except for the quality of the silence. Some difference in it made him take Yerby's gun out of his pocket and slip the safety catch. Across the room he could see the edge of the flush workroom door not quite flush. He went silently to one side of it and kicked it sharply open.

"Come in, damn you. I'm waiting for you."

O'Leary stood motionless a bare instant. "Hold it," he said. He went on in. "What the hell . . . ?"

"I thought you were Dunning."

Nat Twohey's voice was as steady as the barrel of the gun in his hand and his eyes as steely.

Spig looked past him to the table by the wall. On it was a straight-edged razor and a pile of canvas ribbons. Under the table was a heap of empty stretchers.

"The gallery of rural types," Nat said. "And what was left of a portrait of Molly."

Spig glanced at the window. "How'd you get in here?"

"Lucy was kind enough to give me the key. She said I'd like to see the other portrait of Eloise Dunning was painting. The swine . . . not fit for my father to spit on, and raking up a dead man's past. Now I'd like you to get out. I'm staying till he comes."

"You're crazy, Nat," Spig said. "You've lost your mind."

"I'll appreciate that testimony later." The flicker in Nat Twohey's eyes was very like his father. He nodded towards the easel under the skylight. "I left that . . . for him to explain."

Spig slipped the safety catch back and put the gun in his pocket, moving around in front of the easel. It was a long moment before he heard Nat's voice through the

Q

pounding of the blood in his ears, as he looked down at
the paper pinned on the drawing board, trying to shake
off the slow paralysis creeping down his legs and the chill
of the grave along his spine.

" What is that, Spig? "

He heard himself, factually casual. " It looks like a
study of some kind." It was several pencil sketches of a
skeletal hand, a draughtsman's study. " Interested in
anatomy, I guess. But I don't think he'll need it any
more."

He ripped the sheet off the board, took it over to the
fireplace and held a match to it.

" I'm going home," he said. " I'd advise you to do
the same, Counsellor."

" I'm staying. And before you go . . . Miss Fairlie's
settled the problem of the Ashton place."

" She's not buying the Ashtons'——"

" No. She's keeping them from selling it for commercial use. There's a State law that prohibits a
commercial entrance within five hundred yards of a
State-owned bridge. That's why Ashton had to have the
use of your road in from the highway to your gate, and
get you to give him the right-of-way through your woods,
if he wanted to sell to the gamblers. But your road
from the highway to your gate is on Miss Fairlie's
property. She's closing it and refusing them permission
to use her lane. They're bottled up. They can't sell
to any commercial outfit. It'll be a jolt to Anita when
she finds it out."

" She's had all the jolts she can take right now, Nat."

Somehow the whole thing had lost its importance
when he thought about the hands . . . on the drawing-
board, in the shallow grave. And his need to know what
Molly had seen.

She was coming down from John Eden's room when he got home.

" Oh, the poor lamb, Spig! He told me . . ."

She caught her breath, pale again. He shook his head quickly.

" It's something else, Molly." He drew her into the old cottage and closed the door. " You saw something this morning. What was it? It's not Dunning in the grave . . . if that's what you thought."

" Oh . . ." She closed her eyes for a moment. " I . . . was afraid it was. David was . . . dragging something to the graves. It was after the shots. Tip's rifle was gone. I was afraid to tell you. Then when you and Buck were going over I was terrified, so when you were in here I ran over. David said Tip loaned him the rifle and he'd seen Dunning up at the gate and fired, just to frighten him. But . . . he'd been digging—and he'd do anything for Tip. You're sure nothing's happened to Art Dunning? "

" I'm sure he's not in the grave."

The phone rang. He went quickly to the desk. The line was blank at first. Then he heard a click. " Hallo."

" Daddy! It's Miss Fairlie . . . come quick! I've called the doctor. The letters, Daddy—they're under my mattress. Molly A.'s asleep. Hurry, Daddy! "

He turned back on his way to the door. " Yerby's coming. Wait for him, tell him to come to Eden. Get the dog in with the kids. Lock the doors and come with him. Something's happened to Miss Fairlie. Molly A.'s all right."

CHAPTER XXIII

He took the children's stairs in two leaps and tore up the mattress on Tip's bed. Flattened under it was his old army knapsack, Tip's now. He grabbed it and dashed down and outside, pounded across the bridge and up between the borders, seeing the first lights he'd ever seen at Eden except in the kitchen, light on the porch spattering through the chinks of the downstairs shutters, the front door open.

"Here, Daddy!"

Tip was calling from the parlour to the left. A single drop bulb in the centre of the chandelier was spraying the lovely room with rainbow drops of crystal light. There was a door open beside the fireplace across the room, beyond it dust-covered steps leading down into the closed hyphen, a single-room brick floored passage that connected the main house with the vine-sealed wing that balanced the kitchen wing on the other side. It was pitch-black down there except for the ball of Tip's flashlight. Miss Fairlie was lying at the bottom.

"Oh, Daddy, she can't be dead! She can't! she can't!"

Tip's face looking up at him tore his heart. He went quickly down and knelt in the dust, his hand to her pulse.

"She's alive." He lifted her up, a tiny fragile thing, and carried her up the steps. "Where does she sleep, do you know?"

" In there." Tip pointed across the hall. Spig carried
her over. There was a four-poster bed there, at its foot
a child's trundle bed, with a real child really asleep in it,
Molly A.'s dark curls on the pillow, a rag doll in her arms.
He laid Miss Fairlie gently down on the huge bed. The
bottom of her white wrapper was black. She did not
speak except for the vague smile in her blue eyes for an
instant before she closed them.

" There's a car, maybe it's the doctor . . ."

Tip ran out and down the steps to open the picket gate.
Spig followed as the car came around the boxwood
and Yerby and Molly came running up through the
garden.

"—In here."

He went back with Doctor Parker. " She'd fallen.
Tip found her." He turned away as Molly came quietly
in, bending quickly down to touch the sleeping child's
flushed cheek with her lips before she went on around the
bed.

" It looks like a stroke. We'd better get her to the
hospital."

Spig saw Miss Fairlie's eyes open in agony to his.

" No. We'll keep her here. Molly was a nurse's aide,
just tell her what to do."

He went out into the hall again. Yerby and Tip were
talking on the porch.

" Come on, Buck. Have you got a light? You stand
by, Tip."

He took his own flashlight out and closed the parlour
door behind them. The knapsack was where he'd dropped
it by the open door down into the hyphen.

" Tip said he didn't have a chance to tell you," Yerby
said. " He got over here and she told him to stay with
the kid while she went some place . . . the noise might

frighten her if she woke up and heard the hammering.
Then she went down here." He played his flashlight
down the steps and around the brick floor of the hypen.
" He heard her fall then."

The dust on the bricks was heavy as the velvet pile of a
rug, thick with mould. There were tracks across to the
open door into the wing that balanced the kitchen.
Yerby's light rested on Miss Fairlie's footprints and the
blurred trail of her wrapper. Then it moved to a second
line of prints, of a work shoe, leading to the door, coming
back. The ball of the flashlight followed them methodically.

" Easy enough to trace her—and those. You better
tell me what's on your mind, first."

" Just a guess. We'd better look."

" Let's go, then."

They went down the four steps, across the summer
mould and the seeping dust of forty years, the cobwebs
like black stalactites hanging from the ceiling, crêpe
festooned along the cornices and over the shuttered and
barred windows, already sealed tight with the ivy and
creeper through which no light passed and no air. By
the open door through the thick masonry walls into
the sealed wing a corroded iron bar that had been taken
down from it leaned against the wall, flakes of rust on the
floor.

" Watch out for spiders," Yerby said. " You get the
black widows in closed-up holes like this."

It wasn't the dust and the turgid air catching Spig's
throat. *The spiders. The black widow spiders were all she
was afraid of.*

He followed Yerby through the door into a single large
room, their lights on the floor. The tracks of the work
shoes went to a great fourposter bed in the corner, and

back to where they were standing in the doorway. Miss Fairlie's tracks went to the hearth of the fireplace, and from there to the bed, and to the door again. But there were other tracks of small ribbed rubber-soled shoes, criss-crossed over the room, between the fireplace, the bed, the doorway, to the windows, where the inside shutters had been opened and the panes smashed to let air seep through the matted ivy and creeper, pale green shoots growing through the dilapidated louvres of the outside shutters still barred, held intact by the thick growth of the vines. From the outside there'd be no sign that the sealed room had been disturbed or entered.

" He needed air," Spig said evenly.

" Who? "

" The chimney sweep."

The white ball of his light followed the criss-crossed rubber-soled tracks into the corner of the room. A chair had been pulled up to serve as a makeshift easel, a canvas propped on it, another chair drawn up for the Tattoo Artist to sit on. On the table beside it was a box of oil paints, a box of tacks, a hammer and an electric lantern focused on the fourposter bed, as the chairs in the corner were angled to face it. The far side of the bed, the head and the foot, were a screen of spider webs, a fantastic net woven around it, completely enclosing it, torn open where it had covered the near side, as if the sleeper waking had thrust the curtain of them aside as he rose and before he drew back in its place the faded patchwork quilt that covered the bed. Lying on the hearth was a broom, the straw black with soot and webs.

The witch with the broom.

Yerby's flashlight rested on Miss Fairlie's tracks again, following them from the hearth to the bed, on to the door. He brought it back, raising it to the great overmantel with its rack of rusted guns, and brought it down until the white beam filled the fire chamber, littered with dead leaves, soot, rubble and the scaly rust of the damper-plate that had held them before it was broken through. On top of all of it was one blackened-soot brick, or part of a brick, the mark of a ribbed rubber sole on it. It had been broken off, the end a fresh rosy-mauve, not sooted.

"That old ivy outside's dead easy to climb," Yerby said.

The two of them went towards the fireplace then, moved by one impulse, their lights on the fire chamber, stooped down, the lights raising, jerking suddenly and coming to rest, as they saw what Miss Fairlie had seen. In the white glare the blackened tennis shoes, one scarred red from the broken brick, the sooted denim legs, flesh between sock and trouser cyanosed blue from asphyxiation, hung limp and motionless, the body still imprisoned in the flue. Yerby thrust his light into Spig's hand. He knelt down, on the hearth, moved in, grasped the legs and pulled. He pulled again, lifting his whole weight, and jolted back as the body gave and came down, soot and brick pouring after it. They pulled Dunning out on to the floor, looking down at the bearded face, the black eyes glazed and staring, lips swollen and blue-black. The rope, knotted under his arms, coiled wire-tight around his wrists, had brought down at the other end a piece of iron. Yerby reached in the fire chamber and picked it out of the soot and leaves. It was the scroll-shaped metal, pin snapped off, driven into the chimney to hold the brick.

He looked down at the rope. "That didn't give when the brick snapped off and he fell," he said somberly. "It caught on this iron. He was holding it with both hands over his head. Slipped a noose round his wrists. My God, what a way to die."

"He knew Miss Fairlie was alone here at night," O'Leary said evenly. "He knew she could hear him. God knows how long he'd been coming, getting that stuff down the chimney, hammering his stretcher together and the canvas on it . . . It didn't matter to him. He was getting another painting for his gallery of rural America . . . a companion piece to the graveyard scene he was starting last night. He knew she was helpless, in more ways then one. There's the evidence he had for Mrs. Twohey and her friends."

He forced himself to cross the room and turn his light on the canvas propped on the chair, knowing what it was he was going to see, knowing now why Dunning was laughing when he sat down to paint his picture of Ammon Fairlie's grave without a stone, and why he'd said he wasn't hurting a soul . . . not a soul. Old David's work-shoe tracks in the dust to the now empty bed, the torn curtain of spider webs, the fresh-dug grave, the burden Molly had seen the old man dragging, the luminous white bones Spig had uncovered, thinking it was Dunning he'd find in the unmarked grave, the sketch of the skeletal hand on the drawing board in Dunning's studio—all of it added up. Ammon Fairlie's grave was unmarked because it was an empty grave—not a soul in it for Dunning to hurt, or a body either, not until old David had dug it that day and placed Ammon Fairlie's bones there under the white myrtle for their final rest.

He turned his light on the painted canvas and stood there, Yerby beside him, the silence growing intense, until he could hear his heart beating cold against his ribs. It was a painting of the bed, the front curtain of the spider webs not torn, finely, intricately woven, with a brush stroke so delicate it was itself a web. Behind it, the patchwork quilt was spread out, covering the sleeper, long dead, the bare skull resting on a pillow laced black with dust and cobwebs, the arms outside the quilt, sleeves of a tattered coat flat, the skeletal hands folded, not carefully painted but blocked in to show where they had rested. That much Spig had known he would see. What he had not known was that Ammon Fairlie had not died of a heart attack. In the centre of the painted forehead a spider sat in a splintered bullet hole squarely between the hollow sockets. Echoing in Spig's ears was Dunning's laughter, its devilish malice and evil delight. *I'll crucify Miss Crazy Fairlie.*

Yerby's voice, deliberately matter-of-fact, broke through the silence as he reached down and switched on Dunning's lantern, its broad white beam on the empty bed.

" Am I crazy, or was he? I guess you call it creative imagination. If that's what he thought he saw, he ought to have come to me."

He put his flashlight on the table, reached out to the painting, calmly ripped the canvas off the wood, rolled it up and handed it to Spig.

" Let's go. Tip says you've got the letter. I'll get Parker in here."

The rip of the canvas from the wood had sounded to Spig as Anita's voice had sounded. " Those kids, Buck . . . at the hospital? "

Yerby stopped at the door. He was silent for a moment. " Only one of 'em made it, Spig. Lucy. Maybe it's fair. She was out for kicks, Charlie was out for dough. It was him rigged poor old Ramey. Harlan knows it now. And Lucy's going to have a long, long time to think. I guess we all lie for our kids, Spig. Like Tip's rifle with Molly's initials on the stock. And Anita . . . she said to tell you you can have the place, in trust for Molly A. Lucy's father's coming down. He's never married again—maybe they can get together on the kid now. And Harlan's taking his For Sale sign down. He's blaming himself for the Death Strip. So your damned highway's safe—if it was worth all this. Come on, let's get out of here."

They went back and up the four steps. Spig took the letters out of the knapsack. The one Miss Fairlie had given Tip was a single sheet with a brief note on it.

" My dear Tip—My will is at Judge Twohey's office. I am leaving Eden to your parents in trust for you at their death. If I am ill, if it isn't too much to ask, I would be happy if your parents would move to Eden and let me stay here. I'd like the house completely opened and renovated. There is a trust for each of the other children, and for Eden and my care. I love you very much. Thank you for coming into my life.—Sincerely, Celia Fairlie."

Spig handed it to Yerby and picked up the old judge's letter. It was written with the same pen that spluttered, the same heartbeat pulsating in the fine uneven strokes.

" Dear Spig," it began. He stopped as the door opened and Dr. Parker came in.

" It looks pretty hopeful. Not too much paralysis. She'll need care."

" We'll see she gets it, sir."

Yerby gave him back Miss Fairlie's letter, dropping his hand for an instant on his shoulder. " I'll be back. Give me your flash. Come on, Sam. You won't need your bag." At the door he looked back. " You've got matches, haven't you? " he asked. He closed the door carefully.

Spig put the judge's letter down. He took out the

canvas he'd stuck in the knapsack and went over to the fireplace. It burned easily, with very little ash. He went back to the letter.

" Dear Spig—Call Buck Yerby at once when you have cause to read this. Take him to Eden with you. His father was with me the day Ammon Fairlie, Celia's father, shot and killed George Sudley. Tell Nat and Harlan. I'm afraid they always thought it was I who killed him.

" Ammon Fairlie was a stern and passionate man. He found the post box and a letter telling Celia that George would fall in the river as a ruse to meet her at the cottage, to decide what to do about the baby she was carrying. Ammon let her meet him, and shot him down while she fought to save him. David called me. I got the blood on my overcoat dragging Celia from his body. None of us knew she and George had been secretly married. She'd returned from an ostensible visit to tell her father, who was violently opposed to that or any marriage for her, found him seriously ill with his strained heart and decided to wait until he was well to tell him. David was the only one they told. Yerby and I assumed Ammon Fairlie was avenging his daughter's dishonour. Harlan, I believe, made the same assumption on my behalf—knowing his brother was conducting a clandestine affair with Celia, George was handsome and gay, and we assumed the worst.

" It was to avoid exposing Celia's presumed dishonour that Yerby and I concocted the story of the accident and allowed Ammon to return to Eden. We counted on his love for his daughter. A month later in a frenzy of rage at her condition and her grief he threw her down the stairs and brought on a premature birth. It was the morning of the snow. David was bedridden with an

injured back. He sent the boy down as I've told you.
The boy thought Celia was mad. When David got it
out of him and crawled down to Eden he found Celia
with her dead baby. She said. ' My father shot and
killed my husband. Now he's killed my baby. I've shot
and killed him, David. He's in his bedroom. The gun's
beside him.' She collapsed then. He got her out of that
terrible house where she'd been those days and nights,
without heat or light or food, a creaking house of death,
with Ammon's old Gordon setter howling, scratching at
his master's door. It was in her delirium David learned
the story of the baby's birth and death. He didn't dare
call a doctor, but he couldn't have got one through that
snow even if he had dared to send. He buried the baby,
and piled pine branches up to look like the grave I saw
when I finally came. He put the gun back on Ammon
Fairlie's rack over the mantel.

" I have before me a transcript of the testimony at both
inquests. Perhaps it is because I know the truth, or it
may be that forty years of experience with witnesses has
given me insight . . . but the testimony we gave, and
that is solely my responsibility, not David's, is so palpably
false that it amazes me anyone ever credited it as they
did.

" It describes Fairlie as a very large man. It's humanly
impossible for a tiny creature like Celia to have got him
into the house out of the snow, to be there with his dead
body until David came. It's humanly impossible that this
tiny creature and a small man with a crippled back could
have moved Fairlie's body through the snow to the
graveyard. If they had buried him, they would have done
it near the house. With the weather of that winter it is
fantastic to believe that they could have thawed the
ground deep enough to bury so large a man. It is

fantastic, too, to believe that a man who knew guns as George Sudley did would blast out his own heart in that way. My kindness immortalised in Gus's classic sermon is equally dubious.

" It is because all of this seems such a transparent fiction to me now that I have a strong feeling that, at some time, someone hearing the story of George and Celia from the tongues that have never stilled will decide to investigate the mystery of Eden. An objective eye is all that is needed. It is that possibility that I have in actuality had in mind in both my letters to you. Beyond that: unless David has found the opportunity he never had, because of Celia's almost constant presence in Eden and its grounds through all the years, you will find Ammon Fairlie's remains where he died . . . where his daughter raised his own gun and shot him as he sat on his bed to change his snow-wet shoes and David managed to move him and cover him with a quilt for the long sleep. Your son will inherit Eden, through you and Molly, at Celia's death, and if David is gone by then, there will be no one to tell you the truth of the strange tenant you will find.

" Monstrously culpable we may have been. The responsibility is solely mine. As I come to the end of this journey and start the infinite journey to the Court of Last Appeal, my love for Celia my only defence, my prayer is for your long life and happiness at Eden—for the happiness and saving grace your children have brought to her. So may God in His wisdom be with you and in His mercy with me and all mankind. Sincerely, Nathan Twohey."

Spig was still there when Yerby came back. He roused himself, handed Yerby the letter and went across the room, folding back the carved shutters, opening the window and the green slatted blinds, and stood looking out along the silver path of the moon on the river. He stood there a long time before he heard Buck Yerby move and heard a match strike. When he turned, black flakes of carbon were fluttering softly up the chimney.

" You tell Nat," Yerby said quietly. " I'll tell Harlan. I never knew they thought it was the judge. I'd have told them." He went to the door. " We're going to open the outside door in the hyphen and get Pete Greenway and Anita's father and Mrs. Twohey out here. Especially Mrs. Twohey. Nobody's going to say Dunning was murdered if I can help it. You better lock this."

He went down into the hyphen. Spig closed the door and turned the key in the old lock Then he went out into the hall. Molly came from Miss Fairlie's room, her face lighted.

" She's asleep, but she can speak a little," she said softly. " I'm so glad . . . so glad." She came into his arms. He held her tightly a moment, the Sea King's daughter, cool and crystalline, all his.

" David was here. He's gone to stay with Kitsy and John Eden. He said to tell you Miss Fairlie came before he could move the chairs and things. What did he mean? "

" I'll tell you later." Dunning could wait. " Where's Tip? I've got a letter that's his to read."

" He's in the dining-room. Finishing Miss Fairlie's report on the rabbit."

O'Leary moved back, looking at her cautiously. " Not . . . the red rabbit? "

" Certainly." Molly laughed. " Darling, if you'd just read the things your children give you . . . It was Tippy's Conservation Magazine two months ago. The dyed rabbit project—to trace where they go, how far . . . you know. Like banding birds. Good heavens, you didn't think they were all crazy, did you . . . Mrs. Twohey? "

" Which reminds me," said O'Leary. " She's coming." He glanced out at the picket gate. " We don't happen to have a bushel basket of rotten pears right handy, do we, Mrs. O'Leary? "

THE END